THE NEW DISCIPLES

THE NEW DISCIPLES
A NOVEL

Anthony B. Pinn

PITCHSTONE PUBLISHING
Durham, North Carolina

Pitchstone Publishing
Durham, North Carolina
www.pitchstonepublishing.com

Copyright © 2015 by Anthony B. Pinn

10 9 8 7 6 5 4 3 2 1

Library of Congress Cataloging-in-Publication Data

Pinn, Anthony B.
  The new disciples : a novel / Anthony B. Pinn.
     pages ; cm
  ISBN 978-1-63431-008-6 (softcover : acid-free paper)
  1. Clergy—Fiction. 2. Penance—Fiction. 3. Serial murders—Fiction. I. Title.
  PS3616.I576N49 2015
  813'.6—dc23
                                        2014037615

CHAPTER ONE

It had never been completely clear to James Ford how he ended up in the priesthood. Perhaps he felt something that people would say was a calling from God, or perhaps it was simply an easy career option that smacked him in the face. He'd always been comfortable in the church, enjoyed the services, and admired the robes worn by the priests. Maybe that feeling of comfort—the feeling this stuff is sufficient to mark a good life—constituted a calling?

The reason might be mundane, but he always had a question in the back of his mind. Why not a more spectacular something, a more fantastic push into ministry? He'd read the Bible on his own and as part of his church education, and he couldn't help wishing for the same type of connection to God—some marker of him being special. At times he found himself wondering why he didn't experience something like the vision Moses had with the burning bush and the booming voice in the wilderness. He could ask these questions and have this wish, but ultimately there was no way around it.

His entrance into ministry wasn't very dramatic; in fact, it was rather pedestrian and somewhat boring. He'd been an altar boy—and he'd relished the responsibilities that had gone along with that title. He knew he was an essential part of the service, and his role was key to the development of mass each Sunday. He felt a little important, useful, noticed, and maybe it was a desire to maintain that feeling that pulled him into the ministry.

Ford's family had always placed importance in the Roman Catholic Church, and had expressed deep regard for and obedience to the priests encountered over the years. His mother admired the priests because they were committed and well spoken; they expressed a certain type of stability, a presence that was sure and steady. His father had a healthy respect for authority—and who could trump the guys who work for God? So there was no surprise that Ford's parents were pleased when one morning he awoke and at breakfast told them he wanted to be a priest. He'd never seen his mother or father so happy with him, or at least a bit relieved that their son would make something of his life.

They kept these thoughts quiet, but at times they wondered what would become of him. He wasn't as intellectually gifted as his sister, and didn't have the self-assured presence of his older brother. In fact, he followed the lead of his brother and sister, and it didn't strike his parents that he did this simply because he was younger. There was more to it than that, although they couldn't quite articulate what they had in mind.

Even at a young age James seemed to them one in search of something—a mission and purpose—that would give life meaning and importance, and perhaps the priesthood would offer exactly that. And they hoped that something once he found it would give him the strength and the insight necessary to accomplish great things. His parents expressed these thoughts and their relief with smiles and hugs. And their smiles made him happy and he thought maybe life in the priesthood would give him that same feeling of satisfaction and accomplishment over and over again.

Encouraged by his parents—his siblings gave his announcement little thought—he told the priest in charge of the parish his desire to devote himself to the work of Christ. The priest wasn't as excited by the announcement as he assumed (or hoped) he might be, but Ford did begin to receive some attention and new opportunities to learn informally what it meant to be a priest.

Some of what he observed seemed uninspired, just a bunch of guys in black who went through a range of motions. Other times, Ford believed he felt a spiritual connection to something greater than the men in black suits. Ford paid careful attention to his responsibilities at the church. After this informal training and the first few phases of his education, Ford entered seminary where he encountered other young men like him, who'd also told parents and priests of their desire to serve.

He studied hard, and met with modest approval from his professors who spoke of him in a general way—as they would of any student— although they were not particularly impressed with his intellectual abilities. Many of them thought of him as unspectacular; he wouldn't become a leader of the universal Church; but, they'd seen worse and, after all, the Church needed priests. And the number of volunteers had decreased over the years.

Although it was not said during those moments of conversation and evaluation, the professors understood that many priests in training were like Ford. One professor was fond of calling Ford the Church's equivalent of white rice—a useful staple, but rather bland and unimpressive on its own. A few thought more highly of Ford, believing that a strong push, a certain type of opportunity might just change him and result in him doing for the Church things of which no one thought him capable. Yet, even in this belief there was an assumption Ford's best accomplishments would be modest when compared to those of others. Still, for them, the more encouraging professors, there was something—in class papers and in his conversations with other students and with faculty—about Ford's reaction to sin and punishment that marked him as different. This response to the dark side of humanity was a rare sensitivity in young men who entered this seminary.

Just one member of the faculty put more thought into Ford than this, and he believed there might be something dangerous for the Church in this reaction to sin. If this were actually the case, he prayed nothing would happen to bring this wicked potential to Ford's conscious mind and make manifest a problem hard to control.

Ford sensed at times his odd relationship to his training, to the Church, and to its leaders. But his sense of marginality didn't end with Church related persons and activities—at least all of this church-related business existed within the context of the familiar known as religious devotion. He also recognized his odd relationship to the outside world. He'd entered training for ministry early and never experienced life as those his age typically did … when not seeking ordination.

Ford was no wiser concerning the workings of the world as a result of his education; in fact little of what he learned had anything to do with what it meant to be a flawed human with desires, wants, and fears. But he did learn prayers, theology, rituals, some philosophy, and the general workings of the Roman Catholic Church.

After graduating from seminary, Ford was assigned without much explanation a series of unimpressive (and modest) parishes, all within urban areas of major cities. His stays were long enough to learn some of the workings of ministry—how to engage community service opportunities, how to interact with his people. But, these assignments, often a matter of months rather than years, didn't last long enough to foster deep connections on a personal level with members of the various congregations.

Ford knew other priests who had great friendships with members of their congregations, and friendships with people beyond the Church—but not him so much. He'd get together socially with some members, share a laugh with some, and develop relationships with a few that resembled friendships. He went to dinner in homes when invited, and worked to make pleasant conversation about things of which he knew little—politics, the economy, and relationships. He cursed on occasion, and drank particularly when he was anxious, but that didn't seem to bother his parishioners. And he certainly wasn't the only priest with these weaknesses. He had the occasional cup of coffee when the offer was made, and learned something about the everyday concerns and experiences of those trusting him with their spiritual well-being. Ford avoided the conflicts and dilemmas that destroyed the career of many—no sexual misconduct of any kind, no stealing, nothing that would bring disgrace.

Ford, during times of contact with those outside the priesthood, always knew in the back of his mind that he could say little of real substance to them because they lived in a world he hadn't really experienced firsthand.

He was pretty much alone, without deep connections and too far from family to maintain good relations with them. In each case the diocese had limited expectations for those parishes, but simply needed to keep them open for the time being. Ford did his best to meet the needs of those in his charge. Baptisms, communions, sermons, counseling sessions, and community service—he did it all, and the people around him seemed to appreciate it (or at least expect this work).

Many days he made an effort to enjoy his work—not as much as he'd imagined when he sat with his bowl of cereal and told his parents about his calling. But he struggled to feel at peace with his ministry, although at times it was far from satisfying. Even the people—the real Church—held, although he'd never say it, only limited appeal for him. He went through the motions as best he could, despite the moments of doubt and regardless of the loneliness.

One Monday, at one of these many churches, he'd been in his office going over the typical Monday stuff—schedule of counseling sessions, thoughts that might form his next sermon, recovering from the demands of the previous day.

The boredom was broken by a knock on his door. It was Cristina Gomez. She and her husband were members of the church and had been active—attending services and special events, and giving an offering each service they attended—and they made certain to bring their small children along. Cristina made it clear she hoped her son would become a priest, that at least would take him away from the dangers of their neighborhood and maybe their daughter would become a nun—although she was really smart and both her parents hoped they could somehow get her through public school and into a good college.

She needed to speak with Ford about her family. After taking her seat, she told him about her husband's increasing use of alcohol. He'd lost his job, and they would soon lose their home. She wanted help, any type of assistance—at least some way to make sense of it all.

"Is God punishing us, father? Did we do something wrong, commit some type of sin?"

Ford listened to her questions, and studied her face. He wanted to admit ignorance, but he knew he had to come up with answers. Drawing from his school days and set of stock responses to such questions, Ford smiled and told her, "Sometimes God tests us, Cristina.

Think about Job ... he committed no sin. He was good, and God allowed him to be tested. Perhaps you are being tested. Stay strong and prayerful."

She seemed comforted by this, but Ford felt a bit numbed by it all. On some level, he realized this type of conversation was a part of his responsibilities, and he would handle those moments. Even then, he didn't see himself as being any closer to Cristina or the others who came with similar problems. At times, as he talked to them, it was almost as if he hovered above his body, watching and listening as he spoke. He'd wonder if this was all there was to ministry. Should it even be called ministry?

It was assumed this limited and uninspired ministry would also mark his time at his new parish—St. Barbara, where, unlike earlier assignments, he'd spend a good number of years.

Ford tried harder at this new parish. In fact, he came to think highly of many of the determined and gentle people he taught, coached, and counseled.

The people at St. Barbara worked as best they could, but with little chance for financial traction, or security really of any kind. Parents pressed to keep their children safe, and an opportunity to advance beyond high school to college was a rare gift. One face, one story, above all others made this real for Ford.

Black mother and Hispanic father, Joan Douglass marked the best of what the United States had to offer. Her bright, brown eyes seemed so hopeful whenever Ford saw her, and Joan's light brown face, wide smile, and small frame seemed somewhat unflustered by the grit of her neighborhood. She was a stand out, and he thought as much from the day of her christening forward. Her family, like many families in the neighborhood, had its trials—including an uncle who had a dangerous interest in his young niece. The uncle was jailed, and Joan got over the physical trauma. Ford and her counselor provided by the state worked to help her address the spiritual, emotional, and mental damage.

Joan was special. In spite of the brutal moments in her life constituting experiences from which many would not bounce back, Joan kept her faith, did well in school, and stayed out of trouble and determined to go beyond high school to college. She wanted to be an attorney—corporate law because she said she had to understand what made the world work in order to change it. Joan was going to fix her country from the inside out.

He could close his eyes and hear Joan sitting in his office explaining to him the outline of her future. Ford smiled and thought, "Boy was she determined, and when she got going … it was hard not to share her enthusiasm. She'd make a dynamite attorney."

She'd picked her schools—small liberal arts colleges because she wanted to be out of the city, have the attention of her instructors, and learn networks generations of "legacy" students could provide. Her grades were good enough for college, her letters of recommendation coming from teachers and community leaders, including Ford, were outstanding. Joan was accepted at four of her six schools—her top four picks—and she decided to attend Williams College.

It was a long way from the city she called home, far away from the noise, the confusion, and she assumed from the challenges. Everyone, including Ford, was so proud of Joan. There was a party before she packed her stuff to go. Small gifts and big wishes for success were given to her. And she was on her way.

Joan loved Williams College, the safe feeling of Williamstown, the history of the area, and the green space. She could walk for what seemed miles without confronting a speeding car, without rude words from lowlifes on street corners.

The first year went well. Her bills were covered. She was making friends, doing well in her classes, and growing. Joan stayed on campus that summer because she remembered what her neighborhood was like during the hot months. She got a job at the local Your Food Groceries, and took a class in first-level French. Joan planned to travel someday. She'd need the language skills and money—so she'd not waste her paycheck on prepared foods at the store because even with the discount they were expensive. Instant noodles—four packages for $1.50 would do. She'd call home every Saturday morning to report on the week, and to share all the wonders of life in Williamstown. Her parents were proud, and her siblings anxious to have the experience she described. The family didn't have much to share with her, but they'd send letters expressing pride and offering a few dollars to help out.

Joan financed her education through fellowships, work-study, and federal loans. But that second year there were issues with her family finances that made completing all the required forms problematic: her mother had to take a different job, working at a drycleaners "under the table"—no W-2 forms and income that couldn't really be reported. The school financial aid officer asked questions and the federal government had regulations.

During registration, Joan was called to the financial aid office, and told her federal loan application had been rejected. Between the tears, Joan tried to find out why—but nothing the stone-faced officer said made any sense to her. All she knew was that without the loans she couldn't enter her sophomore year. Joan asked about additional support from Williams, maybe more work-study. Nothing could be arranged, even her state support couldn't be increased enough to make up for the loss. Her formal appeal of the decision amounted to nothing more than a rehearsal of school and federal government regulations.

With her dreams falling apart, Joan went back to her room, called her parents, and cried. There was nothing to do but pack up, try to save face with her friends on campus, take the long bus ride back to her city, and plan a new strategy.

The priest remembered a conversation with Joan shortly after her arrival back in the neighborhood. She'd had some time to think it through, and had some plans in the works. Her smile wasn't the smile from years ago, the one that lit up a room. Yet, it was a smile—a glimmer of hope and an expressed desire to figure something out. She wasn't giving up and that gave him some relief.

Ford didn't see Joan again after that meeting, after seeing that smile. Schedules were busy. He wondered how she was doing. He hoped she was well, or that at least she'd made a new life that was worth living.

That thought was quickly overwhelmed by pressing news he couldn't keep hidden in the back of his mind. He was pulled from memories of Joan back to uncomfortable church business. And he'd have to find a way to share it with the members of his parish.

Every bit of concern for these people, every ounce of compassion he felt for them and for this church and his ministry, Ford would have to express clearly. He wasn't certain he was up for this. Couldn't the

Bishop share this news? But, no, Ford would have to do his best. He'd figure out a way to say what he needed to say, what he thought people needed to hear.

He dressed that Sunday knowing things were changing forever—and although he knew he couldn't predict the future, he had a feeling his ministry would be transformed as well.

"OK," Father Ford said, looking in the small mirror on the wall of his room, "this has got to start just right. I've got to nail the first few lines perfectly."

"Your children have been christened here and have come to know the grace of God in this church. We have cried together; laughed together, and fellowshipped within these walls. But, the connections we have made as a church family are not defined by our limited physical building. God's church is more than this. We are stronger than these bricks. We are more than this space, and … the Gospel message will have meaning after this building no longer exists."

Father Ford was standing there, going over his outfit—his best black suit and newest collar—and practicing his sermon. This was going to be a special Sunday; in fact, it would be the church's last meeting. The Bishop had made a decision to streamline. All congregations that could not support themselves would be forced to close, and Ford's church was the first to fall victim to this new policy. This is what Father Ford had been told by his superiors; he remembered the lack of emotion in the Bishop's words; the emptiness in the eyes of the others.

Ford paused, and awkwardly pushed his hand through what remained of his hair. "I don't even buy this shit," he thought to himself.

Ford walked slowly out the door of his room, down the hall. He had taken more time in his room preparing than usual, and service was just about to begin when he walked through the office that connected to the sanctuary and took his position in the pulpit.

Church service began.

After the songs were sung and prayers rendered, Father Ford took a deep breath and started his last sermon in front of the people he'd come to know over the course of the years. Ford looked around the sanctuary for the last time and reluctantly began, "Your children have been baptized here and have come to know the grace of God …"

Ford fought his way through the sermon, smiling, gesturing, and attempting to speak with an energy that would—hopefully—suggest confidence. He was almost able to convince himself that things would be fine; parishioners would find new church homes and he, of course, would be assigned to another church where he would work to increase the size of God's kingdom on earth. He continued to speak, to preach the closing of his church, and as he attempted to convince parishioners and himself of the ultimate purpose of this plan, its fit with God's grace, he punctuated his words with volume and passion.

"God's hand is on even this plan! Sometimes the faithful experience afflictions, situations that are difficult to understand and accept; but God's presence is real and we will survive the closing of this place …"

After the sermon, Ford moved to the back of the church to shake hands with his members.

"Father Ford, why? Why our church?" Jane Johnson asked. Father Ford answered Jane like he answered the twenty who asked the same question before her.

"The Bishop thinks it is best," he said with a forced smile and a pat on the back.

He hugged members of the church—the Petersons, the Smiths … all those who'd spent so much time in that space, and had given so much energy to the safeguarding of that place. He'd miss them, but in an odd way he knew the people had never been his full concern. Thinking back on his years of ministry, there always seemed something missing, that there had to be more to his ministry than sermons, prayers, communions, and counseling sessions. As was the case with all his other churches, he believed he, for the most part, liked his parishioners—even felt deep affection for many. But at other times they seemed a bit of an annoyance, a distraction from something more important—some dimension of his ministry he hadn't yet discovered.

Ford made it through that service and walked back to his office, removed his vestments, and continued the lonely walk back to his small room. He'd made this transition as easy as he could, considering the fact that he had not mentioned what the church building would soon house.

"Damn," he thought. "How could the Bishop do this? Sell the

building to the state for use as a state-run halfway house ...There's got to be some irony in there somewhere."

The police had never been much of a positive presence in the community, and he'd spent too many Saturdays visiting relatives of parishioners who were in the local jail for one reason or another. Now, their church was going to be turned into a halfway house? Ford sat in his room, thinking about the paradox: God's house, the church, meant to free souls and uplift spirits would now storehouse bodies and limit the hope that feeds character.

It wasn't his everyday practice, but during times like this, Ford indulged in a bit of scotch. He sat there, with his collar still on and his best suit hanging off his limp body, sipping his scotch and hoping he'd never have to share the full story.

"There has to be another way ... baked good sales, auctions, a bank loan, tapping into the rich citizens who might need a tax break," Ford thought to himself. But he knew these things wouldn't change anything. The church was as good as gone. Thinking these thoughts, and holding his glass of scotch, Ford fell asleep and dreamed of better days.

He awoke the next morning feeling no better but with an added pain in his neck from his awkward sleeping position. His pants were still wet from the scotch that slowly leaked onto him during the night.

Ford put the glass on the table next to his chair, stood up and tried to stretch out his aching body. It was going to be another difficult day. His congregation had the evening to think about the loss of their church and he just knew confessions would be particularly difficult to hear this morning. He prepared himself for his duties—morning mass, followed by time in the confessional. This is what he dreaded, being plied with questions about the church, questions he couldn't answer. Questions he didn't want to think about—all masked by the pretense of a confession.

CHAPTER TWO

He sat in the darkness of this box, the confessional, dark wooden walls, and a red curtain that had seen better days separated his space from the space where parishioners came to confess. It had always been an odd situation for Ford, perhaps for most priests. He would find himself thinking, over and over again—"What the hell do I say about things my religious life is supposed to exclude?" This was his mantra, used in most cases regarding sex stuff, acts that he wasn't supposed to even think about. But today was different, he was certain they would come, one after the other wanting answers, wanting him to say a prayer or prescribe some action that would allow parishioners to keep their church.

With dread and fear in his heart, Ford sat in the confessional as Michael arrived. He'd been attending the church for a few years now, but was an unassuming figure, one coming across as the type wanting a contained and manageable spiritual experience—service on Sunday and a few community service programs when his work schedule allowed. Michael, who usually dressed in a conservative suit and wingtips, was the type of guy who came to mind when the term "yuppie" was mentioned, but with a twist—beyond the fact that he was living in this neighborhood. There was something those who met Michael, heard him talk and watched his eyes, could not fully understand or explain.

With nervousness bleeding through his words, Michael sat and began his confession. "Forgive me Father for I have sinned. It's been months since my last confession ... I usually depend on my wife to take care of this for me, let her handle her sins and mine during one session. But ... ah ... not this time."

"What do you mean?" Ford replied.

"Well, Father. It's not really a sin. At least I don't think so. I'm planning to abide by the Bible on this issue, so it can't be a sin, can it?"

Wondering what Michael could be referring to, Ford shifted his weight, steadied and said, "You'll need to explain before I can answer that question."

"I heard your sermon about plans to close this church, and I'm going to do something about it ... at least that's my hope. I've been reading the Bible and I've come across a solution to my problem ... or, uh ... I should say our problem."

Ford was anxious and curious. He wanted a solution, had hoped the scotch and deep thinking the night before would have produced some possibilities rather than just a pain in his back. He wanted to know more, but was cautious, even guarded in his response. "I'm not certain I know what you're talking about."

It was a noncommittal response, but it was one Ford hoped would entice Michael to say more.

His being in the confessional was difficult enough without this priest slowing down the conversation. "OK, Father," Michael continued, "I've been reading the book of Matthew, and I can't get past Jesus and the moneychangers. You know this story? Of course you do. You preached about it—the story where Jesus punished the greedy. Well, I'd like to follow that model."

Father Ford's anxiety increased. He could feel his heart beginning to beat faster and his throat became dry. He thought to himself, "This is just what I need. Random quoting of the Bible. What the hell is this guy talking about?" But he kept this thought to himself and instead replied with as much control as his stressed body could muster up, "Please, I'll need to hear details. Vagueness won't help."

"Well, Father, it's simple. You know ... word gets around, and I know what they plan on doing with this church. Middle management has its benefits—information. Information."

"Please get on with it," Ford responded, raising his voice above the usual whisper.

"I know that the church is becoming a halfway house," says Michael boldly. "And I think I know a way to stop it."

The verbal dance was over. Michael had Ford's full attention. He began to explain that he had once considered the priesthood, going so far as to start seminary training. He decided the religious life was not for him, too confined, too distant from what he admired most about the world. He hadn't had a real opportunity to apply his perspective until now, when he felt there was something real at stake. Michael believed that there was a beauty in Jesus' violent attack on the moneychangers who polluted the temple. On the surface, it might appear to be an act of vandalism, but that's not the message, Michael argued, we are supposed to get from it. It's a justified action because it maintains the values and concerns that should motivate our existence, our reason for being. Jesus' vandalism was righteous because it maintained the purity of God's relationship with humanity and it kept sacred the space marking that relationship.

Michael wanted desperately to follow this example—to strike out for a righteous cause. And what better cause than this one, the welfare of his church home and all it represented? And what better way than to take violent action? He knew, hell, most of the community had heard through the grapevine, that church officials were selling the church, trading sacred space for cash. He'd left behind the idea of religious life years ago, still Michael was certain: he wouldn't sit by and allow this to happen. Yet, Michael knew protest would prove useless. Who pays attention to signs and catchy slogans shouted by a faceless crowd? What had to happen was clear, and so Michael tightened every muscle that covered his small, pale frame and said it. "Father, the Bible teaches us that money is the root of evil and we have an obligation to prevent money from contaminating the Church. Turn this church into a halfway house, the temple into a den of thieves? They've got to be kidding ... Isn't this why Jesus punished the moneychangers? The same should be done now."

Ford was chilled by what Michael suggested. How far was Michael willing to take this?

"What are you planning? What are you talking about?" Ford asked, his heart beating fast, his mouth dry.

"Father, it's simple … I'm going to destroy the church, set it on fire. I'm going to save it by destroying it." Feeling more comfortable having finally spoken the words for the first time to any one, Michael continued. "Don't you see the beauty in my plan?"

"What? You can't be serious!" he screamed. The conversation's location no longer mattered. Michael was talking about a crime—wasn't he?—committing an evil act under the illusion that it was actually beneficial and righteous.

"Please, Father, keep your voice down. And try to understand the poetry in my plan. Don't you see? It's the only way. There's nothing left to do but this."

Trying to get himself together so he could speak as calmly as possible, and hoping it might help Michael see the danger in his plan, Father Ford responded. "That plan is a mistake. If you can't see the uselessness in destroying property, think about the children, the families. What about them? How can this possibly help them?"

"Father," Michael said moving closer to the curtain that separated them, "don't be a hypocrite. Really? I expect more from a man of God. You said in one of your sermons that the true church is not confined to a physical space. It's a community of like-minded people committed to God. Did you mean it? Or was it just meant to make us feel good as the prisoners are unloaded into the church … uh, I mean, halfway house?"

There was insult to injury for Michael. The state wasn't going to simply use the land, but it was going to literately use the church in its current state—with only necessary changes. Was it a budget decision, or a direct insult against God's people? For Michael, any use other than as the House of God was unacceptable, and he wanted to do something about it. Ford too didn't like the idea of the church closing. And to the extent a halfway house stood in the way of it remaining his parish, the halfway house was a problem. In theory the priest took no issue with helping "ex-cons" transition to life outside of prison. In the abstract, halfway houses served a purpose. They made sense to him, but should helping that population mean closing his church? Who was the church meant to help? What function should a church building play? No matter what, his parish coming to an end troubled Ford. It hurt him, but not primarily because of the halfway house situation, that was an easy target. Transition in the building's purpose was only a sign of a deeper problem Ford would struggle to recognize fully. Not lose of physical space, no; but instead a graphic symbol of the Church's lose of its way, the surrender of its primary purpose and its embrace of superficial interests and de-spiritualized agendas that point to its failure to fully appreciate the nature of sin.

Michael's words hit Ford hard. A truth ran through them, but it was a harsh and clumsy truth, one he could not easily embrace. There was a fine line between righteous action and criminal behavior; he knew this, had been taught it throughout his years of study and ministry. But didn't this push it too far, and cross the line? Michael spoke of an action that Ford found hard to reconcile with the actions of Jesus, the Christ who rebuilt lives and morals; created hope and enlivened possibilities. Didn't Jesus preach peace to a troubled time? To give more of one's self in the aid of others? Yet, when he opened the inner doors to his desires and sensibilities, this was worryingly attractive to Ford. Why allow the loss of his church? Why replace prayer with "ex-con" conversation? Why substitute the stages of the cross for politics? But couldn't this be God's will? Perhaps this was just a time of tribulation out of which God would bring about ultimate good—make them more faithful, bring them greater comfort and closeness to the faith. Was this the season of pain that led to the budding of renewed commitment to God, to a deeper understanding of Christ's sacrifice through a sacrifice of one's own? He'd had a hard time believing it when first told of the plan and he found it hard to preach it, but now Ford desperately wanted to believe that the surrender of this earthly temple was not the end of the story, but rather removed obstacles that prevented a deeper connection with God.

"There's got to be another way," Ford responded. "God works in mysterious ways to bring into our historical moment, our limited time on this earth, a richness that is beyond our imagination. We must be open to God's plan in even the most distressing event."

Ford wanted to believe this, but did he really have a choice? The decision had been made without his input and he was left to explain it to his congregation, and help them live through it. Ford understood that he lived between two worlds—the Church and its vision of life and the historical moment and problems that confront those to whom he ministered. Hadn't he always been taught to believe that God's purpose is worked out in unlikely ways, through improbable events? And wasn't it true that God's plan for those who have faith is found in events that appear tragic with our limited knowledge? Recognizing this requires a willingness to venture forth with faith, to challenge the obvious and uncover its glorious potential.

"God always works through confrontation, Father," Michael responded. "Think about those who got in the way of God's chosen children of Israel. Didn't they die? Didn't God demand violence? Why not now? Why not, Father?"

Michael's questions and persistence were getting to Father Ford.

"That's enough!" Ford left the confessional, clumsily navigating the elaborately craved interior, leaving Michael behind.

CHAPTER THREE

Ford wanted to know who was on the other side of the curtain, but more importantly he wanted to quiet the voice, to keep the plan it suggested from echoing through his mind. He'd encountered aggressive plans to transform the Church before; they were discussed in the books he'd read in school; they were part of casual conversation with other students; and, on occasion, he'd toyed with them sitting quietly when church work seemed less than satisfying and church hierarchy problematic. But Michael was trying to force the issue in a way that troubled him, while also seeming a bit intriguing. Ford wasn't certain exactly why he was torn, why he didn't just forget about the idea and move on.

Forgetting about his other obligations for the day, Ford moved as quickly as he could, his heart still pounding and his head aching from the conversation. Ford tried to run away from Michael's voice and its haunting message. Ford tried to forget the conversation in the confessional; he fought to remove the images from his mind, images of a church destroyed, a ministry perverted, and a community left in chaos. But he couldn't shake it; not even more of the scotch that helped on those other painful occasions helped now.

Ford went through possible reasons for this anxiety. Nothing he could conjure up solved the problem. No, nothing about the voice made him long sexually for Michael. The priest wasn't open to Michael's ideas because he was sexually aroused. It wasn't a matter of acting in accordance with Michael's plan as a way of flirting with him. And, he didn't believe his changing perspective was a result of him being naive, and just so unfamiliar with the ways of the world. That wasn't it. Still he'd never considered himself radical; he wasn't a huge fan of liberation theology, and he wasn't very engaged in politics. But maybe there was some embedded meaning in those earlier moments of discomfort with ministry when he wasn't certain how much he really cared for the people or saw interaction with them as the focus of his ministry, those moments when the people seemed a distraction from what should be his real ministry. He did have a strong sense of sin, and the need to address sin beyond the more generic practices of his faith.

Ford thought Michael's words might be tapping into these feelings, and might be exposing subconscious thoughts about the Church—all its workings—and his place in it. Michael might be offering Ford a way to finally express both his disappointment with the Church and his deep longing for the true Church beyond all the hierarchical foolishness and stale traditions he'd encountered from his days as an altar boy to the present. All of this was possible, but Ford wasn't certain, didn't think he could be certain. He wasn't convinced being certain really mattered in that maybe only God really knew and understood the human mind. Whatever the reason, Ford found himself unable to forget his conversation with Michael, and found himself increasingly open to Michael's words. He kept hearing the voice from the confessional: "There's nothing left to do but this ..."

Sleep caught Father Ford, sitting at his desk, in his small room, still dressed in his clothing from the confessional. But not before Ford got up, reached for his Bible, and read the passage the voice spoke about. Matthew 21:12: "And Jesus entered the temple of God and drove out all who sold and bought in the temple, and he overturned the tables of the moneychangers and the seats of those who sold pigeons. He said to them, it is written, 'my house shall be called a house of prayer'; but you make it a den of robbers.'"

"Shit," Ford said to no one in particular. "What do I do with this? Jesus rides into Jerusalem, preparing for his crucifixion and glory, but first ... the temple must be cleansed."

Chapter Four

It was Tuesday, the next morning, when Ford awoke with that familiar pain in his back, and a headache from the scotch. He was running late, but he was in no rush to return to the confessional.

He went into his bathroom, splashed water on his face, and brushed his teeth. Too tired and emotionally drained to worry too much about his appearance, such concerns had never played well with him those who knew him were wont to say. He pushed his thin, pale hand along his skinny, narrow face, shook his slight frame as if to dislodge his troubles. He slowly walked out of his room and back to the confessional, resolved to make the best of the day, and to better handle his responsibilities before church officials turned the building over to its new owners.

"Hello, Father." Father Ford slowly sank into his seat.

"I've been waiting here ... skipped work again today ... but ... this is important business isn't it, Father?"

Ford recognized the voice.

"Please forget this plan of yours. It's not God's way." Ford said the words, but he wasn't convinced. Those old thoughts of a less than satisfying ministry, and the feeling something more awaited him made it difficult to rule out completely this possibility. He simply felt that was what he was supposed to say.

"But it is," Michael responded, "it is God's way. You should have read the passage in Matthew I mentioned."

Ford interrupted Michael, moving closer to the curtain, so close that his lips touched it and his words caused the red curtain to shift

24

and move like a gentle flame. "I know the passage, and you're wrong." He hoped moving closer to the voice and making this statement with passion might emphasize his point, change Michael's mind and end this plan. But he also knew, deep within, that this wouldn't be the outcome. Ford sat there, speaking these words, knowing the response would only push him deeper into violent possibilities.

"I'm just an instrument, one who has finally come to realize the risk involved in devotion. For too long, Father, and listen carefully, I've been content to pretend. I've come on Sundays, sure, and I've given some money. No problem. But nothing in this relationship with the Church entailed risk, the type of risk that Jesus encountered and his disciples embraced ... not the kind of risk that Jesus showed dealing with the moneychangers ... What's wrong Father, afraid to be like Jesus?"

Ford felt he had no choice but to go where the voice was leading, to expose himself to the voice's anger, and in so doing to recognize his own anger and frustration. But he refused to take the bate. He wouldn't respond to Michael's question. He'd pose one instead. "So, you are holding on to this plan to destroy this church?"

He realized this was a weak statement. Here's someone planning to burn down the church, and he can only muster a ridiculous grasp of the obvious. So he quickly tried again, before the voice could respond. "Uh ... you think destroying the building will prevent the dismantling of the congregation, the end of church? You can't really believe that."

Michael was beginning to sense openness in Ford, a flirtation with the idea of destruction as regeneration. "Sounds like you're looking for me to convince you," Michael responded sarcastically, "but it shouldn't be necessary for me to play that role with a man of God ... But, hey, I'm willing."

Michael explained his perception of the required action with a calmness and assertion not present earlier in the conversation. God did not merely condone this violence; God required it. God is far from squeamish when it comes to destruction of peoples and property.

Ford couldn't take this calmly; he couldn't sit and be lectured on the merits of violence. Yet, it was oddly attractive to him. This was the problem. "How can you be so certain about this? The consequences are staggering. What if you're wrong?"

Who had the upper hand was clear to Michael, and so he replied to Ford's frantic questions with an ever-growing sense of certainty, not only that he was right but that the priest could be convinced to participate as a new dimension of his religious life.

"Relax, Father, relax," Michael began, his words oozing with confidence as he concluded his point. "It's got to be done and in the end we'll know we were right."

Ford tried, but he couldn't put his finger on the moment when it became plausible in spite of his questioning tone. All Ford knew for certain was that it didn't seem as offensive today; actually, it was rather sensible. He could appreciate the biblical irony involved—perhaps God could work even through this. Hadn't he always believed and preached that God's grace and will could be manifest in the most unlikely ways? He told his congregation to be open to the possibilities, so could he close off this option? No matter how much he wanted to dismiss this conversation, to forget about it and make the most of the remaining days before the closing of the church and his transfer, it compelled him and captured his religious imagination and political sensibilities. Perhaps because Ford couldn't explain his growing attraction to this plan, he started to think it might be a plan from God. It's the voice of God or it's madness. A link or dependency between destruction and construction, between virtue and violence was becoming undeniable.

"Isn't it obvious to you? I'm here for your help, Father. You and I ... we. And," Michael continued, "by the way, Father, you might as well use my name; I think this conversation blows away illusions of indifference and distance. The name's Michael."

Michael knew he had to get a commitment from Ford now. Time was running out and the plans had to be made, the work completed. The sale would be finalized and the church closed in three days.

He needed Ford's participation not just because Ford knew the layout of the church, nor because it was a plan that required four hands. No, he wanted Ford's participation because it would signal a much stronger relationship between the deed and religious life; it would make Michael more comfortable with the idea that God was working through him if a man of God was also involved. He was certain enough to bring the plan to Ford, but carrying it out required Ford's presence as the physical representative of God.

"So, Father ... what do you say? Are you willing to risk God's work?"

Ford thought for a minute. Time for debate was quickly coming to an end. Decisions had to be made. Was he in or out?

"My name's James ... James Ford."

The decision had been made. He'd take a chance and destroy the building in order to prevent the diocese from selling itself to the state. Was it the righteous thing to do, a part of God's will? Perhaps yes, perhaps no. But one thing was increasingly clear for Ford, standing still couldn't be God's way. The church would not be turned into a den of thieves, and he'd risk doing the wrong thing in order to prevent it.

"I have it worked out, James. It's amazing what information you can get off the Internet."

"Not too fast," Ford cautioned, "I'm still making the mental adjustment."

"OK. Fine. Meet me here tomorrow. What time do you lock the door?"

"Shortly before dark," Ford replied.

"So, I'll be sitting in the last pew with all the supplies, around nine. I'll tell my wife I need to go to the office to take care of something."

Michael left the confessional and Ford sat there for a few minutes, thinking through what had just occurred. It was too late to change his mind, so he slowly lifted himself off the seat and made his way through the assignments and tasks for that day, all but one.

Most members of the church weren't around, but a few made plans to help Ford pack. He'd have to think of a way to avoid suspicion.

"Father Ford," Mimie paused as she took some books from the shelves in his office, "will you be okay?" She didn't worry about herself; she'd miss St. Barbara but she'd move to another location. Yet, she didn't think it could be that easy for Ford. St. Barbara was his life and it must be more difficult for him.

"I'll be okay, Mimie. Thanks for asking."

"I imagine you've already been assigned to another church." Brian, Mimie's husband—a pragmatic man, a business man—asked assuming the Church was something like the company for which he worked.

Ford didn't like having this conversation. He wanted to concentrate, but knew he had to provide answers. "I don't have the particulars yet, but I'm to meet with the Bishop soon. It's not unusual for there to be a short delay between parishes." This seemed to satisfy Brian.

Fran stepped around Mimie, grabbed a box, and readied herself to enter the conversation. "Father, I … we will miss you."

Ford knew the right answer, although he wasn't certain how heartfelt it was, "I will miss *all* of you as well."

This polite conversation went on for an hour or so, before Ford was able to come up with what he considered a good reason for not finishing more packing. "I think this is enough for today. You have other things to do, I'm sure. We don't have to finish right now. There's still some time."

There was no need to pack up all his belongings and the church items that were to be moved to another location. The fire would take care of those things he didn't pack. He'd need to put some of his belongings in boxes because it would look suspicious for him to not at least pretend to be moving at the time of the fire. He and the others filled seven boxes and positioned them in his office.

Although Mimie and the others were happy to help, the situation was tense. Everyone liked Ford, but this kind of time with him, and under these circumstances, was a departure from their normal interactions. Everyone welcomed an opportunity to leave. Palmer followed Ford's remark and said what the others were thinking, "Sure, Father. Just let us know when you want us to come back."

"I will." Ford began moving toward the door and signaled through his body language that they should follow him. Handing off the coats, Ford opened the door, shook hands, and smiled as his helpers exited.

With them gone, Ford spent time thumbing through the Bible, looking for nothing in particular but everything that might give him that deep sense of comfort with the decision he'd made.

CHAPTER FIVE

Michael spent the evening with his wife, Susan, showing her tenderness that hadn't defined their relationship for some time. It seemed so long ago when they'd first met—her stroking her short blonde hair, blue eyes glued to that book she was reading. He still remembered the dog-eared book, James Baldwin's *The Fire Next Time*. It was a book for class at the local college. He walked over. He was a much younger and more hopeful man then—one who believed college would actually change his life. Coffee in hand, he asked if he could sit with her— seeming somewhat disinterested, she agreed. That was the beginning, days together, nights together ... planning a future together. Could ten years really seem so long ago? They were no longer in college, and plans had changed. Both had jobs, new responsibilities, and a limited number of friends. They spent time with those friends some evenings, but for the most part they kept to themselves. They went to work, came home, watched a bit of television or read. And this was the pattern repeated day after day.

This night was different. They talked, held each other, and shared a connection that pleased and troubled her. She was left with a sense that something was wrong, but why disrupt closeness that was so pleasing and so long in the making with questions for which she really didn't believe she could withstand the answers? She decided to just enjoy it.

Evenings usually move quickly for Ford, so many small things to accomplish for a priest without an assistant, whose parish couldn't afford a housekeeper or church clerk for that matter. This day seemed to last forever. For Michael, the hours didn't matter any more; hours were no longer the way to measure time. As of this evening, he would measure it in terms of risk taken and deeds done, and clocks couldn't capture such moments. After this evening, he would measure time by memories of flickering flames.

CHAPTER SIX

It was shortly before nine o'clock. Ford locked the door and looked around the sanctuary to see Michael's outline on the last pew on the right side. Michael sat close to a depiction of one of the stages of the cross, but Ford couldn't make it out and his mind was too full with what was about to happen to remember which stage. "Does it really matter anyway?" Ford thought as he moved toward Michael.

Michael caught Ford's form but he couldn't make out Ford's expression, couldn't tell much from the shadow's movement; it was too dark for that.

"Father ... I mean James ... are you ready?"

"As ready as I can be to commit an act I'm not certain about," Ford responded, finally reaching Michael and seeing his face clearly for the first time. He thought back as he looked at Michael, trying to place him in the context of worship, church meetings, church events, but he couldn't.

Their bond was an odd one; both seeking to save a church through the destruction of a building. They would save it from what it would become otherwise. They were chasing their own moneychangers out, preventing God's temple from a use that would only soil it. Past connections, a handshake, a pleasant word, prior to this moment mattered little. In committing this act, Ford wanted to believe they were the new disciples of Christ, and the prior lives of the disciples were overshadowed by the task before them. Wasn't this the case? Anyway, it was too late for entertaining substantive doubt.

"James, this may sound odd," Michael said with a meekness that

31

startled Ford, "but can we have communion before doing this?"

"I imagine so," Ford said a little confused and wanting to move through the deed as quickly as possible, "but why?"

"It's a closeness to Jesus, isn't it? I mean it is taking in his body and blood and in a way becoming one with Christ, isn't it? It's like taking Jesus in before the fire consumes him."

"A bit more complicated than that, but I get the point." Ford went to the room where the elements were kept. Pushing past the vestments, he gathered the wine and wafers and headed back to the sanctuary where he found Michael on his knees at the altar, next to him a container of gasoline and rags. He stood in front of Michael and handed him the cup of wine.

"This is the blood of our Lord and Savior Jesus Christ shed for our sins." Michael drank and looked up at Ford who took the cup back and drank.

"This is the body of our Lord and Savior Jesus Christ broken for you and for many ..." The wafer dropped out of Michael's hand, but he picked it off the red carpet and ate it. Ford took a wafer, paused, and ate it.

"Thank you," Michael whispered before standing and gathering his goods. As he moved from the pew where he'd stored the supplies he poured gasoline—making a liquid trail to the front of the church, along the same path members used when approaching the priest for blessings.

Michael moved toward the wooden altar. Ford, not knowing exactly what he should be doing, but wanting to be active, to do something, walked toward the altar and collected sacred items, kissing them and putting them on one of the pews.

"It's too late to turn back. Lord I hope this is right" he thought as he walked back toward the altar. He wondered if his steps that evening toward the altar were anything like Jesus's steps in the temple as he pushed aside tables and moneychangers. Did Jesus feel any of what the priest was now feeling?

By this time, Michael had poured gasoline over the altar and along the carpet and choir pews, with gasoline soaked rags strategically placed.

Michael handed Ford a box of matches. As the priest lit a match Michael whispered to him, "and Jesus chased the moneychangers out of the temple, saying this temple will not be turned into a den of thieves."

Ford looked around at the stained glass windows only dimly lit by the moon. He looked at the pews that once held members of the community who came to this church for guidance and comfort. Thinking about the children who had been baptized and the couples married in this sanctuary, Ford looked at the wooden crucifix above the altar and touched the match to the gasoline that bathed the altar. The flames jumped, quickly caressing the crucifix and moving down the base of the altar. They wanted to watch as the fire consumed all in its path, but they knew they couldn't stay much longer. The flames were moving fast, so the two men ran through the supply room to the back of the church, through an exit that would allow them to remain covered by the night.

"It's done," Ford said out of breath and not knowing whether to celebrate or mourn. Michael didn't reply. He didn't know what to say. Instead he looked at Ford and motioned for him to follow.

Michael led him through a hole in the back fence. Looking around, they cautiously walked to Michael's car and climbed inside. The smell of smoke and gasoline quickly filled the car. It was now ten o'clock and, although it seemed to take forever, the process had gone fast.

"Look," Michael said, "you can see the flames through the windows. The fire's spreading."

Ford turned his head slowly afraid to look, but needing to see the outcome of the risk they had taken.

Slowly and deliberately, Ford spoke. "And Jesus went into the temple of God, and cast out all them that sold and bought in the temple, and overthrew the tables of the moneychangers, and the seats of them that sold doves."

He paused as the flames began to break through the building and lick the sky.

"It is written, my house shall be called the house of prayer; but ye have made it a den of thieves."

"That's the scripture," Michael said interrupting Ford. "That's the call to action, the demand for people like us to do something." They sat there looking at the church burn.

It took some time before the sound of fire trucks broke the silence and people began to look out their windows and step into the street. Ford and Michael were far enough away and the flames too engaging for anyone to take note of them.

The old, poorly maintained church began to collapse, sending flames high into the air. Ford and Michael sat in the car, watching the flames. Neither man could think of anything to say, no words of comfort, no clichés. They sat there—each waiting for the other to speak wisdom.

Outside there was noise and frantic activity, but inside the car they were still, thinking about a passage of scripture, and an act that had changed circumstances, while somehow leaving everything much too familiar.

CHAPTER SEVEN

Ford felt odd, but better than he had ever felt before. He felt new—not without some lingering questions—just new. He understood he couldn't mention this out loud. It would sound much too strange. But for the first time he felt alive, really alive—feeling his body touch the world. He had hidden for years, the black robe of the priest was not without meaning—it hid the body and all it entailed, making it invisible to view—a shadow without much substance. But now, in the car he was present, visible. He burned with feeling and he knew he couldn't let that feeling go.

"How do you feel?" Ford asked. He had to say something, and maybe these words—that sounded so stupid as they left his mouth—would give him an opportunity to explain this new feeling taking over him.

"What … what did you say?" Michael responded. He'd been in his own thoughts. He wasn't remorseful, didn't regret, didn't even fear discovery by the authorities. He just felt … and for the first time in a long while. Michael was soaking in that feeling when Ford asked his question.

"How do you feel?" Ford repeated.

"Okay, no … pretty good." Michael responded. "We did it. This makes a fucking difference, doesn't it?" The feeling of feeling was even stronger now. "Things won't be the same around here. Those other priests you work for have to understand now."

Ford knew what he meant. The Church, the institution beyond this now destroyed building, would take note of this righteous action.

Stop *The* Roman Catholic Church? Ford knew better than that. He'd been involved too long, had seen and experienced firsthand the way doctrine bleeds into life and shapes it, arranges it, and makes the most odd and belittling requests and actions seem spiritually necessary. Now that it was done, could this one act change the thinking and practices of an organization that is centuries old?

Ford responded, "Don't get me wrong. I feel like I've never felt before, but I'm not certain. It transforms our relationship to the Church … that's for sure; and maybe that's what's most important. But changing the Church, or even ending the plans for a halfway house …" Ford said this, thinking as he spoke—"but I believed it enough to go through with purging by fire."

Michael pushed. It wasn't the answer he wanted. It seemed to him so distant from the act they'd just committed. "It's important. It will make a difference." And he took a long pause before completing the thought: "Because it won't be our last move. This is the start of a mission."

Ford continued to look straight ahead, out the car windshield.

Michael turned to Ford and asked, "Where will you stay tonight?" Michael felt awkward asking the question. They'd destroyed a place for worship, and also Ford's home.

Ford would speak with the Bishop next day about his new assignment, but for now he knew he needed to stay near the church. People would look for him. Members of the church would want to make certain he was okay. And, he needed to be available to remove suspicion. He couldn't just vanish. How would that look, the priest—the shepherd—in charge nowhere near his flock?

"We will need to talk soon. The police will probably ask you questions and we need to figure out the right story, Ford." The priest knew this was right. He didn't want to give anything away by mistake.

"That sounds right," Ford replied without much concern. He got out the car, and closed the door. Ford would speak with the fire fighters, the police, and people from the neighborhood. He'd express concern, answer questions, and all this should take him through to early morning, and then he'd prepare to meet with the Bishop.

Michael started the car, and rolled down the window. "Talk

tomorrow?" Michael asked.

"After a meeting with the Bishop … the coffee shop two blocks south. 'Coffee For Goodness Sake' is the name."

"I know the place, say, 2 p.m.? I'm not going to work tomorrow."

Ford thought about the longwinded Bishop, and all the topics that would need to be covered sitting in the Bishop's mold-smelling office, with pictures of Saints neither could name with great certainty. And he said, "better make it 4."

Michael drove off, and Ford watched the car move down the street. When Michael's car was beyond view, Ford quickly and quietly joined the crowd. Once he was noticed, people approached and tried to comfort him; the fire department captain noticed him and began to ask questions. Members of the police department also had questions to ask.

CHAPTER EIGHT

Things had gone as planned. Ford had conversations with the appropriate people. He'd spent some time with Mimie and her husband in their home, talking about the fire and their memories of good times at the church. No one could sleep, and so they talked through the night. Ford hadn't been in the church building very long, but there was still a faint smell of smoke on his clothing. Mimie and Brian were willing to ignore it in their home, but they thought the Bishop might find it problematic. They made available use of their facilities, but Ford refused their offer of a shower, a change of clothing, and a ride. He said he was okay, but what he couldn't tell them was that something about the smell of smoke on his clothing gave him comfort and he wanted to keep that feeling.

He'd make his way on foot to the meeting with the Bishop. According to his watch, it was 8 a.m., and the meeting was to start at 11 a.m. He'd need to walk fast. He had no interest in eating, so food wouldn't delay him.

Ford arrived at the Bishop's office, and he walked inside. He took a seat. He'd be silent and wait. Ford didn't care for the Bishop. Never had. The Bishop was a show without substance—a religious leader who worked based on smoke and mirrors, and who loved all the elaborate rituals and church hierarchy. The priest was tired of all this formality, the layers of protocol. With the church gone, he realized that he'd never cared for this part of the tradition so much—even when he'd been the beneficiary of the reverence.

"Come in, Father Ford" the Bishop said. He was standing in the doorway, looking unfit in so many ways. His black suit a bit too tight. The Bishop was a large man, slightly bent, and with so many creases in his face that Ford thought they marked the atrocities he'd witnessed on behalf of the Church. The creases were a text for Ford, telling the story of tough years that could only be stored away, hidden from view, eating their way out of him.

"Yes," Ford replied and moved past the Bishop trying not to touch him as he stepped into the office. Ford took a seat in front of the massive desk. "Did the Bishop actually do any work behind that desk?" Ford wondered.

"Ford," the Bishop started, slowing drawing out the word in a way that annoyed Ford. FOORRRDDD. The Bishop continued, his body spread out in his chair, and his hands folded on top of the desk as if he was trying to hide something in the palm of his hands.

"Ford, we … ah … the Church is troubled by how you've behaved regarding the plans for the church on Hopkins Lane." The Bishop thought explaining too much might compromise his authority, but he couldn't leave it with those words.

"The plans for it are … ah, *were*, consistent with the needs of the Church, and you behave … ah, *behaved*, as if to suggest that one congregation supersedes the designs of the larger Church of Christ." It was an awkward pronouncement. The burning of the building took away the impact and purpose of his words, but the Bishop could think of no other way to start the conversation. He adjusted his tone and verb tenses to reflect this development, but the Bishop was determined to make his point. He'd thought long about what he'd say to Ford. He couldn't drop it. He was in charge and Ford would be dealt with.

"There has been a tragedy with that building, I understand," the Bishop continued, "but I am speaking to a larger point, to a larger concern."

Ford sat and listened, tensing up, and keeping his mind on what he and Michael had accomplished.

"We are concerned that you are forgetting your vows, losing perspective on your obligations and as a result doing damage to your ministry."

Ford jumped to his feet and exploded at the Bishop. Something about the fire, the way it made him feel different, emboldened Ford to respond to the Bishop as he never would have before. "What are you saying!" Ford countered. "Are you saying I won't have a ministry?!" Ford had never been so confident in his ministry and in his place with the Church, but he didn't think the Bishop was really in a position to say anything about it. Ford was angry and he couldn't hold it in.

"Forgetting my vows!"

The anger threw the Bishop, who now had to change his demeanor and try to calm Ford. He leaned forward, and countered Ford's explosion with a quiet request. "Ford, please, take your seat. I understand you are upset, and perhaps my phrasing wasn't the best. Let me restate my point. We both know you haven't always performed at your best. Some members—two, three, ten, or some other number didn't matter for the Bishop's point—of your church have raised questions concerning your commitment. This isn't just me, Ford. We think you have potential, but you must admit that at times you've lacked focus and passion."

There was some truth in the Bishop's words that Ford had to acknowledge. He stopped his rant, took his seat and composed himself.

"I'm sorry. I shouldn't have reacted like that."

The Bishop smiled with relief, and continued. "No, you will have a ministry. But you need to make certain you are following the leading of the Lord *and* the demands of the Church. You have obligations. Responsibilities that extend beyond what you may think the right thing to do." The Bishop talked with some confidence, enough, he hoped, to hide his discomfort with Ford.

"What do you have in mind?" Ford spoke trying to give the impression that he really cared what the Bishop thought. The fire, his fire, made the Bishop's concerns seem so small.

"First things first, Ford," the Bishop said as he shifted his hands to his lap—out of Ford's sight. "We have an additional issue to address—the fire."

The Bishop didn't seem to suspect anything. Should he? Was the Bishop hiding something? Covering up what he knew, waiting for Ford to slip up? Ford needed to control himself and let it play out.

The priest explained to the Bishop that he'd left the church as quickly as he could as soon as he began to smell smoke, but only after trying—without success—to find the source of the destruction and gather a few precious items. This explained the faint smell of smoke, the odd look Ford just knew was on his face, and his unusually angry response earlier to the Bishop.

"The fire has, well … temporarily altered plans for the local church."

The Bishop hoped the coded and indirect language suggested the deep importance of what he was to say, and that it had the type of vagueness needed to generate intrigue and awe—the stuff he thought might keep Ford under control.

"So, of course you can't go back there, even though that would have been temporary." Ford waited for the rest of this assignment. "The Roman Catholic Church won't suffer too great a loss. We are a spiritual entity with saving souls as our mission and that requires material resources. The good news is, in spite of the loss of the physical church, the land has the real value."

"What do you mean?" Ford was nervous and angry, but he sat trying not to show either. He couldn't afford to lose control again. The Bishop was in a position to do whatever he liked with Ford, and Ford knew this.

"It means, Ford, the deal with the state will continue. The land was purchased from us, and now the plans can move forward without the sticking point of modifying the physical building." The Bishop responded, feeling that he was in control. He had information that Ford didn't. It wasn't a matter of theology; they had both been trained the same. Church theology changed slowly, but he knew the workings of the Church in a way Ford didn't—could not.

Ford knew the fire had meant something, still meant something, but he had been in the priesthood long enough—had heard too many conversations, some not actually meant for his ears—to think the fire would end everything in his favor. But there was always hope … hope against hope. An impossible possibility of a kind was a thought that crept into his mind as he talked with Michael in the confessional, as he sat in the car with Michael after doing their work, and it stayed with him in the Bishop's office.

"So we aren't concerned with the building, Ford. We stand to collect the insurance money and the proceeds of the land sale ... It's complicated Ford. Too complicated to explain. The church isn't an issue. You, my friend, are an issue."

The priest had to know more, "How am I an issue?"

He wanted to jump up and grab the Bishop by the collar and shake him, but he couldn't. The priest would have to maintain his composure and listen.

"Well, Ford ..." the Bishop wanted to sound authoritative, "you are now a priest without a church." There was a pause meant to make certain both absorbed the full meaning and intent of that sentence.

He was Ford's bishop. In theory that said a lot; yet, in light of their interactions over the years, it meant nothing of importance to Ford. As far as the priest was concerned, for most of that time, he'd been bishop in name only.

"You can't go back to a church that doesn't exist." The bishop paused again for effect.

Ford wondered way the Bishop wasn't more emotional about the loss of the building, and why he'd repeated that obvious point about pastoring a church that had burned to the ground. It was in some disrepair, but it was still a beautiful building. And shouldn't a custodian of the Church be more upset? Shouldn't the Bishop show signs of concern and loss? Not wanting to give it too much thought, Ford shrugged it off as another sign of a Church gone wrong—the inability to demonstrate loss, regret ... humanity. Perhaps too many centuries moving between spiritual rhetoric and political maneuvering had made the Church somewhat callous?

"We believe you have some talent and energy, but you need to learn to control it." By this he meant learn to play by the rules and do as "we" say. "And," the Bishop continued, confident his pause had had effect, "we want to keep you in this city because you know this place, and we believe you can have a useful ministry here."

Ford was relieved a little, but only showed it with a small smile and slight shift in his chair.

"So ... we are thinking you might be most effective and have the most productive ministry by serving the parishioners at St. George

Church. You know the church, correct? Some miles from your former charge, a different neighborhood, but with its own set of challenges."

Ford wasn't clear why he was assigned to this church. Hadn't he been a problem for the Church? Disruptive? Rebellious? Now this church with economic resources and position in the community? He wouldn't ask the Bishop why.

Ford had heard of the priest who'd been in charge of that parish. He'd been too busy with his own parish's needs and challenges to get to know this other priest well. But still he had to ask the question: "And Father Connors, what will happen to him?"

The Bishop didn't like that question, that much was clear in the reddening of his face, his fidgeting in the chair, and the change in his voice.

"Father Connors … uh, has run into a spiritual challenge and will need time away from parish ministry to work on it."

He understood this was code for an increasingly visible problem facing the Church. Ford had his questions about doctrine, but at no point did he see these questions as an easy justification for this type of abuse. Sin should be dealt with, on this point he was firm. What troubled him, however, was his inability to consistently know what constituted sin—with a capital "S" and evil with a capital "E." The priest wouldn't entertain the possibility that he was also somehow responsible, somehow implicated. The blame could be isolated better than that. Connors was an easy example of what was wrong with the Church, and Ford hated him for that. Connors' actions damaged the Church. Ford respected ministry enough to want to protect the Church from predators of all sorts. He and Michael had given themselves to that effort just the night before.

This hatred could be useful, his animosity toward the Bishop instructive. He would figure out a way to combine the energy and passion generated by the fire with this new parish assignment.

"When do I begin my parish work?"

"This coming Sunday. I will be present to aid with the transition."

Ford knew the neighborhood. It was inside the loop, a place in transition. But this wasn't the same type of transition as what marked St. Barbara—not a move from one color of poverty to another. This inner city space around St. George was becoming the new domain of the mobile with means—with all the markers: Starbucks, fine dining carved out of old buildings. Lofts, townhomes, luxury cars parked in driveways across from lots awaiting renewal. These were the homesteads of urban pioneers, or so they liked to call themselves. They brought with them their own angst, their hidden gems. And Ford was going to have to deal with them.

"Is there a staff in place?" Ford asked with a smile.

"There's some assistance ... someone who cooks and cleans but doesn't live there and some other help." The Bishop didn't know all the particulars. This hadn't been one of his favorite parishes to visit, so he tried to end this part of their conversation. "Details can be worked out over the next few weeks."

The Bishop was thrown by what appeared something akin to happiness on Ford's part. He seemed okay with this new assignment. The Bishop expected some fight, if for no other reason than Ford was being moved away from the neighborhood he knew to one that stood in opposition to it.

"If there is nothing else, sir ..." Ford threw in the "sir" for good measure, to confuse the Bishop a bit—one last jab at him before leaving.

"That's all ... for now" was the reply.

Ford stood up. The Bishop, with a little effort, moved from his chair toward the door, shook Ford's hand, and moved aside.

Ford left the office, aware of his odor—sweat, smoke, and a bit of something else.

As he walked, he heard the Bishop call out, "Go to St. George Church. There's space for you. We can't have you living on the streets."

The priest thought about those words ... "living on the streets." Sleep outside. Jesus said the "foxes have holes and the birds of the air have nest, but the Son of Man has no where to lay his head." If Jesus could handle homelessness, as a minister of Christ he could expect his own discomfort, his own challenges.

Once outside Ford felt relief. He was away from the Bishop, undiscovered, and with a new charge from which to work. What would he do? This question pressed on him. He had a vague idea based on the sense of joy, of purpose, that came to him watching the church burn. It was now 2 p.m. and he would make his way to the coffee shop with a little time to himself to process it all.

Chapter Nine

"*Coffee for Goodness Sake.*"
Ford saw the sign and made his way through the wooden doors covered with flyers and signs—the typical "we are a community institution" markings of exchange and services available.

Ford had been in before, but he'd never come in smelling like smoke and looking so … bad. But they got all kinds in there, so the young woman near the door—with so many other things to occupy her thoughts—paid his condition no attention. Shop policy—as long as they pay, and don't disrupt others; no worries.

He was mindful of his appearance. He hoped it didn't say too much, didn't speak the wrong thing. Ford had never been so aware of his body before now. It wasn't the Christian way. His body had always been present. He knew this. It had always been part of his movement through the world and his work, of course. But he'd never really felt his body, understood its weight and work, until now. Ford liked it, but …

As he walked in, he was met by the strong smell of fresh coffee—the kind of coffee that wakes you up and keeps you up. And the shop had a good number of people all looking like they needed that type of jolt. Students from the area college—hair combed to look unkempt, tight jeans, and T-shirts that spoke their political views. And a few nonstudents stopping by to catch a break from whatever their day might include. They all sat at well-worn wooden tables, some round and others square. These were not Starbucks tables. They showed age—the markings of life. The floor was warped wood. Ford thought about all the other feet that had moved across that floor. Did any of those feet carry people who'd done anything like what he'd done?

The walls could use some paint, it had been awhile; but much of the wall space was covered with posters and old concert announcements for jazz musicians and rap artists, both matching the music played but overpowered by the conversations, orders taken at the counter, and the sound of coffee drinks being made.

The shop was dimly lit with small lamps for those wanting them. Ford liked that and found something comforting today in being a shadow.

It had been a long walk, and he was looking forward to some time to sit and think before Michael arrived.

3 p.m. ... he had an hour. In the hurried activities of the night before, he hadn't taken much of his property—had let it burn. But he did have his wallet and there was enough cash in it for a snack—some coffee and a sandwich. Ford hadn't eaten for a good number of hours, and now he was beginning to feel it. The burn in the pit of his stomach from excitement and nerves was replaced by the pang of hunger.

"Large coffee and one of those sandwiches, please." He pointed to the wrapped chicken salad sandwiches.

"Anything else?"

"No." Ford handed her his money. She placed the change on the counter, and Ford noticed the black nail polish ...

"Cream, milk and sugar are over there." The young woman—red hair, green eyes, small frame, and no tattoos under her white T-Shirt and faded jeans—pointed to a corner of the shop but her mind and attention seemed elsewhere, not on Ford.

Without paying much attention, he grabbed his items, and headed to a table in the back, away from windows and listening ears.

He thought the sandwich and coffee would taste better because of his new take on life, but they tasted the same. Nothing special. But it was good to be off his feet, and away from the Bishop's office. He sat there, in the corner, away from the others. He'd just be there, not thinking too hard, just sorting his thoughts, processing his new church, and wait for Michael.

Ford sat—dirty clothes, sore muscles, the fire on his mind and his mind on fire.

CHAPTER TEN

4:01 p.m.

Michael walked in. Unlike Ford, his clothes were clean, hair combed, and a confident stride led him through the door. He looked around for Ford and discovered him hunched over a cup of coffee, in the corner, in the back. Giving little attention to why Ford selected that location, Michael walked over and took the seat opposite him.

"You look like shit, priest." Michael said with a laugh meant to speak to the humorous nature of the situation but also to avoid more substantive remarks.

Ford saw the humor in the remark, but also found it a bit offensive. After the night before, shouldn't this conversation begin with something more penetrating? He wasn't certain what he expected Michael to say, and he had nothing groundbreaking to contribute. Michael, Ford remembered, had been more provoking, more compelling, more penetrating in the confessional when they first talked. Now … not so much. Ford smiled an awkward smile, and shifted in his chair.

"Yea, well. My home is gone remember?" This seemed inadequate, but he said it anyway. "Have you heard anything else about it? What are they saying on the news about it?" Ford asked hoping that nothing had destroyed their cover.

"Nothing to worry about … By the way, what the fire didn't get the firefighters' effort to save the church got."

Once Michael finished, Ford knew it was his turn. He'd need to share the information the Bishop provided.

"I met with the Bishop earlier." Ford said this knowing it wasn't

THE NEW DISCIPLES · 49

news to Michael; he'd mentioned it yesterday. But he wanted to provide context, to get Michael on the same page, get him to see the connections as he made them.

"I know."

"You won't believe it …The Church seems positioned to make even more money with the building destroyed. Now there are fewer PR problems and more money—insurance and the sale of the land. The land is the big deal here."

Michael listened, assuming Ford was hiding the lead.

"Besides that," Ford was getting to it … "I've been assigned to a new church, St. George."

"I know the church," Michael interrupted. "It's in a different type of neighborhood."

Ford nodded his agreement, and continued. "Seems like what we did was for nothing." He said it but didn't actually believe it. "The Church gets more, and the people in the community get a reminder of how shitty life can be."

"It's not that simple," Michael reminded him. "Yes, the Roman Catholic Church marches on, but maybe we need a different target, a different way of trying to do something that will last. No grand designs, no one event that changes everything. Instead, maybe we do smaller things—deeds that might go unnoticed initially but they add up to have a major significance."

This was the kind of thing Ford wanted to hear. So he leaned forward and took it all in. "What do you have in mind?" Ford thought this question was an appropriate response. It was inviting. Interesting.

Michael was thinking it through, and outlining a question … more like a game plan on the fly. That seemed okay to him. "Well, rather than trying to change the Church, we change the people— remove the problems." Michael had more to say, and he'd let it flow. "I remember reading Thoreau's *Walden*, and I remember the part about being good people as opposed to simply doing good stuff." Ford remembered the book as well, but not those details. It was about a vague transcendentalism for him, although he wasn't certain what to make of that philosophy.

"Maybe," Michael continued "we weed out the people who can't be good and in that way slowly—one church at a time—leave behind only those who stand a chance of doing good because they are good. Do you see what I mean?"

Ford wasn't certain he understood, but he thought those years of seminary training should count for something—if nothing else he'd been trained to at least pretend he understood things. After the fire and the conversation with the Bishop, Ford found it difficult to imagine another ministry like he'd had at St. Barbara and the churches before that one. Sin and evil remained important to address, but there were limited opportunities to address these in any significant way in those ministries. He thought there should be more for him, an opportunity to address the only dimension of the priesthood that held ongoing but unfulfilled interest for him. What Michael offered might not be the answer, but he could think of nothing more compelling. He'd take a chance, and perhaps—he hoped—find that element of ministry missing for so many years. "Sure," he replied, hoping Michael would say more.

"Rather than setting fires, we try people by fire. Rather than destroying property, we destroy people who've proven themselves unable to be good."

The air was thick, and although the crowd in the coffee shop had increased over the minutes they'd been in place, in the back, they got lost in conversation—talking quietly enough not to call attention to themselves, although they had no real concern for the others in the room. The customers were just background noise.

"Maybe we kill, Ford." Michael concluded with this simple statement and he waited for Ford's reaction. He knew based on their initial conversations that it could take Ford some time to come around. So he waited.

"Kill ..."

Ford was taking it in but had to hear the word again—this time from his mouth. He wanted to feel affronted; he wanted to be disturbed. He wasn't. He had destroyed in the name of the Lord, destroyed to protect and restore. Was there much difference here? Removing opposition to the will of God, how could that be a bad thing? Didn't the Bible condone death for the sake of the greater good—God's plan for human beings and the world in which they live? Yes, it did; and, so, why not now? So many communities had been destroyed, with their demise recorded in scripture. If God is consistent through time and is protective of God's people, how could the removal of those opposed to righteousness be wrong? Violence was a part of salvation history, and it was typically brought about through human agents working on behalf of God. Blood sacrifice in so many forms was part of the story—from Hebrew Bible stories of punishment and scapegoats, to the Christian story of the sacrifice of Jesus the Christ for the sins of humanity. Yes, blood, pain, suffering, death—all part of the story of human advancement consistent with the will and aims of God. No way around it, killing wasn't necessarily a problem for Christians like he and Michael. In fact, it might be a requirement of contemporary disciples of Christ.

"Thou Shalt not Kill," Ford was familiar with that scripture. But it had to be placed in context. It had to do with proper treatment of those within one's group, and it clearly never ruled out murder. After all, the Children of Israel secure the Promised Land by killing those in their way. Maybe he and Michael had a similar task—clear the way of all who work against the will of God.

Ford was working to make theological sense of what Michael proposed. This is how he'd been trained to think through life—to put it in line with the sacred text, church doctrine, and tradition. Those things were flexible. That had always been the case for the Church—why not its disciples? He needed to work through this, and he realized he had a limited amount of time. He needed to respond to Michael in real time. Yes, violence and murder—deception and the like littered the Bible (and the Church for that matter). They were an important, a vital, story within the saga of human salvation.

Perhaps God was calling them—he and Michael—to continue this process? He and Michael were the unlikely, the new disciples of Christ who would take up where other disciples had fallen short. They would do whatever was necessary to weed out those whose words and deeds damaged the meaning of being Christ-like. The fire, his conversation with the Bishop, and now this challenge from Michael sparked something in Ford.

"Maybe we are a new type of disciple," Ford finally spoke. "We will do the work of Christ that others can't or won't … bloody work, the mission of Christ, and a divine charge that involves inflicting pain to safeguard the body of Christ. To kill, in order to save."

Ford paused, and then continued with the idea. Something about perceiving himself a new and bold type of disciple pushed him forward, urged him beyond his comfort zone. "We'll be disciples who are serious and assured … the type not impacted by things that cause others to freeze in place; the type of disciple, like the Bible says, who can handle serpents without harm, drink poison without effect. Powerful people of God."

This was more risk, more bodily involvement than Ford had known before. Until the other night, the communion with fire, Ford had never put himself on the line. There had been a clear distinction between what he thought—or preached—and what he did. Both were rather bland. Some emotion but only when appropriate. No risk. Nothing lost, no threat of personal involvement. If not for the fire, even his protest against the selling of the church and its transformation into a halfway house would have just been so much talk—self-righteous theology to be sure; but, impotent ethics as the end product.

"A time for killing, Michael. All for the glory of God and the subduing of dangerous men." Rather poetic, Ford thought as he spoke.

"That was much easier than I thought it would be," was Michael's response but only to himself. Out loud he said, "I don't know what to say." He thought this was odd, but it was also on his mind, so he said it.

Ford was relieved because he wasn't alone in feeling some anxiety. He was certain committed actions were demanded, but he was anxious nonetheless.

There was silence after Michael's comment, and Ford could stand it only so long. He had to say something, and what he said needed to carry their mission forward. His confidence was growing, slowly but growing. Whatever he said needed to demonstrate this.

"We've said enough," he lingered over the words for effect and affect. "We started something. It didn't accomplish everything we wanted. But we were naive, really naive. It was a baptism by fire."

His comment had the desired effect. Michael felt more assured.

"We need to be careful," Michael continued the momentum of the discussion.

"Of course."

"I mean really careful. Who do we kill, and how do we decide?" Michael wanted to be certain death came only to those who deserved it. Even if they could work this out, Michael understood, there was another consideration.

"Ford, have you ever killed?" he asked although he knew the answer.

"No."

"How can we do it? The church was different. I mean … we've never killed before. How? Using what? Overpower the victim? What?"

Michael knew these questions were important, and he needed to ask them although the idea of killing had been his. It seemed to be their process: a bold statement, a series of questions, affirmation of the bold statement, and so on. After all, Michael reasoned to himself, he wouldn't be the first person of God wanting to act on faith, wanting to do something radical for God, and being committed to doing it; but, still having some doubt and moments of uncertainty that require affirmation. Moses, David, Peter and a host of others also had these times of human frailty in the face of a grand mission. These questions he now asked all pointed in one direction: Could they actually get it done, and without getting caught? Did they have the heart to do it? Could they develop the skill to take life from someone who desperately wanted to keep it? And could they do it without a great deal of mess and commotion?

They were both firm—as much as they could be and at least for stretches of time—about what they needed to do but now the mechanics of murder had to be addressed. This wasn't theory anymore, no "what ifs." How would they select and dispose of their victims?

Pulling from his years as a priest and the way in which questionable activities took place without much notice, Ford began to think through Michael's questions.

"They need to come to us, Michael."

"What do you mean?"

"They need to come to us," Ford repeated.

As he spoke this statement again he thought of all the people who'd come to Catholic churches, and Catholic priests, for assistance of some kind. Many received help. Others were damaged by priests who'd turned predator, and who had motives other than spiritual healing. But this one thing was certain, priests—regardless of their various agendas—did little to recruit or find their confessees. They came to the Church looking for a priest. Some found priests who had an interest in the well-being of the soul, and who gave them a formula for getting themselves together. Other priests took people coming as an opportunity to meet their own needs. The first type of priest treats anyone, and the other model of the confessor looks for a particular type and then covers their actions as priest with the authority granted by their suits, white collars, and religious words. Of course, he and Michael weren't predators. They would be doing God's work by helping to move out of the way those not committed to a righteous path, and so they would get rid of predators and others incapable of being good. They would pick carefully, and depend on the damned exposing themselves. Ford even had a theological rationale for this decision. He'd learned about it as a seminarian—redemptive suffering.

Everyone who believes in God asks questions about God and about what God is doing with and for humans in light of suffering in the world. What can you say about God's justice in light of systematic oppression and destruction of life? Some people, the professor told Ford and the other students in class, respond by denying God. According to the Church, these are the unfortunate ones who will never know eternal life. There are others who try to avoid the question by filling their minds with other thoughts and their hands with work enough to keep them busy. Their answer is really "I don't know," whispered from tight lips. Those who answer this way can't deny God, nor can they affirm God's work in the world with great certainty. The last group can. They find in human suffering opportunity for goodness. God, their reasoning goes, uses suffering as a way to teach people, to make the faithful recognize that true contrition in some cases comes only through pain and perhaps even surrender of physical life. It was this last possibility that Ford connected to this new mission he and Michael would undertake.

"They will come for contrition and penance, and the pain, the suffering endured will be the completion of their deserved punishment. Certain mortal sins destroy the soul, and words of absolution won't end this, their redemption will require more. For them, forgiveness requires surrender of the physical body. In this case, the only way to come to Christ is death. Contrition and penance, in some cases, require death."

Ford knew he had to say more. He couldn't stop.

"These are people of deep guilt, who can't be redeemed ... their only hope is the cleansing power of death."

Michael listened, and was glad—or at least he suspected he should be glad—to have a theological reason for what they must do. Yet, deep somewhere in him where theology means only so much, he didn't really need this justification. If nothing else, he believed telling this story of deserved suffering was beneficial for Ford. It would keep Ford focused. Less concerned with theology and more concerned with ethics—what they should do, not what they should say or think—Michael pressed on. He accepted the idea of deserved punishment in the form of death, and he believed with all the faith he could muster that God called them to the task.

Ford's words—penance and contrition—suggested something, but Michael wanted clarity. He had to know precisely what Ford had in mind. He drew himself up, sat firm in his seat and asked, "Yes, Ford, they come to us, but exactly how do they come to us? Mass? Weekly meetings? They come looking for help, but come to what exactly?"

"The confessional," Ford said slowly, carefully. He was thinking through all the hours, all the days, weeks, and years sitting in the wooden box.

"You know," he continued, "contrition, confession, satisfaction ... the sacrament of confession. The confessional. They will need to come to the confessional to lift the burden of their misdeeds. It's the practice of the Church. They kneel, and whisper their story."

Michael didn't respond. He wasn't certain what to say, so he decided to listen.

"The confessional, it's perfect." Ford's excitement was increased. "Think about it, we first talked in the confessional. People tell the priest things they tell no one else because the confessional is a special place—a place of deep consideration, a space of special reflection, a sacred place."

Michael remembered conversations with Ford in the confessional, and he wanted to know more about what others told him in the box. But, he thought, could Ford really see the person, wasn't that part of what made it anonymous? The priest can't see the person, right? He had to ask. "Ford, how will that work? You won't see the person and you can't remember the voice and place it with a face later. You may never hear the person outside the whispered conversation in the confessional."

Ford knew this could be a problem in some Catholic churches where the physical structure of the confessional space prevented the priest from seeing. Even this never stopped a priest from putting together sins and faces. How many stories had he heard from other priests about the sexual practices, petty thefts, and other practices of congregants? He also knew some work had been done on St. George, since Vatican II made Roman Catholicism more user friendly. (He remembered being annoyed that St. George got work done on it while his St. Barbara was ignored.) The confessional arrangement had been changed. He'd train himself to make out faces through the screen, and he might be able to pull the screen so that it isn't completely secure—leaving some of the facial features outlined.

"I can figure that out. The confessional at St. George isn't Fort Knox. People create the security, people can compromise the anonymity when a higher good requires it." Ford had more to say. He knew Michael expected and needed him to say something else. After all, he was the priest, not Michael.

"I listen to the confessions, push for details, and tell you about the people who deserve our attention. They come to us, Michael. They come to the confessional, and basically ask us to fix them. But only we know that fix is death."

Ford needed to place this ministry he was outlining into the context of their initial call to ministry back at St. Barbara. He had to point out the spiritual connection between then and now. "Michael, God is requiring something different from us. St. Barbara involved a destruction of the church's mission, a surrender of its people for the sake of money. It was a type of mortal sin, I think, but on an institutional level. It wouldn't be the first time a religious institution called into question its connection to God—its ethical standing—for the sake of material gain. God wanted us to attack failings through the purging effects of fire. The church continued, as the Bishop made clear; but we did what God wanted. And now, although the larger Church continues its relationship with the state, God wants to use us to address the people who make up the Church. The parishioners who in various ways mirror the worst aspects of behavior, who, perhaps in their private and professional dealing, are also perverting the gospel of Christ and our obligations to live a Christ-like existence."

Ford paused, collecting his thoughts and seeking more inspiration before continuing, "They seem different—institutional church against individual parishioners; still they point to a similar problem of challenging God's will for human life in its fullest and in relationship to the best of the faith. God started us with attention to the institution, that's what was needed at the time, what we could understand at the time. Now God is directing us, calling us to address the problem in another way. But the same God, the same calling on us to be good disciples."

Michael sat back in his chair, crossed his legs, and an odd smile lit his face. The kind of smile that creeps up when you find something funny that shouldn't be. It's the type of smile when someone falls, or slips. Michael's was a smile that was about someone else in pain, and the joy knowing it can be a productive pain. It's the joy of distance, but at the same time being close enough to help or harm. This feeling was strong and moved through his whole body. It shouldn't be fought; it was a gift.

He felt like God's special mercenary, with a special relationship to God's will—a relationship involving a willingness to do what others fear. He was certain Ford must be feeling the same thing. He was seeing the connection between the two—St. Barbara and St. George.

"When do you start at the new church?"

"Soon."

Ford and Michael finished up in relative silence. Enough had been said. Their last words were brief.

"I'll see you at church." Michael knew attending St. George would be easy enough, a different route, but easy. After all, it wasn't a matter of finding a service that appealed to him, that met his spiritual needs and desire for community. He was going for work, to do God's work.

"Yes," Ford replied before picking himself up, and heading to the door. He knew it wouldn't be good to have Michael give him a ride. He'd need to walk, but it would also give him time to think, to further embrace the new phase of their ministry.

CHAPTER ELEVEN

Ford arrived late, tired, disoriented, and broke. He knocked on the door and someone answered who he assumed was assigned to care for the house after the former priest's quick departure. He paid no attention to the person—a woman, maybe mid-fifties. Black hair? Gray hair? Heavy? Light? It was a blur. He was tired and had a lot on his mind.

"Good evening, sorry to arrive so late … I'm Father Ford."

"Yes, I know. The Bishop called today. Your room is ready. Follow me," she said and moved away from the door, and down the hall. She was making every effort to be polite, but she did want to get home and a priest in dirty clothes, unkempt in general, wasn't what she expected. He no longer smelled of smoke. That had dissipated, but he looked no better than he had earlier in the day; in fact, the hours had only made his appearance more haggard.

Ford followed her, and, as he moved, he thought about all the events that brought him to this evening in a new ministry. He was happy, tired, anxious. He moved behind her feeling the full weight of his body in the world. And it mattered; it would make a difference.

They traveled past a study, past a kitchen, another room, another room, and finally the bedroom that would be his. The spaces he passed were dark, but not simply because it was evening. There was another reason for it, just the drab nature of the place.

His room had an old double bed, with new sheets and big pillows. There was a wardrobe, a chest of drawers with a large mirror. He saw no pictures or paintings on the walls, and the bathroom was easy to ignore. The rug on the floor had an odd design, not flowers, yet something like flowers in shades of blue and red on a faded tan background.

"The basics are here," she said holding out her arm as if she were some game show hostess pointing out a prize to be won. It was awkward. "If you need anything else, let me know. The Bishop said I should take care of you … for as long as you … I mean I am here."

"Thank you," Ford replied, trying to be polite but just wanting her to leave.

"Is 7 okay for breakfast? I can arrive earlier, but is 7 okay?"

"That's fine."

"And lunch, at 12, and dinner at 6:30? It would be helpful if I could leave for home around that time … is that okay?"

"That's fine."

"Okay. It's late and with your permission, I'll be on my way."

"Fine, thank you."

With that she left. It was all odd, and Ford just wanted to sleep. He closed the door, and faced his new home.

He didn't have a toothbrush, comb, pajamas, or anything else that would constitute the raw material for calling it a night and getting ready for bed. Pulling off his dirty clothes, it hit him again that St. Barbara was gone, consumed by what he knew was healing fire. The members of that church would feel loss, but with time that would end and they would enter new churches. Some had said as much in the days before the fire; they said it in a way not meant to offend Ford by lessening his value to them. They meant to assure him they had the ability to move on.

He took off his glasses and the world was a blur. Pushing back the covers—it was the beginning of summer and no need for so many covers—he crawled into the bed, curled up, and waited for sleep.

He wasn't certain how long it took, but he felt himself drifting off … thinking about the conversation with Michael, wondering if Michael was also nodding off, and knowing first thing in the morning he'd need to walk through the church and study the confessional. It was now 9:30 p.m., soon to be another day.

Ford slept.

Chapter Twelve

Ford slowly opened his eyes and looked at the blank, off-white walls. He got up, washed his face, and used the washcloth to clean his teeth. He dressed in his dirty clothes, sat on the bed, and put on his shoes before moving out the door.

Looking at his watch—the old watch his father had given him when he said he was going to become a priest—it was later than he thought.

9:00 a.m.

Moving down the hall, he stopped at the kitchen where he could smell coffee and could see a plate with toast and jam on the table. He wasn't hungry, stomach still in a bit of a knot. But the food was there and the coffee, and he didn't want to offend. The day couldn't start with him ignoring her efforts in the kitchen. Ford sat down at the old, wood table in one of the large ebony chairs. He pulled the plate near him, grabbed toast and then put it down to open the jam. Spreading the strawberry jam on the toast he thought of blood; he poured the coffee and thought of dark blood. Why blood? He thought maybe God was preparing him for work that had to be done. Maybe he was just nervous, or overly tired.

Ford drank the coffee and ate the toast. He placed the cup, saucer, and plate in the sink. Food in his stomach, dirty clothes on his back, he moved down the hall looking for a door leading to the church—or something that would point him in the direction of the sacred space. He'd worry about new clothes and other items later. But for now he wanted to walk the church, get a sense of the space where he'd minister.

The priest wasn't certain how much activity there was at the church during the week, but he wanted to take advantage of the morning. After seeing the church, he'd looked for staff—anyone who could get in the way of the work he and Michael needed to accomplish.

As he walked he thought to himself, St. George Church ... St. George, patron saint of soldiers, slayer of the Dragon. "Rich, too rich," the priest said softly and smiled.

Ford came to a door, somewhat reminiscent of a door at St. Barbara that led into the church proper from the parsonage. He turned the knob on the big, ebony door and opened it. Entering a set of offices, Ford pushed forward. The spaces were empty. Nothing special about these spaces—desks, chairs, pictures of saints on the walls, pictures of church leaders where there were no saints, rugs worn from so many footsteps for whatever reasons. Ford wanted to limit his thinking about these rooms, these quiet spaces, because he remembered the conversation with the Bishop and knew why the other one was no longer priest-in-charge.

How much pain had that other priest caused young bodies behind these closed doors? How many times had he tried to quiet that pain and end the tears that dripped down those cheeks, and ignore other bodily fluids evidencing the deeds conducted? Young ears in these rooms had heard how many passages of scripture, taken out of context, and how many pieces of Church doctrine warped to meet his erotic needs? He'd had similar thoughts concerning the bedroom but eased his mind with a thought. It wasn't the former priest's bedroom; it was a different space. No one would put him in that other priest's old bedroom.

These destructive moments weren't anything Ford wanted to consider for too long. He pressed on trying to convince himself that what he and Michael planned would help to make up for the damage this other priest, one the children called Father, had done.

Chapter Thirteen

After walking for a few more minutes, trying to remove from his mind those unpleasant thoughts of hurting flesh, Ford found the sanctuary.

It was a magnificent space. There were images of St. George for whom the church was named, upon his horse, killing the dragon. Stained glass windows of Jesus that told the story of the savior from birth to death, and resurrection. Columns marking out the sanctuary and elegant chairs lining it, facing the grand marble altar, spoke to new wealth spent on worship rather than more mundane dimensions of the church—living quarters and office spaces. Gold candlesticks and other items were arranged on the elaborate cloth covering the white marble altar. Ford, just feet from the altar with the space for the choir behind it, turned 360 degrees to take it all in. And as he turned, words came to him: "Take off your shoes, for the ground upon which you stand is holy." But this was quickly followed by another thought—one carried over from St. Barbara Church and just as relevant here—"you have turned this into a den of thieves."

Ford would preach in this space, introduced to the parish by the Bishop, and without much comment on the whereabouts of the former priest once in charge of this flock. He assumed the Bishop would bumble through some remarks that made little sense and he would need to say something as the new priest to introduce himself . . . There was time to work on the sermon. If needed, he could always use something from his days at St. Barbara. How likely was it that people at St. George Church would have heard one of his sermons before? It was a chance he was willing to take, if it meant something useful in terms of his larger mission. His work revolved around the confessional, not the pulpit.

After taking another look around the sanctuary, Ford moved toward the confessional. Everything hinged on this; he'd had this feeling even as a seminarian thinking about the nature of sin and evil. The sermons weren't the most important part of his ministry because they couldn't really redeem or transform lives. Not even communion, with the body and blood of Christ present, could counter the deeds of humans committed Monday through Saturday, and most likely Sunday after service as well. There weren't enough hours in the day for people to read scripture, theology, and church creeds with energy sufficient to redeem themselves. All this was really the work of the confessional—where the things we hide from all others are spoken in the open and acknowledged, and where, Christians assumed, mortal sins were absolved with the proper ritual motions, and a limited commitment to the body.

The confessional. He'd study the confessional. Feel its dark wood, know the patina on the few pieces of metal and the sheen on the wood. The carvings on the confessional he'd also remember. The priest pushed the screen to see how it felt and how much energy was needed to slide it. Ford moved the screen with great care to figure out just how much space could be left before the confessor realized the priest was watching. He'd memorize the smell of that odd box, and map out the bend of his body as he sat inside it, and the shifting of his weight and the tilt of his head as he heard those inevitable words—"Forgive me Father for I have sinned. It has been …"

Ford wasn't certain how much time he'd spent sitting in the confessional thinking, studying, and planning. He looked at his watch. 11:30 a.m.

Ford thought he'd work his way back to his room, rest for a moment to put his thoughts of the confessional into relationship with everything else with which he needed to be concerned. Included in these other things was purchasing supplies. He'd use his credit card to get a suit or two, and other things a priest starting work at a new parish should have.

Ford made his way back to the room, and upon entering found

that the woman—he didn't know her name—had provided some basic supplies, things like toothpaste, toothbrush, a brush, comb, soap, and fresh linens. The priest would sit for a few minutes, then eat lunch, and finally make his way out.

CHAPTER FOURTEEN

Ford purchased a couple of suits and other pieces of clothing from the store he'd used since his arrival in the city—nothing spectacular. He had everything he needed in order to perform his tasks—meetings, various masses during the week as soon as he was responsible for them, Sunday, confessions to hear …

Once back at the parish house he stopped in the kitchen and waiting for him was another plate of food. Still warm, so he sat, ate, and put the dishes in the sink.

7:15 p.m.

It was too early for bed, too late for much of anything else. So, he turned on the small television in his room and flipped the channels until he was ready to sleep.

Pajamas on, teeth brushed, face washed, into the bed. Ford slept with ease and comfort, and awoke in the morning ready to have a day just like the last.

Friday.

He thought he'd hear from Michael, who might want to gather some information about the church. But Michael didn't call the church. Did he even have the number? No visit. That would have been a dumb move anyway. So Ford went through the day trying to find something to occupy his time, while staying out of the way of the woman he couldn't name. He prepared for sleep as he had the night before.

Saturday morning.

Ford hadn't given much thought to his sermon for Sunday, although he'd had plenty of time for it. No interruptions, no visits, no masses to lead because the Bishop made other arrangements. He wanted Sunday to be the first time the parish encountered formally Father Ford.

Between his meals on Saturday, he worked on a sermon. This was as hard as the sermon he needed to give to prepare the parishioners of St. Barbara for the closing of their church. He, despite his at times mixed feelings about them, found himself thinking that he should be with the people of that church—wherever they were gathering—to ease their minds. But what could he tell them? The Church had betrayed them, and his presence wouldn't change that. He'd try to correct his failure with them through his new ministry at St. George. They are all connected he wanted to believe.

For a moment, Ford felt sorry for himself. "It's the Bishop who is denying the people their priest," he thought. This didn't linger long. He didn't appreciate nor respect the Bishop, and he wouldn't give him that type of authority.

He needed to give a sermon that settled his mind—and if it annoyed the Bishop (indirectly at least) all the better. Just thinking about the Bishop sitting there, face turning red, large round body visibly uncomfortable but without the ability to do anything about the sermon was enough to put Ford's mind at ease for the moment. His sermon wouldn't really have this impact, but the possibility of this reaction was a welcomed distraction.

By bedtime the sermon was in rough draft—good enough—and he would make the final revisions as he delivered it. He'd been preaching that way for a good number of years.

New suit, collar, and polished shoes, Ford was ready for Sunday. Of course his robes were destroyed in the fire, but there were others available for his use. It would be fine. The priest prepared for bed, thinking about the new faces he'd encounter tomorrow. What would these parishioners think of him? What would they know about St. Barbara Church?

In bed, stretched out, Ford wondered what it would feel like to have a knife plunged in his side; to feel a club against his head; or, to feel fire burning his skin. Is that how Michael and I will kill?

He drifted off to sleep.

Morning. 7:05 a.m.

There was a faint knock on the door, and he responded. "Ah …" Ford was disoriented and desperately trying to see the familiar in what was still a strange space. "Ah …" he looked around him, and it hit him. Yes, St. George … my room. Sunday.

"Yes, ah, yes … I am up."

The priest wasn't certain who knocked or why. Would this wake-up call happen every Sunday? It was unusual, but he'd been sleeping hard and long, and could use the help. This was a special Sunday, his first at St. George, and it had to go well.

"I'm up," the priest reported again, as he swung his body around and put his feet on the floor. Ford moved to the bathroom, turned on the light, and opened the shower door. Clothes coming off, he entered the shower and turned on the water. "Cold!" Ford clinched his body, adjusted the water and put his head under it.

"This is a new time for us …" He said, rehearsing his sermon. Was that start to the sermon okay? Did it have enough energy?

"… in the life of this church. We come here for many different reasons, carrying with us our own issues and concerns. And in this place we find forgiveness, healing, community," Ford said as he lathered and washed himself.

Stepping out the shower, Ford felt the words in his mouth, "for some this isn't possible, in another part of town, a church is but a memory …" No. He couldn't say that. It wasn't in the sermon as he'd written it, and he wouldn't say it. He had a different mission. The priest remembered Jesus' rejection of his mother and sister as his obligation. He, like Jesus, would embrace a larger purpose for life—all who do the will of God are his family.

CHAPTER FIFTEEN

7:50 a.m.—dressed and ready.

Ford left his room and moved down the hallway back to the door that lead to the church offices. There was activity, more bodies moving around then he expected to find. Everyone polite and eager to meet him, he was moved from one outstretched hand to another. "Good morning, Father."

"Hello, Father."

"Good morning, Father."

"Everything is in order, Father."

"The Bishop is waiting for you, Father."

Ford entered another room, not paying attention, but led by the voices and outreached hands. "Good morning … good morning … hello … good morning. Thank you …"

Robe on, ready.

Ford's mind wandered—going through the motions, thinking about the sermon and not really hearing the words spoken by the Bishop. He'd been a priest long enough to go through mass on autopilot.

"Good morning …" the Bishop said, and Ford tuned out again.

"God's will shall be done, and the Church under the guidance of God, through prayer, has assigned you a new priest."

Ford caught this and quickly moved back to his own thoughts; he and the Bishop knew the people in those pews didn't want the details, the rather mundane way in which he was actually chosen. They probably had a clue as to the former priest's behavior but that wasn't Sunday morning conversation.

"Father Ford, as you know, led St. Barbara until the unfortunate events of recent days. We have moved quickly, you might say, but not without firm confidence earned through prayer that we are providing you with the correct leadership."

There were more words, and Ford heard some of them. And then he heard the Bishop say, "Father Ford …" A pause, and again, "Father Ford."

This was odd, not the way a sermon was introduced. It caught Ford by surprise. Maybe the Bishop was trying to embarrass him … It didn't really matter. The priest had a job to do. Ford stood, and moved to speak.

Ford entered the space set apart for the word of God, and looked around. How many others had been here, stood in this place? Did it really matter how many—when the Church provided the theological blueprint? How much variation on a theme could there be in a Roman Catholic sermon? How far from the church's script could he be if he continued to be placed in parishes? The priest continued this internal conversation as he prepared to speak, script placed on the large wooden frame of the lectern, body covered in the proper garb and positioned firm with hands gripping the sides of the wooden framed box, looking out at the flock.

There were about three hundred people looking back at him, curious and anticipating what the new priest would say.

Ford looked at them, trying to see faces and placing those faces with particular life stories. Middle-class, college educated, rather lazy on social justice but putting in overtime trying to secure their take on the "American Dream." White for the most part, with a sprinkling of blacks and Hispanics. Suits, dresses, slacks and casual shirts, jeans and T-shirts. No real dress code detectable, but that wouldn't have told him much anyway. The cars in the parking area would be a better indication. Short, tall, large, thin, old, young—some of this he could tell by looking; but they were seated and this evened out size.

He turned his eyes to the sheets of paper containing his sermon. He'd preach, and maybe in the process answer some of the questions they must be asking themselves and each other about him. Recent events freed Ford from some of the restraints he'd felt while working at other churches. He didn't feel as incomplete. The priest was able to separate out church responsibilities from his actual ministry. He knew his work wasn't for most of those sitting in the pews, looking up at him. It wasn't for those who could work out their difficulties hiding behind church doctrines and creeds—those who could easily stumble their way through the week and grab a seat in the sanctuary on Sunday and then start it all again without major damage to others. His theology in practice, what he and Michael would undertake, had no felt consequences for most of those in that church; his sense of sin extended well beyond most in his parish.

Ford remembered a line from a collection of Richard Wright's stories he'd been given some years ago: most of these people were asleep in their living and awake in their dying ... something like that anyway. They would do this without much fanfare, and without major consequences for anyone beyond themselves. Most in their small worlds wouldn't even notice. Ethically impotent and living as theological savants might be the way to describe them. Ethically they were of limited importance in the world, and deficient in so many areas, although they could speak back enough theology to appear Catholic and devout. Ford didn't despise or pity these people. Simply put, they could manage themselves and, even when they failed it would be of limited consequence and reach. He and Michael had more pressing issues, harder work to figure out.

This sermon—not the ministry with only some exceptions—was for those sitting there, the men, women, and children whose lives did little to challenge the grit of Christ-like living. Sunday was for these people. The ministry—the confessional—would serve a different population a more spiritually and physically threatening group.

As he thought these things, the priest looked, and his eyes landed on Michael, sitting near the front, erect in his seat, and an intense look on his face. This shifted Ford's thoughts. And so he spoke, "This is a new time for us in the life of this church. We come here for many different reasons, carrying with us our own issues and concerns. And in this place we find forgiveness, healing, community ..."

These words were followed by other words, written on those sheets of paper, and delivered with little emotion, lots of precision, and some eye contact. Tame ideas. Done.

After the last few ritual items marking service that morning, Ford made his way to the back, to the main entrance to meet those he was to lead. Handshakes, smiles, kind words of welcome were both given and received. He thought Michael would be in line to greet him, but no.

Ford finished greeting the parishioners, moved back to the office and took off the robe that felt so heavy. He'd eat, and go back to his room to think through the schedule for his time in the confessional—evenings and more time on saturdays.

After that he'd go to bed early to be ready …

Chapter Sixteen

7:02 a.m. Up, showered, groomed, dressed.

Ford moved down the hall to the kitchen. He anticipating that breakfast would be there. It was—a pot of coffee, toast, and eggs with bacon wrapped and waiting for him. How she knew when he would arrive and how long to keep the food warm he didn't know, and it didn't matter much. He still wasn't certain of her name.

He'd need to present himself in the office, and begin his responsibilities—masses to conduct during the week, meetings, visits, and so on. This was nothing new. Masses took place on a regular schedule that every priest had memorized. For his congregation it was once each day during the week, Saturday and Sunday.

Back to his room for just a few minutes to pick up his Bible only to realize it was in the church, burned. "Why didn't I remember that? I didn't have it yesterday at service. I hadn't felt it in my hands for some time now." It didn't matter much, all he needed from that book he already had in his head—violent justice, and death for life or life as death.

Empty-handed Ford left his room and moved down the hall. He was less uncomfortable with the empty white walls and more certain of what was behind each door.

It was a good-sized church, and so Ford assumed some secretarial assistance, perhaps someone else in the office as well. Isn't that what the Bishop said? Not a huge staff, times were hard for the Roman Catholic Church—lawsuits to pay were just one drain on resources. Ford heard a voice as he approached the church offices. A woman on the phone—

answering questions. The voice got louder as he approached but then softer as he got closer. Ford looked into the room, a non-descript woman—maybe middle aged, black and silver hair, and modest dress sat behind a desk on the phone. When her eyes caught his, she excused herself from the call and hung up the phone.

"Good morning, Father Ford. How are you?"

"Good morning …" He paused.

"Margaret … I'm Margaret."

"Good morning, Margaret. I'm fine."

Ford looked around, seeming a bit confused.

"This is the outer office, Father. Your office is over there." Margaret was sensitive to the confusion Ford must be feeling. She pointed in the direction of another door, off of her room, to the left.

Ford thanked her, and went into his office.

"Do you need anything, Father?"

"No, I'm fine. Thank you." Ford said these words really just wanting to be alone, to think and plan. Wait for Michael and for their work to begin.

The priest looked around his office. Walls were empty like everywhere else in that place. Bookcases empty too, of course except for one book—something about saints of the church. There was a big, elaborately carved wooden desk in the middle of the room. Off to one side of the massive desk there was a computer—nothing else. Two chairs in front of the desk, a couch with a coffee table, a couple of additional chairs parallel to the couch, and a few lamps for lighting made up the furnishings. Before he could do more than take a look around, Margaret knocked and reminded him of mass starting soon.

Ford conducted mass and took care of some other obligations. The morning was done. More of the same awaited him the rest of the week.

The priest decided to spend some time on the computer and then take a walk around the neighborhood. He looked for information on line about the church, about that area of the city—hoping to learn something more about the parishioners who'd be present for church activities and services.

"I'm stepping out for a while," Ford said as he moved back into the outer office, past the woman whose name he couldn't remember.

"Yes, Father, but before you go may I ask a few questions? I mean, just a few questions to help set up your schedule beyond masses to celebrate."

"Okay."

"In your office, Father?"

"No. I'm out here now. I'll take a seat and you can ask what you need to ask."

"Fine, Father."

Ford took a chair near her desk and pushed it forward some.

"Would you like your appointments in the morning, after mass, Father? Some of the parishioners will want to talk with you after mass and before they go about the day, and morning seems to be a good time."

"Okay."

"Many work, and the morning can be difficult. They will attend mass at more convenient times, Saturday and Sunday …" She corrected the statement. "I mean other times, not more convenient times. Ah, will you allow appointments at other times as well, Father?" Margaret was nervous. She didn't want to annoy the new priest. She was conscious of all the questions; it might come across as probing. She shifted in her chair.

"Should I use the computer? Would that be faster?" She thought these questions but already had the pen and paper.

"Yes … appointments are fine. They are a part of the job." Ford was a little annoyed. Hadn't she just said mornings were good? "Whatever," he thought. Things were changing for Ford. He had a more focused sense of his obligations.

Ford anticipated where this was going, and he wanted to end the conversation as quickly as possible. "Afternoon and early evening during the week, and Saturday morning and afternoon for confessions. I know this isn't a typical schedule, but I want to be available. Also, confessions by appointment as well."

"By appointment?" Margeret thought, but instead said, "Okay, Father Ford. I will put that in the schedule and make that information available."

"Very good," Ford replied hoping he was pushing things along and could leave soon.

"If it is okay, Father, I will just schedule other things as they arise. That might work best. Okay?"

"Yes, that's fine."

"Uhm … I won't hold you, Father. Thank you." Margaret looked at the door leading out, knowing Ford was in the chair but already gone.

"Thank you. I'm going for a walk, see the neighborhood."

"Yes, Father. Enjoy." She hoped that was the right thing to say.

Ford got up, walked out the door and looked for the exit. Finding it, he pushed the door open and stepped into the morning light.

Two blocks, maybe three, from St. George was a Starbucks. This was a clear sign the neighborhood was officially gentrified.

"A cup of coffee might be good," but Ford didn't stop in. He kept walking past, looking in the window at the laptops, nooks, and people finding themselves in expensive coffee drinks.

Restaurants carved out of old buildings, small boutiques, a dog park for the pampered pets, and more. This was his new neighborhood.

Ford walked.

11:45 a.m. The priest saw the time on his watch, and imagined lunch was ready or being placed on the table soon. He turned around retracing his steps and headed back to the church, to the entrance he'd first used the day after the fire.

Down the hall, to the kitchen, the food was waiting, wrapped and warm. Ford sat at the table and ate.

After finishing, he cleared the table and went back to his office. No grand thoughts were in his head, he was just waiting for it to be time to go to the confessional.

Afternoon, and Ford was on his way to the wooden box, wondering about what would happen that day. He knew it in his head and he'd worked it out in his theology, but this time it was real. When does it start? How to select the right ones? Ford and Michael hadn't worked fully through these details. But they had time, right? No rush. This was serious work, and time was not the enemy. He took a breath, tried to center, relax, and get to the confessional.

The priest wasn't certain there would be anyone seeking absolution; he'd just arrived and set the times. Maybe people called while he was gone and the secretary—"Margaret?"—told them of his hours? Waiting for someone—anyone—to arrive he thought about St. Barbara Church; he thought about his conversations with Michael; and he thought about the mission—the discipleship—he and Michael had agreed to undertake. Surprisingly at ease, Ford began to doze off. "How could I sleep?" he thought to himself embarrassed.

Ford heard a noise. He pulled the divide meant to keep the confession anonymous, but he left it cracked. Ford stiffened, leaned forward, and readied himself.

The person entered, and sat down. Ford couldn't make out more than a shadow. He'd have to practice, and train his eyes to see what they shouldn't. In case that didn't work, he would need to consider other options for identifying those in need of special redemption.

The breathing of the person, his or her movement across the cushion, brought Ford back to himself and back to the confessional. Deep breath. Begin.

"Forgive me Father for I have sinned …" Ford recognized the voice. Relieved, he said, "Michael. How did you know?"

"I called, and spoke with Margaret."

"Margaret …"

"I was in church."

"I know," the priest responded wanting to move beyond the niceties to the real business. Ford paused, hoping Michael would get the idea and they could advance the conversation. Michael sensed Ford's anxiety, and pushed forward.

"Still think the confessional is the way to go?"

"No change here," Ford replied, trying to be somewhat casual in tone. He wasn't certain why he'd taken this approach, but he had.

"I see the benefits, but there are problems." Michael wanted to be careful and sensible. There were risks involved and they needed to be mindful.

"Okay. I can see your outline, but can you see me?" Michael asked hoping for a particular answer.

Ford responded. "I'm working on that. I have the screen not

completely closed and I'm hoping I can adjust my eyes to make out the form of the person."

"That worries me. Too many uncertainties," Michael said, hoping for more confidence from Ford.

"Is there another way?" Michael shifted his body weight and repeated the question, "Is there another way? ..."

It came to him. "Yes, I've got it." Ford was excited but trying to keep his voice down just in case the volume carried through the empty church.

"Ok ... I probably won't be able to make out the face, and I can't keep the screen open enough to change what I can see. But, I can make certain the person exposes himself ... or herself."

"What do you mean?" Michael was growing frustrated.

"God provides the occasion, but the priest determines the penance. The priest determines what the person does to make things right with God. And I can require something that will bring the sinner—he liked that word for some reason—into the open." Ford paused so that Michael could gather it all in, and then he continued.

"They will ask for forgiveness, and I will set the terms of that forgiveness. A few prayers and gestures will work for most; but for others ... uh ... I can require something more imaginative."

Ford paused for effect before continuing. "I can require them to, say, go to a particular location at a particular time to pray or volunteer somewhere, or something that allows us to isolate them from the confessional and see them. Get it? The key is *not* providing absolution on the spot—no 'I absolve you of your sins' spoken. A few prayers from them won't be enough. Sure, they will say prayers; but they won't be absolved through such a minor act of contrition. They will carry their sin out of the confessional."

The priest paused again, trying to work things out in his head before speaking. "It isn't likely they will notice the oversight, but for us it makes a significant difference." Ford was getting excited, so he caught his breath. "Even if they do notice and say something, I will indicate the nature of their mortal sin requires a greater act of contrition beyond what they can accomplish in the confessional or at the altar. We, of course, will know their sin has damaged the soul in such a way that requires death for life."

Ford stopped talking.

Michael was gaining confidence. This seemed like a reasonable plan, something that could work.

"It's not perfect," Ford wanted to modify expectations, "but it solves the major problems: we identify those with spiritual sickness that requires death, see them, and put them in spaces we select."

"Okay." Michael couldn't think of much more to say. Then he thought of another question to ask. "When should we start?"

They'd worked out details in theory, but there was a larger issue. Neither had killed a person before.

"Inspiration and faith," Ford said. It didn't make much sense as he released the words, but isn't that the nature of faith?

Michael thought Ford might have this tendency, a slipping into religious rhetoric. But he needed to be patient and hear him out. "What do you mean?"

"Well, we are doing the will of God, what others won't recognize and won't do. But, if we are doing God's work like other disciples in other times, God will provide the inspiration and will guide us and protect us. That's the faith." It all sounded too seminary for Michael. But, okay …

The priest sensed the reluctance on Michael's part and wanted to address it as best he could. "Open ourselves to God, allow God to work through us and do with us what we cannot do with ourselves. The cross is our marker. We will know this is the work of God because it will extend us beyond our comfort zone, beyond what we know to be our abilities and vision. How many disciples had all the experience and know how necessary for the task? That's what God provides. We must provide willing hearts, committed bodies, clear thought, and dedication. God will use those tools for God's purposes. Be open and available. That must make sense." Ford paused, "Had you ever set a fire before?" That question hit Michael hard. He couldn't counter.

"Think of the fire, Michael. Think of that fire. Can you honestly say you really knew what to do when you got to the church that night? I didn't … But, killing can become natural for the disciples of God." Ford was feeling confident, "don't think of it as killing in a traditional sense. It's not a senseless stealing of life; it's not taking away what someone deserves to keep. The term killing might not even capture the full, spiritual function of what we will do." It seemed to Ford he might be preaching at Michael, and he didn't want to do that. So, he stopped.

Michael couldn't argue, and why would he? They wanted the same thing, wanted to be of use, to correct wrongs.

"You listen to the confessions, and you can call me if there is someone sick of soul and in need of death for redemption. Make certain to get as much information about their deed as you possibly can without it seeming odd. Confession is good for the soul, right?" Michael giggled to himself.

Encouraging detail might not be the way most priests handled confessions—just enough information to assess the need and the correction. Ford was a disciple, a new priest, and how others handled confessions didn't matter to him. Any way, people would probably understand, if not appreciate, his particular process for confessions—as long as there was penance through acknowledgement of wrongdoing, and as long as he offered recognizable ways to gain forgiveness. The confessional dulls the senses and suspends reason, and the authority of the priesthood only reinforces this response.

"We can meet the person, make certain it's an isolated place or that the person can be isolated, and … do the work of the Lord."

"Okay, James."

Michael gave the priest his mobile number, and left the confessional some fifteen minutes after he arrived. Ford remained in that box, awaiting others. He wasn't certain he should wait, but he sat collecting his thoughts and envisioning the work ahead of them. None came.

"Maybe tomorrow," he thought as he stood, left the confessional and stretched his back and his legs.

Ford felt a string of emotions, one taking its place after the other. Fear, anger, happiness, nervousness … and he enjoyed everything he felt. The priest wondered if Michael felt the same way, or did the black suit, robes, and other trappings of church life make some type of difference?

He walked back to find the outer office empty and quiet.

"Okay, she doesn't work all afternoon. Good to know." He didn't stay long in that space.

He walked down the hallway to his room. He pushed the door open and entered. She'd made up his bed, and straightened up the few items he'd left around.

Ford sat on his bed, pulled off his jacket and threw it on a chair, took off his shoes and swung his feet on the bed with his head hitting the middle of one of the pillows. He closed his eyes, placed his arms at his sides, and embraced the darkness.

Chapter Seventeen

Ford opened his eyes, and looked at his watch. He didn't realize he was that tired, but he'd slept for a good amount of time.

Dinner crossed his mind. He sat upright, put on his shoes, gathered his wrinkled jacket, and went out the door. Down the hall to the kitchen and again, like magic, the food—baked chicken, green beans, corn, and a roll—along with a glass and pitcher of lemonade covered with plastic. It was cold at that point, but he didn't care.

He sat and ate and, like every other time, he put the dishes in the sink and assumed the woman he couldn't name would take care of them. Why think any differently about it?

Full and dressed, Ford decided to walk around the neighborhood again. It was late, almost 9:30 p.m. He did have some time to kill. "Time to kill," the imagery hit the priest.

It was that point in the year when the weather warms, and people move outside during the evening. On porches, and decks, looking at their neighborhood and trying to forget about that work day. Ford didn't have the same pace of his earlier walk. He moved faster now. He had an odd feeling as people looked at him, and those who'd met him Sunday spoke.

"Hello, Father … good to see you." Ford nodded his greeting, waved, and smiled.

More stores, similar shops, and restaurants … the same look as the blocks of the neighborhood he'd already seen. There were more blocks to walk before turning around and going back.

Once in his room, he decided tomorrow would be the day he'd

give serious attention to the confessional. There should be people coming and he'd listen, find out whose mortal sin required the type of attention he and Michael could provide.

"Lord, be with me," the priest spoke, as he laid on his bed ready for sleep.

CHAPTER EIGHTEEN

"Good morning, Father."

"Good morning …"

"Do you need anything from me …?"

"Margaret, the name is Margaret, Father Ford." Shouldn't he remember at this point? She thought to herself. How many names did he have to learn at this point?

"Ah, yes … Margaret. Anything I need to be aware of today, anything after mass?"

"No, Father, your schedule is clear until confessions."

"Okay, thanks." Ford moved away from the front of her desk where he'd positioned himself during that brief conversation. In his office Ford sat on the couch … then a chair. Bored, and anxious, Ford grabbed the only book in the bookcase. Back at his desk he opened the book on Catholic Saints. "Well, let's start with St. George."

The birth and life of St. George—warrier and martyr—was of little consequence for Ford. How the story of St. George's battle with the dragon to save the king's daughter and end the surrender of children to pacify the beast was told, and when it was told, didn't matter much to him. What gained his attention was St. George's slaying of the dragon in exchange for the conversion to Christianity of the king and the people of that area. Known as a soldier, had the saint taken life, and on how many occasions?

There was a quiet comfort in that image. Ford thought of himself in that role, destroying evil for the sake of the larger community and in keeping with the demands of God on disciples. He wasn't armed with death-dealing iron, no shield, but an idea and the confessional.

Ford put the book on the desk, with the image of St. George on his horse face up. He leaned back in the chair, crossed his arms, and thought for a moment. Then he was off to mass. He didn't mind mass during the week; it required little of his time and energy. He didn't really give a sermon, just brief reflections often developed on the spot.

No lunch today, he would just sit and think in preparation for the afternoon. No food would center his mind and control his body—a type of fast in preparation for a great work.

Over the past few days, the priest had surprised himself with his ability to sit with his thoughts, and to do so with limited distractions. Maybe this was God preparing him? He wasn't certain. Still he'd take in the moments, and try to clear his mind of unnecessary things.

Chapter Nineteen

"Lord, make me truly worthy of the discipleship and service before me. Make righteous the actions Michael and I will undertake for your glory ... Amen."

Ford heard a voice. He hadn't noticed the soft movement of the person into the confessional. It was too late to try to adjust the closed screen. Something about the voice threatened him.

"In the name of the Father, Son, and the Holy Ghost ... Forgive me Father for I have sinned. It has been six months since my last confession."

Ford was silent.

The confessor spoke to break the silence and because, in certain ways, he found additional joy in saying what he'd done.

"I want to share something with you, Father."

Silence. Ford's heart was pounding; this was it.

"I want to share something with you ... Father."

Ford caught himself, and this time responded, "What is your sin?"

"Well, Father, is it a sin when you can't help yourself? What if what I do is a matter of genetics?"

"You've come here because you know what you've done is a sin. Why else would you come to the confessional? The name says it all."

There was an uncomfortable giggle, and the stranger continued. "Okay, Father, I will admit you are correct. You know more theology and church teachings than I do. I am a Catholic, but ... you, of course, know more."

"Your sin?"

"Greed is natural, Father. It's part of who we are."

"Your sin?" Ford wanted to move to the important conversation, enough with the preliminaries.

"Okay, I'm a contractor. I'm responsible for much of the new construction in this area of town. Actually, I'm responsible for most of the gentrification in the inner loop ... It's about making money, Father, not spending it. I have to keep the profit margin high. Sometimes, you cut corners. For me that has involved, well ... some workers with questionable employment rights. You may have read about this."

He paused to give Ford an opportunity to think about what he'd read and what he'd heard.

"On a construction site a week or so ago, workers were killed. We didn't use all the safety mechanisms required by law. They were illegal, so no one raised too much dust about it. I couldn't afford press over it, so we hid the bodies and cleaned the site before the authorities arrived. Once they were gone, we put the bodies in the foundation." He had a thought, a question he needed to ask before moving on. He knew his employees, as guilty as they might feel for helping him, wanted to keep their jobs and wouldn't speak about what had taken place; but what did he have on the priest that might buy silence?

"Say ... Father, you can't report this, right? There's confidentiality here, right?"

"It's not that simple," Ford thought, but instead he whispered yes, and that was enough.

"You should have seen those mangled bodies. They almost didn't look human anymore. Crushed bones, and on what could be recognized as faces were marks of terror." There was a pause as he gathered himself and tried to get rid of the images of bodies. Then, he continued, "It was business, Father. Probably wrong, but business."

"Are you sorry for your deeds?" Ford asked trying to maintain his cool. He had to remember his larger mission.

"Sorry is a strong word, Father."

"Have you changed your practices as a result?"

"It's about money, Father. If I'm making money, and those around me are making money, it's okay." He thought about those bodies, and continued, "I just feel a little bad about it, and I need you to tell me what to do for forgiveness."

No regret in his voice and in his words. Ford thought this is the first case, the first spiritually dead confessor.

"How many died?"

"Three."

"And they are all in the foundation? Any effort to locate their families?"

"Why?" the confessor seemed confused and annoyed by the question.

"They were human beings who deserved consideration." Ford had another question, one he and Michael would need answered. "Where is this building? What's the address?"

Without thinking, he responded, "1606 Grand Avenue." Then it hit him. "Father, with all due respect, aren't you going beyond what should be happening here? I need to know what I should do as penance? Which prayers? How many times? ... What?"

This was a crime, and part of Ford simply wanted to report him. That wouldn't solve the problem and it was his mission to do what church and civil authorities couldn't and wouldn't do.

"You should go to the authorities, but I know you won't. Think about it, and as you do you need to say a series of prayers—I'll tell you which ones—and give to the less fortunate all of the wealth made on that building. You are to say those prayers every night for a week, starting tomorrow, at the building site, as the sun is going down."

He expected more of a challenge, thought he'd have to do more. With some relief he said, "Yes, Father." Not wanting to linger and give the priest opportunity to think about what had taken place, he moved quickly from the confessional and left the church.

Father Ford heard other confessions that day—shoplifting, and other tame activities—but this first confession was the one that stayed with him. It was the one he would need to share with Michael. Ford was convinced this first confession was a sign from God. Putting that person in the confessional was God saying "Yes" to his new ministry. And the fact that it was the first confession of the day only strengthened his sense that God wanted them to do this work ... beginning with this contractor. Whoever said discipleship was without violence?

Back in his room, he called Michael and shared the story. They agreed the last day of the penance would be the day they would finish the work. Ford and Michael would be there waiting.

Everyday would be the same until then—meals, a few meetings, walks, and confessions. Going through the motions, the week passed.

Ford connected with Michael at the coffee shop where they first met after the fire. They ate although not hungry. They had to pass some time and couldn't just sit there.

As they left, the sun was beginning to go down. Grand Avenue wasn't far away, but they couldn't afford to walk. They needed to be able to leave the building quickly and without calling much attention to themselves. Michael drove.

They arrived at the building, a mid-rise building a bit out of place in the current landscape. The area would fill in as the middle-class moved back into the city, and the industrial feel—the paint shops, plumbing supply shops, and auto repair shops—left. Stepping out of the car and looking up at the building, they could see a figure. Fairly certain the person couldn't see them, they moved around to the back and began climbing the skeleton of the building using the unfinished stairwell. Ford was surprised that the person had actually followed instructions. However, it was a small price to pay for what he'd done, so—then again—why wouldn't he?

Moving carefully to avoid noise that might alert him, Ford and Michael approached the third floor where the contractor was kneeling. Michael moved ahead, holding what seemed to Ford a tire iron from the car he must have pulled out and placed in the back seat in easy reach. Ford hadn't thought to bring anything. Confident he would do better next time and that Michael's tire iron would do the trick this time, he pressed on behind Michael.

The stranger was still on his knees, hands folded in front in the posture of prayer. And he rocked back and forth a little.

Michael had the weapon—the sword of Michael, the lance of St. George. They approached with caution. There wasn't much activity around the building, so no strong noise to drown out their movement. Be careful. Quiet.

When they reached the stranger he turned and saw the tire iron rise above Michael's head. It was too late to move, too late for pleading or any sound. His hands meant to guard his face had little effect. The tire iron crashed down on his head with a cracking sound, splitting it open. The blood splattered on them and made an odd design on the cement floor—something that reminded Ford of a symbol he'd once seen when a seminary student, almost like an exploding sun. One blow and he was dead. Michael grunted as he brought the tire iron down and breathed a sigh as he pulled it out of the split head. Ford stood there, not frightened. He felt a bit of relief, a feeling that a difficult task had been completed, and God was pleased.

Ford looked at the mangled head, then the limp body. He knelt down next to it as Michael watched. And then the priest spoke softly, as if for only he and the lifeless body to hear, "I absolve you."

Michael looked at Ford, and without saying a word handed him the tire iron and began to pull the body toward the stairs. Ford stopped him. "We should carry him." Ford grabbed his legs, trying to balance the body and the tire iron. Michael grabbed the arms. Neither looked at the body they carried. They didn't feel the need to look; the work belonged to God, and it was dark. Carrying the body down the stairs would strain them, but they couldn't leave it.

Michael had thought to bring some type of weapon, but they hadn't thought about disposing of the body. They were determined to take this man's life, although there was something about the process they felt to be out of their hands. At least subconsciously they needed God to play an active role.

As Ford thought about their failure to plan the removal of the body, to think about how to dispose of the body, he put down the man's legs, and said out loud, "Michael, maybe this is God? We didn't plan on what to do with the body, because we knew God would provide inspiration, would work something out because this is God's will. And … maybe that's why I didn't even think about a weapon … the will of God is my weapon. God always provides. Abraham got a ram to replace his son as a sacrifice, and Moses had his staff … God gave us a tire iron and a willing spirit."

Ford paused thinking through what he'd just said. It was trite, but he felt it strongly and so he continued, "I know this sounds like too much, but God has inspired, has done, stranger things."

Michael hadn't let go of the arms; he concentrated on the work at hand, just nodded his agreement and said, "We need to get it to the ground, behind the building, and out of view." He'd let Ford have his theological theory, but for him the real test was the blood they'd leave behind as they moved the body. God would need to prove God's self by shaping how people thought about all that blood. That was the real test.

Feeling drained and barely able to move, they reached the stairs, adjusted their hold on the body, and began the climb down.

It seemed to take hours, and it may have. Neither looked at the time. The priest had no restrictions, and Michael told his wife he would be very late ... some work to do. They reached the ground and exhausted they carried the body to the back of the building. This was a zip code under rapid development—townhouses, condos, and stores. Next to them was another construction area, but one less developed. It was a brown field, with plastic piping sticking up like tentacles on some giant insect.

"That field over there," Ford pointed, "we can bury the body." For the priest, this thought that popped in his head was just another sign that God was with them. He had never done any construction of any kind, but pipes were in place, and he had a deep feeling that meant they wouldn't be doing any more digging. Michael was tired, and agreed without question. Together they carried the body to the brown field, away from most of the pipes, and laid it on the ground.   M i c h a e l went back to the mid-rise construction project where the murder had taken place and looked for something with which to dig. Construction workers don't tend to leave tools around, and he wasn't certain what they'd do if he couldn't find anything. It took a while but he was lucky that a couple of damaged shovels had been left on one of the floors. They were in bad shape, but he and Ford could make them work.

"You were gone a long time, Michael." Ford was nervous. He'd seen dead bodies before, lots of funerals, but this was the first time he was responsible for the death and the first time he could provide no words of comfort.

They both moved away from the body, and began digging into the dirt. Both threw dirt to the side without speaking a word. Neither was used to that type of labor. They were sore, tired, drained of energy but feeling an odd sense of joy. Ford wanted to say something, to talk about the murder, but he wasn't certain how to start.

"Grab his arms." Michael pointed toward the body and positioned himself over it. Holding both legs, he waited for Ford to get in position. With a rhythmic motion, they shifted the body toward the hole. "On three ... one, two, three," Michael initiated the count and they used what remaining strength they had to swing the body into the ground. It landed with a thud—arms twisted, legs bent, as if it were doing some desperate dance.

They took the shovels and filled the makeshift grave with dirt.

"Pack the dirt down." Michael followed the instruction with an example. He banged the shovel against the ground trying to flatten the earth out. Looking over, he saw Ford pounding the earth, removing signs of their presence and the body.

They stopped. Looked at each other. Both were satisfied they had been careful burying the body and covering any sign of their shoe prints.

"We're done. I imagine the first will be the most difficult. We learn, and get better." Ford talked as if they were taking a test, not disposing of a body.

"It's God's work, and like other disciples we'll get better because we'll grow in this work as our faith statement."

"Do you think he will be missed?" Michael asked trying to remember something of the humanity that once occupied that body.

"I would imagine so. Everyone is connected to someone. Everyone matters to someone." Michael wanted to clarify his question. "Do you think people will suspect murder?"

"Yes, they will suspect a murder took place because of the blood. We were careful to remove signs of blood on the ground leading to the grave, but it's all over the stairs and the fifth floor of the building. But I think you mean will we be suspects."

Ford looked at Michael, tried to study his face before continuing. "I don't think so. People with sins like his to confess don't tend to tell people they are off to the confessional. To admit that is to admit too much, to open the door for questions and suspicions. If he told his wife—if he has one—or his friends—if he has friends—it would be to own something wrong, to attach it to his body as a weight and to bare it in front of others. The Church doesn't require this. Both the Church and the parishioner have too much too lose if sins have to be shared beyond the sinner, the priest, and God."

Ford paused before finishing his thought. "The police will look for him, but no one will connect him with penance. He had too much to lose to draw a straight line from his private and professional life to the confessional. It isn't really likely the police will come to the church. They will probably assume he was robbed and that the thief destroyed the evidence. Even if they find the body, there's no way to connect it to us."

Both thought without saying it aloud God could allow them to be discovered as a way of testing them, or for some other reason beyond their ability to grasp. Not likely, however. This ministry was just starting and why would it end with only one sinner punished?

Michael listened, looked at the ground, and then looked at Ford. He could feel the blood drying on his skin. It was darkening and pulling at his hair and flesh, but it felt good as a sign of righteous work.

"We should clean off." Ford nodded his agreement.

"Can you get in the church without being noticed?" Michael thought they shouldn't waste more time around the construction site, a kind of sacred site.

"I … I think so." Ford was trying to follow Michael's logic. Should they ride in the car with blood on them, getting it in the car—on the seats, the door handles? "But what about getting blood in the car?"

"It's drying, and by the time we get to the car it should be completely dry. Lucky it's cool this evening."

Michael said it but he wasn't content with this reasoning. He'd return to Ford's assurances.

"After all, you said they won't look in our direction. No reason for the police or anyone else to think of me. So I can clean my car without a problem. And my wife will be asleep and won't notice me taking a shower. I'll dispose of the clothing. Burn them maybe."

Ford didn't speak. He just turned in the direction of the car. Looked around to make certain no one was watching.

Michael dropped the priest off at the church. He was worried about doing that, but it seemed the best way to proceed.

Ford looked at Michael with the same look he had when they sat in the car after the fire—at peace, deeply committed, and needing few words to express it. "I'll be in touch."

Michael nodded. Ford got out the car, looked around and moved to the door. Opened it and closed it behind him.

Walking down the hallway Ford thought about what they had done. How easy it had been to justify theologically without guilt.

Blood is often cleansing. Church teachings and scripture support that understanding. Discipleship can require the strength of our muscles and willingness to risk. Wasn't this what the theologian Dietrich Bonhoeffer taught? He said, and this line had been burned into the priest's memory from the first time he read it, "when Christ calls a man come, he bids him come and die." But perhaps, as Bonhoeffer's participation in a plot to kill Adolf Hitler suggests, this call to discipleship also means come and kill. He and Michael, he knew this, had been called to discipleship and this was a demand to kill in the name of the Lord and for the sake of justice.

There was something about extreme penance he enjoyed, and he hoped that feeling would only grow more intense.

There was also a feeling in Ford that he was changing the importance of the sacraments—moving against the teachings of the Church in certain ways. According to the Church, the Eucharist—communion—was the central sacrament. It was a physical and spiritual marker of God's presence with us, through Christ. Being prepared to take it required confession, but it was the acceptance into one's body of the body and blood—no longer wafer and wine—that marked in action and symbol the story of the Christian faith: God surrenders Godself for the sake of humanity, to restore humans to proper relationship after their sin. It was not, according to the Church, something imposed by humans for their benefit—a story they tell and reenact to safeguard their sense of their importance in the world. No, according to Church teachings Christ instituted it. And Christ commanded that this practice be continued in remembrance of the sacrifice he would make.

Ford understood, he had been trained to understand this, that communion was the most important, the most pure and perfect way to remember God and affirm one's relationship with God. All other activities or rituals simply point in the direction of communion, even the confessional. Communion was important because it spoke to a vital sacrifice made by God; but the best way to appreciate and give adoration with respect to this sacrifice was to acknowledge shortcomings, to confess, to make one's body and soul acceptable before God. Communion, in actuality, is real for the faithful, is available to the faithful, only by means of confession.

The priest pushed past communion: Confession is the core, the fundamental element. It speaks more forcefully to one's acceptance of the faith. It is more active than communion because it requires more from us. Pulling on both the body and perfecting the soul through the enhancement of spiritual life, confession gives a better indication of what it means to be Christ-like—to sacrifice, to recognize the beautiful link between death and life through one's own body.

Watching that evening it seemed to Ford that Michael was more advanced in his thinking about their mission. He wondered if this were a problem. Should a priest have the theological and ethical tools needed to make the transition easier than it is for a layperson?

Ford reached his room, turned on the light, and moved to the bathroom. He would need to clean himself off, and do something with the clothes. Looking in the mirror, he saw the bits of blood, bone, and what he assumed to be brain, splattered on him. The priest wasn't troubled because these were the marks of his calling. In fact, he, in an odd way, was saddened to remove them. He took off his clothes, turned on the shower and stood under the hot water watching the signs of his calling move down his body toward the drain.

"I'll worry about the clothes tomorrow. I have other things to wear." Ford decided to bundle them up and put them under the bed until the morning. Before ending the evening, he polished his shoes, and this reminded him to look down the hallway to make certain there was no blood or dirt tracked in. He'd thought wiping his feet before entering the house had been enough but he'd need to check.

Looking out the door, and down the hall with a flashlight, he saw nothing of alarm. Mind at ease, he closed his door and got in bed— wondering if Michael had gone through a similar process.

Michael had gotten home, quietly moved inside the apartment. Stopped to make certain he hadn't woken his wife. Bathroom. Clothes off. He turned on the shower, and stepped in without looking in the mirror and without paying attention to the look of his clothing. He showered and noticed bits of the dead man around the drain. He'd pick those up and put them in the toilet when he finished showering. He turned off the water, listened for his wife, and picked up all his clothing. After drying and putting on his pajamas, he quietly went to the kitchen, took a garbage bag, and shoved his clothing and shoes in it. In the morning he'd take them far away and put them in a dumpster … but first he reached under the sink for the bleach, opened it, and poured a healthy dose of it into the plastic garbage bag, and then doubled the bag so it wouldn't leak. "That should do it," he said as he put the bag in the closet. "She'll never look in there," and he was up first anyway and would be out of the apartment with the bag before she was out the shower.

In bed Michael moved close to his wife, and she close to him. Both slept.

CHAPTER TWENTY

Ford awoke remembering his first task for the day. Get rid of the clothing. He knew he could dispose of the evidence this time, but he couldn't do this every time. There wasn't money for that, and it would be suspicious to continuously replace clothing. Maybe some wouldn't be as bloody? Or, maybe he should get a set of clothing just for this calling?

After breakfast, on his way to the office, it occurred to him that he could simply wrap the clothing in plastic and put them in the dumpster. No one would suspect the church, and the dumpster would be emptied long before the police ... if the police even came.

With the clothing in a bag, Ford walked outside to the back of the church, opened the dumpster and pushed the bag to the bottom, as far to the bottom as he could with his sore muscles.

It was a quiet day. He sat for a while just thinking. He'd need a couple of additional outfits to wear ... maybe another suit and some casual stuff. The priest knew he was also entitled to a car. He didn't really need the car, but it might prove useful at times. He'd also need to follow the news for the next week or so, just to see what was said about the missing man. Reports would give his name and particulars, but those things didn't matter much to the priest. The man was defined, named, by his sin.

After confessions and mass Ford ran errands and went back to his office to work on this sermon for Sunday. He'd put limited time into it. His preaching would simply need to be decent, good enough to pacify. So he'd give them what he thought the middle-class members of the congregation (and those wanting to be middle class) wanted to hear—nothing too challenging, and nothing that hit home too hard. "I'm okay, and you're okay … something like that."

Sunday came and went, and Ford handled it as he planned.

Monday bled into Tuesday, Tuesday into Wednesday, Wednesday into Thursday, Thursday into Friday, and Friday into Saturday when he'd prepare his sermon and ready himself for Sunday. Weeks went on like this—uneventful for both Michael and Ford, except for news concerning a missing man. Mr. Charles Pope, age 54, long-time resident, businessman, and pillar of the community, was missing. He was last seen leaving a downtown restaurant. The family—his wife and three children—were offering a reward for information concerning his whereabouts. The police were involved, but had no leads, although the work site held evidence of foul play. His blood had been found, the reporters noted always with a stern look. While there were no clear enemies, it was likely he was dead. Despite this, local papers and family appearances on local television programs held to the little bit of hope available as the days passed without word or sign.

Ford looked carefully at the work site behind the reporters who nightly mentioned the disappearance. Where they'd placed the body was now framed out. He could easily see this on programs reporting the case. A mid-rise building was in the works. The blood trail might have encouraged police to stop the construction and dig up the area, but they didn't. There were lots of possible reasons for this oversight—too many cases, fatigue, or poor skills … For the priest this was just more evidence of their chosen status as disciples. God hardened Pharaoh's heart for Moses, and clouded the judgment of the police working the possible crime scene for them.

Ford held to this thought of specialness, and it helped him through days that were uneventful. There was no communication with Michael to break things up. They'd agreed to only talk when they were called to acts of discipleship, and there had been no sins requiring extreme penance. Only his internal conversations added energy to rather lethargic hours. Even so, Ford, easily lulled into a state of fogginess over the weeks, tried to stay aware and alert.

CHAPTER TWENTY-ONE

"Forgive me Father for I have sinned," the voice, a woman's voice, said.

"What is your sin?"

Ford didn't anticipate what happened next. It was always possible, and happened on occasion, but for some reason he didn't expect it. The woman on the other side of the screen began to cry, more like a deep moan. "With groaning which cannot be uttered," Ford thought. The sound went through him, penetrating him. The priest knew he had to remain balanced. "What is your sin?"

The moaning continued. Ford could hear behind the moaning the moving of a body, a tight, anguished movement against the walls of the box and against the cushion of the seat.

He waited.

After a while, after the initial despair worked its way out her body, she spoke. "Father, forgive me for I have sinned. It has been one year since my last confession." The voice paused. "I have sinned Father ... I ... ah, I have sold young girls."

Ford sat up, stiffened, paused and spoke. "What do you mean, you have sold young girls?"

He was getting sick to his stomach, the wild thoughts going through his head—young girls bound and gagged, stuffed into airless trucks—were lodging themselves in his stomach and pressing. He was nervous, not wanting to hear an answer, but knowing he had to listen for it. Bad stomach, sweating hands, stiffing muscles. The priest waited for a reply.

"I bring girls from South America and Europe to the United

States. Promise them a good life, and sell them off." The voice wasn't firm. It shook, cracked.

"How long have you been doing this? Where and to whom do you sell them?" Ford needed information.

"To the highest bidder … They are transported all over the country. Many stay in this city." There was a pause. And then the voice continued, providing some context but trying to distance its owner from the deed. "It's very organized. It's bigger than me." Telling the story, confessing the crime, was putting the voice at ease. There was a growing calmness.

Ford was trying to remain steady, but he was thinking of the children he'd ministered to at St. Barbara Church. These children had to be like those children, attached to parents with limited resources, wanting a better life, and unaware of how high the price for this dream.

"How old are these kids?" This question was beyond what the priest should ask as a function of the confession.

The voice didn't resist, but answered as part of the confession of sin. "Young … maybe 6 to 11." This wasn't enough. The voice continued, "There is demand, as long as they are young."

"Do you know what happens to these girls, after you sell them?" Ford wasn't concerned with the amount of money made, or what the owner of the voice did with the money. The selling of the children was enough to merit extreme penance. Of this he was certain … just more detail.

"I don't know. I just provide the kids, and that's all. I don't know what happens to them." No stepping away from the crime, so he pushed. Moving closer to the screen to make certain nothing about the sound of his voice or the intensity of the question was lost, he asked, "But you can imagine what might happen, can't you?"

"Yes … but, ah …" The voice went silent. Ford waited.

"I've come to confess. To make it right. What do I need to do?" There was renewed desperation in the voice.

"You have done a lot of harm, destroyed lives." Ford was tense, wanting to strike out at the voice—confront the body next to him and make it pay, make it feel the pain those children felt. Catching himself, he remembered, it would pay a large price in time.

"I understand, Father. That's why I am here." There was anxiety in the voice—was the deed beyond redemption? "What do I need to do?"

The priest paused for effect, giving the appearance of spiritual reflection when he already knew the price the trafficker would need to pay.

"This is a serious offence before God and human law. I assume you've not gone to the police, thinking forgiveness from God is all that your soul requires."

"Will you tell the cops, Father?" The voice was nervous. It was one thing to ground one's spirit in acts of repentance, but it was another to spend time in a prison. Didn't spiritual change cover sin? Wasn't that enough? Didn't God's forgiveness supersede anything authored by humans?

"No I won't."

Ford had the upper hand and wanted the trafficker to understand and appreciate that. He smiled a little knowing that jail would pale in comparison to the price to be paid. No reason to contact the police, not now, not for any of the sick souls with whom he and Michael would work.

Relieved, the trafficker whispered, "Thank you." Wanting to make certain the spiritual cure was measured out in full, the gratitude was followed by a request, "What do I need to do Father?"

He relaxed, allowing his body to shift into a more comfortable position—lower back pulled away from the wooden seat, face away from the screen, hands folded on his lap.

"We will address the spiritual crisis, and I will leave the rest to you." He paused again, for effect. And then continued, "You have done great damage to a good number of God's children, damaged their souls and done exceedingly great harm to your spiritual life. You must correct for this. Although you can't change what you have done to the children already sold into slavery, you can prevent this from happening to others. First, you must stop conducting your business. Give the money you've made to a charity for children. You must also dedicate your life to service, give your time to the safeguarding of children."

Somewhat relieved, this all seemed manageable, the trafficker asked a question meant to show sincerity and dedication to a new way of being in the world, "Okay, Father. I will stop, but where should I give this service and what should I do for money?"

Ford hit his priestly stride. He was in more control than with the man responsible for the death of the workers. The words flowed much easier, and he felt less invested in the moral outrage of the crime— although this was present—and more concerned with the proper ethical conduct required to bring the mortal sin to its theological and ethical conclusion ... death.

"You can get a job. You can find employment. But this isn't really about your comfort is it? No. Why would penance be comfortable?"

This hit hard, and the trafficker wanted some relief.

"I understand Father. I'm sorry for my question. I didn't mean that I should have it easy." She thinks of how to ask the last part of the question again without making the priest angry: "I want to make this right, to redeem my soul. Where should I go to do the work you mentioned? Is there a community center, a shelter, soup kitchen, some place I should go?"

This neighborhood had changed, and he didn't imagine there were any such places near St. George. But for that matter, he didn't know if she was from this neighborhood. He did know of some places near St. Barbara, but he couldn't have this person using his name in his old neighborhood. The people might ask who sent her. Or, she might get nervous and volunteer the information. He and Michael needed to control her location and schedule for at least several days. Then again, would she really volunteer information? What would be the advantage in naming the priest as her contact? That would raise other questions: how did she know the priest? Was she a member of the congregation? Why had he sent her? She wouldn't want to answer all those questions because they would leave her vulnerable. They would invite a look at her life that might expose the condition of her soul and her crime. Like the other one, she didn't want that exposed; she wanted it fixed without having the public know her condition. It wasn't as if she would tell people what she did, and going to the confessional wasn't something she would announce. No, "Hey honey I'm off to the confessional. Be back later." No. That would invite too many questions:

"Why the confessional dear? You've not been to church in a long time. What's wrong?" She couldn't afford that. There was another issue. He and Michael would need to be in the same area as this woman, and could Ford be in his old neighborhood without being noticed? Ford couldn't afford to be noticed, nor could Michael. He'd need a different location. As the trafficker waited, he thought about alternatives.

The silence didn't bother either of them. She assumed the priest was giving her service a great deal of prayerful thought. And that couldn't be rushed. Besides, she didn't want to take a chance on upsetting him. She'd gotten a taste of that already. And Ford just needed time to think, to make certain he was following God in giving her directions. This was important because a misstep could end the ministry and frustrate their role in the working out of God's will. Be careful. He knew he had to be careful.

It took some time to come up with the location, but it eventually came to him. He'd once gone to the "bottom"—a section of town near his old neighborhood and his new neighborhood. It was a location not yet marked for gentrification. Runaways, drug dealers and users, and the homeless frequented that area. The "bottom" wasn't too far from the bus station where ex-cons were transported once they'd served their time. Some stayed in that area, and the lucky ones had family or friends to take them away from it. His old area was rough too, but without the despair and sense of hopelessness marking the "bottom." Ford remembered a shelter there. He couldn't think of the name, but he could recall the address: 6660 Main Street, South. The priest would send her there.

"As part of your penance"—she was glad the priest was talking again—"you will need to perform service at the shelter on 6660 Main Street, South. Because you also need to work, tell them you can volunteer from 7 p.m. to 12 midnight. You will need to work there one day for each child you destroyed."

Although reluctant to give numbers before, she whispered to her self but loud enough for the priest to make it out, "40 days."

Ford listened knowing that she would not make it the full forty.

"I'll go tomorrow."

Ford could hear her moving, one leg hitting the wooden barrier near his leg, her hand touching the other wall as she stood up and moved out of the confessional. He sat there giving her enough time to exit, and then he stretched his legs, stood and moved away from the dark box.

If others came, they would need to return another day. This wasn't church policy but it was his policy today. No more confessions. There was prep work to do.

Ford walked through the sanctuary, looking at the altar and the windows depicting saints and biblical figures as he left. He wouldn't call Michael from his office, just to be safe. So he told Margaret he would be going to his room for the rest of the day. His stomach was still in knots thinking about the young children abused, so no dinner.

Once in his room, the priest picked up the phone—the disposable mobile phone he'd secured some time ago.

"Michael, there is a sin sick soul that needs penance." Ford smiled as he hung up the phone. He knew their work with this sinner would fulfill God's will, and in that act of obedience to God he would find some joy.

Chapter Twenty-two

They didn't want to move too quickly, so they let her work at the shelter for a couple of weeks. That gave time enough to make certain she hadn't spoken of Ford in a way that would generate suspicion. And it was enough time for her to get into a rhythm and for her to begin believing this penance was sufficient. She'd begin to suspect that her work was making a difference by erasing from her soul the marks of her sinful activities. Unable (or unwilling) to do directly for the children she stole, she could make a difference—for 40 days—in the lives of other children.

Michael and Ford talked about it, and they knew they had to be more intentional and more professional this time—while still leaving room for God to direct their actions. After all, they were disciples, acting on behalf of their Lord. They played an active role, and they couldn't afford to perform that role poorly. What if there'd been no tire iron? What then, pray the man to death? Drown him in holy water? Death was the penance and the violence had meaning. And so they committed themselves to prayer, discernment, and time to outline the proper ritual for each sinner in advance of final penance. It was important to remember that God does the work, and they are merely vessels for God. They should never think they are responsible for this work, as if penance comes at their hands. No, it's God through them. Always God ...

Varying their locations, they didn't meet at their coffee shop, or in the confessional. And they worked out their plan, or what they'd started calling the "ritual" over the phone. Ford's calls on the disposable couldn't be traced … just in case.

They connected in the "Bottom." Ford got there on foot and Michael drove—both certain no one noticed them. Anyway, it wasn't the type of place where people let their eyes linger. People moved through the Bottom like shadows.

Ford knew one of the trafficker's duties was removing the trash and putting it in a dumpster a block or so away. The shelter couldn't afford its own, but instead shared one with another business. Having done a little spy work, Ford knew she'd get there about 11:45 p.m., just as her shift was coming to an end. She'd load the bags on a cart, not too quiet but this was the Bottom, and a little noise didn't startle anyone. Gunfire, screams, and other sounds of despair were common—squeaking wheels wouldn't attract attention.

11:35 p.m.—Michael parked a short distance from the dumpster. The priest joined him, and they waited. They had time: Michael made another convincing excuse to his wife, and no one monitored Ford during the evenings.

They didn't talk. Their eyes were fixed on the dumpster, waiting for her to arrive.

At 11:48 p.m. a shadow arrived with bags on a cart. This person had the same shape, the same movement, was the same person who'd been responsible for the trash every time Ford had come to watch. There was no reason to believe this wasn't the body belonging to the voice.

Ford and Michael looked at each other and, without a word spoken, opened the doors to the car and exited carefully. Michael carried a large, cloth bag. Ford held plastic and tape. They covered the distance between the car and dumpster quickly and were on her before she had time to react in earnest. She tried to get away, but Ford held her small frame while Michael put down the bag.

Hand over her mouth, he could easily manage her in that she couldn't have weighed more than 100 pounds.

"This is the frame of a trafficker?" Ford thought to himself. He'd expected something different. While Ford held her and she tried to get free, Michael approached and hit her on the head. This blow wasn't to kill, but to knock her out.

Her body spread on the ground behind the dumpster, Michael emptied his bag. Ford had placed plastic underneath the body and bound her hands and feet and taped her mouth just in case.

She was still knocked out when Ford began to cut her legs—legs that had traveled to steal children. The pain woke her, but she couldn't make a sound with the tap across her mouth. She tried to get away, but the tape was tight and didn't allow her arms and legs to move. She resembled a snake—her effort gave the appearance of a body slithering. Ford made long cuts along both legs, moving the knife he'd gotten from Michael in a zigzag fashion almost mimicking the slithering of her body in pain. He did the same with her arms. All the time Michael whispered in her ear, "This is for the children. You used your legs to catch them, and your arms to deliver them to their deaths."

With her legs and arms cut, blood oozing down and across her body, soaking her clothing and spilling onto the plastic underneath her, Ford stood above her and looked down. His heart raced and his mouth was dry. He could sense her pain, and he found in it a certain type of peace that flooded him with warmth. Her agonized movements, the jerking of her body, the flow of her blood all pointed toward the will of God. As she moved, his attention turned to the children she was responsible for destroying. And as he thought of them and as Michael watched, he plunged the knife into her heart and twisted it. The body jerked again, seized up, and relaxed. They could hear her tortured breathing before the last death rattle.

Ford bent down with his mouth close to the body's ear, "I absolve you."

They had worn gloves this time, and without fear of leaving fingerprints they wrapped the body in the plastic and threw it into the dumpster. It landed with a thud. Michael gathered the ritual items and wiped them off on a rag before putting them back in the bag. The knife would be cleaned and put back in his kitchen drawer. The remaining tape put with the tools, and the hammer used to knock her unconscious back in the closet with the tape and tools. They looked around to make certain there were no identifying marks, no items left behind in haste.

There was no blood on their clothes this time, and so they quickly and quietly carried the bag back to the car and climbed in.

They weren't worried about discovery of the body. She was in a questionable line of work—human trafficking—and was doing community work in a dangerous section of town, a location where a trafficker might store human cargo. Wouldn't the authorities identify the body—they assumed her identification was in the shelter or on her person—and speak to friends and family? Yes, and it would probably come out that she was involved in a dangerous and criminal enterprise. That being the case, she could have been killed because of a deal gone wrong. Or, maybe another trafficker wanted her territory and was willing to kill over it. Nothing would point to Ford and as a consequence nothing would point back to Michael.

They said nothing about the penance and nothing about the ritual during the drive back to Ford's church. There was some casual conversation, but it was without focus and without direction. Little needed to be explained or justified through conversation … at least this time.

Michael pulled up in front of the church, the door Ford had used before. The priest looked at Michael and smiled, touched him on the shoulder, got out of the car, and closed the door. As Michael pulled off, Ford looked quickly at the car and then back to the door. He put in his key, turned the handle, entered and closed it behind him. He had the layout of the place memorized. Past the kitchen, to his room, he opened the door and closed it behind him—off the shoes came, the clothes, and into the shower. There was no blood to clean off, so he got ready for bed as he did every other evening.

Things were the same at Michael's apartment. He walked in, put the ritual items away, listened to hear his wife sleeping, and went into the bathroom. He took off his clothes and put them in the wicker bin for dirty clothes, turned on the shower and got in. Clean and ready for bed, Michael turned down the sheets on his side of the bed and got in. His wife instinctively pushed her body against his. The touch of her body made him guilty. He didn't spend much time at home with her, didn't do much with her. They'd always kept to themselves, but at least they spent that time at home together. Now when he wasn't at work, he was away from home with Ford. Or, when he wasn't with

Ford, he was home but distant. His attraction to Ford only involved their mission, but it had more of him than did his wife. "Does she miss me? Does she suspect anything? An affair? Too much work?" Michael thought these questions as he placed his arm across his wife and pulled her closer. "She might," he thought as he settled in; but it didn't matter. Nothing would change. He was enjoying his discipleship, and it came first.

Michael lay there thinking about the fire and penance. He was warm and comfortable. Relaxed and at ease.

CHAPTER TWENTY-THREE

Ford turned on the television, not in his room, but in the living room down the hall, and sat in an overstuffed leather chair that had seen many years and probably heard many conversations. He'd been up for some time, had eaten breakfast, but wasn't ready for the office just yet.

There was breaking news. Ford checked and it was the same story on all the local news programs: a woman brutally murdered, wrapped in plastic and thrown into a dumpster. Within a short period of time, the body had been identified based on the items in her pocket. She was Stephanie Williams, 32 years old, black hair, dark eyes, slim build, no taller than 5' 5", single, college graduate with study abroad experience and ongoing international connections, employed (but the type of employment not mentioned but something allowing for international travel was hinted), and the daughter of a prominent physician with ties to both South America and Europe through Doctors Without Borders. Her family had a long presence in the city. She was spoken of with great affection by friends and by those at the shelter where she'd recently started working as a volunteer. "She seemed so cheerful, so willing to help others. She was particularly good with little children," one member of the shelter staff was quoted as saying.

There were no leads on her killer and no photos of the body permitted. As with the other—Pope, the family was offering a reward for information.

Nothing pointed to Ford or Michael.

The priest still didn't feel as confident in his mission as he imagined Moses and the biblical prophets must have felt in theirs, but he was growing into it and the pleasure he felt increased with each act of extreme penance. Doubt came less often now. He and Michael were doing the hard acts of discipleship—those works the Church and its champions were unwilling and incapable of performing. It had only been two acts of extreme penance, but with everyday, he was growing more determined. Ford thought about himself, "I've come a long way in God's work since the fire. It burned the church and purged me ..."

Michael was in his car, on his way to a meeting, listening to the news and thinking similar thoughts. He remembered something Ford had said much earlier in passing. God's will was a shield, and they could do amazing things if they were faithful—drink poison, encounter danger without harm.

The church always had those with great vision and tremendous dedication. Ford and Michael fancied themselves of that group. They began to feel within themselves a special spiritual gift, a special connection to the divine—a link to the ministry and mind of Christ unlike so many others who claim leadership positions and titles suggesting power—Bishop, Archbishop, Pope.

Ford detested the Bishop in part for this very reason: he had a title and claimed a certain position within the Kingdom of God without the matching actions. He was not a soldier of the cross, but a jester, a fool who mocks what he claims. The robes worn by the Bishop did not cover this up. He might as well be wearing a clown's nose, flopping shoes, and a bright and oversized suit of clothes. The same for many other church officials and priests. "Fools! Cowards! Mockers of Christ!" the priest would find himself thinking and whispering under his breath. The priest thought of the Bishop in these terms often, but did what he could to cover it up. He believed himself to have a mission that shouldn't be hampered by his feelings toward the Bishop. To have it any other way would be to forsake his sacred calling.

He'd preach as he was doing—without offending the fools and cowards, and the sheep mindlessly following along. He'd hold his meetings and fulfill his obligations—christen babies, marry couples, bury the dead, counsel the distraught, participate in community events, and monitor the general happenings at the church. He'd smile, shake hands, kiss babies, and walk the neighborhood. This was mindless work, requiring little from him.

Ford didn't have the same social outlets as those available to Michael. His life hadn't developed that way. But even so, he began to feel more keenly his distance from people, a lack of interest in people. He preferred to read, to lose himself in the new Bible he'd purchased, the books on saints and other figures, theology and philosophy. All these spoke to his ministry, his mission and how to think about it in line with the mystery that is the mind of God. What was odd about this was the increasingly vivid way in which he felt his body, took note of its movements, its touch of the world. Ford thought this was because penance intensified awareness—the rituals he and Michael developed required firm control of his body. Being in the confessional listening made him alert to the sounds a moving body made—the creak of the wood when a nervous body moved; the squeak when an agitated body shifted its weight from one side to the other; the sounds of an angry body's labored breathing. He couldn't see the body, couldn't read them with his eyes, so he learned to listen to them. "That's what more priests should learn to do," he thought to himself. They need to pay attention to the body that transports the soul around. The yearnings, desires, and needs of the body—he was seeing more clearly—guide the soul through the world and determine the challenges it encounters as well as the damage it experiences.

"You can't address the soul if you don't understand the body. Spiritual life or death has a relationship to the activities of the body." This thought pushed passed Ford's lips and made its way to open air. He adjusted himself in the chair, and let the thought find complete expression, "Churches might have a different structure and priests a different ministry if they understood this simple fact: bodies matter."

He stopped himself, straightened up, and redirected his thoughts. "Maybe," he was feeling particularly alert as the new stream of ideas asserted itself, "knowing this is what sets some apart—and marks them for a special ministry." Ford was convinced the biblical disciples and early Church Fathers, like the North African St. Augustine, understood this. Those who played a great role in the aggressive development of the Church—when the Church meant something—must have understood this and theologized and worked in light of it. Whether they sought to control and celebrate the body, they understood it was tied to the soul and both had to be dealt with. The priest grew in eagerness and devotion and, was confident that if he and Michael remained humble before God and mindful they would bless the world.

Not everything would involve this glory. Breakfast and then the office, then mass, followed by confessions, was his routine and there was no reason to break that pattern.

CHAPTER TWENTY-FOUR

"Good morning, Father. How are you today?" Margaret was her cheerful self.

Ford tried to reciprocate as best he could, "I'm fine Margaret. How are you?" He heard her answer—"Fine Father, thank you"—as he moved to his office.

With plenty to read and a sermon to begin considering, Ford had enough to keep himself occupied until time for the confessional. He took a seat on the couch, grabbed a book—Nella Larsen's *Quicksand*—and began to read. Ford had purchased an array of books from the local shop; he wanted to expand his understanding in a variety of ways but he quickly realized that almost every book he picked up and carried to the counter had something to say about bodies in the world. The priest crossed his legs, slouched just a little, and began to read.

He was following Helga Crane to Harlem, thinking about his own work through the lens of her body-related dilemmas. He continued to read, and traveled with her beyond Harlem and back. He was with her as she stood in the rain about to enter the storefront church. His body tightened as Nella Larsen described the enchanting sway of the churchwomen. Helga was just about to surrender to a spirit she didn't understand as Margaret knocked on his door.

"Sorry to disturb you, but there is someone here to see you and she says it is urgent." Margaret didn't enter his office but stood in the doorway pressed against one side of it. He could almost feel her anxiety.

Ford didn't get many visits. He was still new and for many in the parish not quite their priest yet. And when they did come it was for routine issues, nothing frantic and nothing that troubled Margaret like this.

The priest wanted to ease Margaret's mind. "Not to worry, Margaret. It's okay, please show her in."

Margaret extended her hand in the direction of the woman, and signaled her to move forward into the office. As she approached, Margaret stepped aside, looked at Ford and then the woman, before going back to her desk.

Ford stood to welcome her in, and then moved to the desk chair. He motioned her to take a chair in front of the desk, directly facing him. He strained to recognize her, to place her in a pew during one of his Sundays as priest in charge. He couldn't. That didn't mean much to him, though. He'd not been there very long, and had to admit he hadn't given much time and energy to recognizing faces and remembering names.

Sensing Ford trying to place her, she spoke, "I'm sorry to bother you, but I really need your help." She had trouble getting these words out. The tears fell and her body jerked violently. Ford handed her a tissue from a box on his desk.

Her breakdown made Ford all the more concerned to place her, to remember something about her. The short almost round woman, graying hair, and stubby arms didn't look familiar. She was clearly concerned with fashion: the tasteful, probably linen, black suit—skirt and jacket—brooch in the shape of some type of flower, and shoes that looked sturdy enough to last for years with a style that would keep them appealing. Even the priest could tell by the fit of the suit, the sparkle of the brooch, and the soft leather of the shoes that she could afford quality and had classic, good taste.

Working hard to pull herself together and make her request, she took a moment and then continued. "There's no reason you should know me, Father. I don't attend your services." Her shifting in the seat told the priest the statement embarrassed her, but it explained to him why he didn't have the slightest clue as to her identity when she walked through the door. "I don't attend services anywhere very often. I was raised in the Church; my children were christened and took first communion. I, ah, I am Catholic. Just for a variety of reasons I ... my family has not been particularly active." As she spoke she thought to herself she wasn't making a good case for the priest to help her. She shifted gears and got to the point. "My name is Anita Pope ... My husband is Charles Pope. Maybe you heard about him on the news?" The hope that this priest could and would help her was in her voice, the change in octave, the slight tremble.

Charles Pope—the missing man who'd come to his confessional with spiritual sickness requiring the sacrifice of the body for redemption.

"Yes, I've heard about your husband on the news. My prayers and the prayers of the church are with you and your family." The priest wanted to make certain his tone and his words reflected pastoral care. "What can I do to help you?"

The question gave Anita Pope little comfort. She was still tense, collapsing into herself. "Thank you, Father. I'm not certain why I'm here actually." She paused. "I'm going around to all the churches, all the Catholic churches and some of the others, simply making certain churches know about my husband being missing. I guess I'm just hoping one of the churches will know something about it, maybe have seen him before he went missing. Just something to help me and my children ..."

"Okay, she didn't suspect anything ... just looking for any help she can get." Ford thought this but said, "I saw the picture of your husband on the news, but I can't place him around here. I've not seen him. I can ask members of the parish to be on the lookout and to notify the authorities should they have any information. But ... you and your family have already done that."

Mrs. Pope cut him off not wanting the priest to dash the little bit of hope remaining. He had been missing for some time now. "Sorry to cut you off, Father. I understand. That would be greatly appreciated."

Ford smiled and asked another question, just out of curiosity. "Mrs. Pope, did your husband say anything to you about where he was going that day?"

"No, and that's what makes this so difficult. He just vanished. No call, no message ... nothing." She couldn't fight back the tears. Again her body jerked back and forth and she let out a moan that reminded him of that moan from Stephanie Williams. He'd have to shake that connection off and stay focused. "Absolutely nothing from him?"

"No, Father."

With a somber look on his face, Ford said, "This may seem like small comfort right now, but know that God is with you and your family. And the members of this parish will pray for you. Please try to take comfort in the love your husband has for you and your children." Ford had no idea if this was true. Perhaps Anita Pope and Charles Pope did not get along; maybe they were together only for the children— only tolerating each other for the sake of their children? Then again, would she have this reaction to a missing spouse within a loveless marriage? The priest had no idea what particular demons haunted that marriage, that family. But what he said was a small bit of comfort—the stock and trade of the priesthood.

"I really appreciate your prayers and your kind words. I hope the good Lord will see fit to bring my husband home. And if not … that he will have eternal rest."

Ford nodded, but he couldn't bring himself to verbalize agreement—not when he knew Pope's actions had produced spiritual sickness. Eternal rest … this might not be the way to think about Pope.

The priest stood to his feet and Anita Pope followed his lead. "Thank you for your time," she said as she walked toward the door.

"Not to worry," Ford responded. Where those the right words? Well, it was too late to change them. "I will be certain to announce your desire for prayer and for any available information."

"Thank you." With that last comment she was out the door and Ford was left alone.

The priest closed his door and returned to his desk chair. He'd have to share this conversation with Michael.

How connected to the church were those who came to the confessional? His years in ministry taught him that most who come to the confessional are attached to that church and to the penance that priest offers. Clearly, this wasn't always the case. Geography shifted, and the urban context involved both commuters and residents. This would be reflected in how confessionals get used. In addition, he saw over the years a growing pragmatic approach to confession (to church in general for that matter), and this involved less loyalty to any particular church or priest. While this allowed for the misdeeds of a priest to go unchallenged, if not ignored, it also generated flexible boundaries of religious loyalty. My church? My priest? Go where it's convenient— on the way to or from work, to or from the gym, the grocery store, and the list goes on. The time and the fit of the location were what mattered most. Confessions on the go ...

"Hell," Ford complained at times, "there are even phone applications for confession!" Stepping back for a moment, the priest realized it wasn't just the parishioners; a diocesan priest can also hear confessions anywhere in the diocese. Priest and the faithful are mobile. Community church didn't have the same meaning, didn't inspire the same connections and obligations of involvement. There had been a time when loyalty to the Church meant loyalty to the priest, but now this seems to only be the case with pastoral counseling. The uniformity of the Church and its practices played into this drifting away, if not encouraging it. There was little variation in the mass, little variation in the confession—pray, go in, acknowledge sin, absolution, penance— something along those lines—and leave without being known. This was mechanical—the parts easily replaceable.

These circumstances reduced the likelihood that the police would become suspicious because all the victims had a known link— membership and participation—to St. George Church. Suspicion had to be avoided. If nothing else suspicion combined with the tension between Ford and the Bishop could result in the Bishop suspending his privileges to hear confession on grounds of questionable character. But he had to remember this scenario was a long shot. Outside of rare cases, he'd never have to answer significant questions and the Church would support him because of the seal of the confessional— penitents are anonymous and their comments are confidential. And these conversations between priest and penitent are to be guarded inviolate even with death. To break this can result in removal from the Roman Catholic Church—no ethical slippage with respect to the confessional. Worse case, the police might press him, but the Church would support him and he would be the only authority, the only one—with the exception of God—to know what was actually said in the confessional. He could never be forced to share the content of the confessional conversation. He didn't even need to share the content of the conversation with Michael. He knew a sinner needed penance. He might slip on occasion with Michael, but he'd never mention more than the type of sin—no details—and this was only to provide the proper form of the ritual of penance. He was still a priest, a priest in communion with the Church.

Ford left his office; he spoke to Margaret briefly, and put on his robe. Through all the rituals of mass, Ford thought about his conversation with Pope's wife and went over the ideas generated by that meeting. As soon as mass was over, and he'd said hello to the parishioners, shaken enough hands, kissed the babies presented to him, he'd call Michael.

This couldn't wait until he was back in his room with his mobile phone, so in his office Ford picked up the phone and dialed Michael's number. He had it memorized now. "Hello." No need for identifying comments, just straight to the point, "We need to talk."

Michael listened as Ford described his conversation with Anita Pope. He told Michael his guarded concern that they be careful so as to avoid suspicion, but he also shared his sense that the privacy of the confessional and its other arrangements would pretty much prevent this problem from happening. They were fairly safe and their mission sure. They were careful, humble, and committed. Rituals, if bodies were discovered, must highlight the sin addressed and not call attention to the ritual's connection to the church … to him, and to Michael. Up to this point, this hadn't been a problem.

Michael stepped quietly away from his desk, down the hall, and out of the building to a bench nearby to complete his conversation with Ford. Michael wanted to be careful—no telling who might be listening—trying to piece together bits of information.

Ford was concerned to tell Michael enough, but to spare him some of the detail for fear too much detail might have the opposite effect intended—produce anxiety as opposed to promoting guarded assurance.

Michael had little to contribute to the exchange, just the occasional question for clarification or "huh ha," "okay," "sure," and "that's good" to demonstrate engagement, understanding, and support.

The mere fact of his background, his training in the Church, his understanding of Church doctrine and theology, gave Ford a certain standing in this ministry. Michael recognized that fact. He'd initiated the work through his first contact with Ford; he'd nurtured this gift in Ford. But he knew and accepted that Ford with time would take the lead. Borrowing loosely from biblical stories, Michael was something of a John the Baptist trying to prepare the way for another. Not Jesus in this case, but one who would work for Christ and God's will with an eagerness and recognition of blood, pain, and violence as vital. This was enough for Michael. He had no envy, no jealousy.

Chapter Twenty-five

"Boom … slide, boom, slide, boom, slide."

The footsteps were loud, determined, and belabored. Ford could hear what must be a large body moving toward the confessional, almost being dragged as if it were suffering under its weight. One side of the body working harder than the other—"boom … slide … boom … slide." He imagined the look of the body that would have this gate, this stride; and nothing was certain to him other than its girth. "This man, this woman … this person is big," he thought not knowing what to do with that information.

He heard it as the body entered the confessional—hit the seat with a "bang!" and breathe out relief. "Whew!"

"Forgive me Father …" a long pause, grabbing for air, "I," another loud breath, "I have sinned. It's been some weeks since my last confession."

This was an uncertain number, a statement lacking commitment, but Ford said nothing about it. He sat taking it all in—the sounds of the body, the troubled breathing.

Finding the silence too great a burden beyond tension associated with being in that sacramental space, the person spoke again. "Forgive me Father …" Ford cut in, unable to keep to this slow and tortured pace of conversation, and asked him, "What is your sin?"

Surprised by this interruption, he thought for a moment before speaking, wanting to make certain he was completely understood. "I confessed my sins on a regular basis. As I said I was in a confessional weeks ago. Contrition, penance, and reconciliation—I've worked

121

through each with a priest. But there's one I've not mentioned, one I've kept to myself. God knows, of course, but not the priest."

Ford shifted in his seat, and this caused a break in the man's thinking. He paused and then continued. "I waited, Father, because you are new to this parish, this is my home church, and I needed to be certain of a few things ..."

The priest was intrigued and showed it by moving his body and head closer to the screen as he spoke, "Exactly what things did you need to be certain about?"

The man knew he had the priest's attention. He'd studied the priest as best he could and he was comfortable thinking the priest did not share his particular, ah ... inclination.

"The last priest, Father Connors," he moved the conversation to context for a moment—"his name is no secret Father. I can use it, correct?" Without waiting for a reply he continued with his statement. "He didn't hide his secret as carefully as he thought he did. Some knew, and I found out. Needed to make certain you weren't the same."

Ford was a bit frustrated. Why was the man beating around the bush? "Get to the point!" He said this only to himself.

"Father Connor had an interest in children—little boys and little girls. How could a priest like that absolve me of my sin? See what I mean?"

His frustration was quickly replaced with a burning rage— the anger he'd experienced when the Bishop first mentioned his assignment to St. George Church. Ford's body tensed up, his hands became fists, and his legs twitched and shook making a squeaking noise on the wooden floor.

The man would hear him, and perhaps stop talking, or worse yet, leave the confessional before Ford could set the penance for the sin. Still, it took all within him not to push into the other side of the confessional. Straining, he sat and listened.

"In plain English, Father, I desire children. My children when they were young, although they've said nothing about it. Children on line ..."

Ford interrupted, "You are a pedophile. Child molester. That is the mortal sin you've not confessed before today?"

Silence.

"You are a child molester. That is the sin you want to address today?"

"Yes, Father."

Silence.

"Why now? If this has been going on for that long, why now?"

He moved away from the screen, hoping that would provide a little cover, some distance from the self he'd hidden from other adults.

"My children are older, Father. They have children now. I'm not old … 56. It's not an end of life confession. Not that at all. I need to tell someone about it, not just about the physical side of it. But what it does inside, where people can't see. Coming to you … you understand both sides of this thing. And God already knows … I see that, but it's been a long time and I need to acknowledge to myself that God knows. Only a priest can do that. You get it?"

Ford sat still—just the faint sound of him breathing. He waited.

Silence … Silence.

"You see what I mean, Father? I don't have the theology stuff down like you do. Can't even say that I really know or understand church doctrine. But who does?" There was a long pause before he continued. "I mean, besides people in the Church like you. But I do know, have known all my life, the confessional is where this stuff gets worked out, and it doesn't have to go public. This is confidential. And of course you know you can't say anything to the authorities." He kept pressing the point, "I'm right about that, Father."

The man also knew that abuse of children could be taken to secular authorities, and he could go to jail. He wouldn't go alone, though. If he faced prison, he'd make certain to go public and expose Father Connor. That would surely embarass the Church and result in lawsuits from Connor's victims. Big money and a major blow against the Church's image. The man assumed that Ford, as a representative of the Church, would want to avoid that situation, and so he was fairly confident Ford would say nothing, and would keep the man's conduct between the three of them—the man, the priest, and God.

Ford saw how the confidentiality could cut both ways. Church regulations, his duty as a priest, required silence to the outside world concerning the destruction of young minds and bodies committed by this faceless man. Silence even when secular law demanded justice. In this way, there was an element of compliance and a twisting of communal obligations.

The confessor's assumption affirmed the soul trumped the body—that the Church's form of punishment superseded other modes of correction. It sickened the priest, but he'd have to confirm the man's assumptions. "Yes, you are correct. I won't provide information to civil authorities. I can encourage you to submit to legal authorities and seek legal recourse. But…"

The man cut Ford off, "I've come to you, not to the civil authorities, as you named the cops. This needs to be handled a different way, Father, in line with the Church's rules. Beyond my contrition, what is my penance?"

Ford had been thinking as the man spoke, and he was ready with a response. "This sin is a mortal sin. Prayers in the confessional won't restore proper relationship with God and the Church."

"Okay, I thought so."

"You'll need to surrender more. You'll need to give more of yourself."

"What?"

"This is your act of penance. You must stop your behavior. Whatever it takes to do that. And you must help restore the innocence of children by giving time to the youth shelter on California Avenue."

"I work, Father." He thought about it after saying it. Did it sound callous? Would those words change the priest's approach and the required penance? He wasn't sure why he said that. The penance seemed minor … in light of what he'd done. Why not just go with it? Why say anything?

He wanted to explode, but he held himself and instead told the man "I understand the need to meet your monetary obligations, to care for your family—although I don't have one and you have damaged yours. So you can make arrangements to go after work. But you will need to give significant time, after 5 p.m., for the number of weeks corresponding to the number of lives you destroyed." Ford realized that what he described was similar to the penance for the trafficker, but he had little reason to believe it would suggest a pattern to police investigators. The penance—giving of time to those in need—was similar but the way in which penance took place would distinguish the two.

"Seven weeks, after work. Must I tell my family what I'm doing … that I'm working at a shelter?"

The compliance in the question surprised Ford, after the man's earlier defiance. The priest thought and responded, "You don't have to tell your family. I assume you didn't tell them you were coming to confession today, right?"

After a nervous laugh, he responded, "No … no I didn't."

"Seven weeks, beginning tomorrow." Ford was firm in these instructions. There would be no debating the points. Seven weeks. Penance started immediately.

"I'll go tomorrow, and I'll sign up. But for now … are there prayers I need to say? Something else I need to do—or you need to do—before I leave? I have a general sense, Father, because I've been to confession before. This just seems a bit different, and I thought maybe it required something different to happen before I could go."

Ford smiled to himself, knowing what was to come next. "No, I've assigned you your penance. You need to complete the assignment. That's all."

"Okay, Father. Thank you." And Ford heard the noise again as the body stabilized enough to leave the confessional.

"Boom, slide … boom, slide." The sound grew faint and then the door opened and closed.

Ford sat for a minute, taking it all in before calling Michael.

The priest dialed the number and paused, thinking again about the sounds—"boom … slide … boom"—and imagining the other noises that body made outside the church, when it thought it safe to act.

"Yes …" There was no need to use names. "Yes …"

"There is a sinner, Michael, in need of penance." Ford relished those words, and imagined the good feeling they generated in him must be similar to the joy the disciples felt when Christ called to them—"come and follow me."

Chapter Twenty-six

California Avenue is one of those streets that seems to cover the entire length of the city, one that cuts through so many neighborhoods and sections of town that it is something of a lifeline cut deep. Moving down that avenue one gets examples of the "look" of the city as it shifts ethnically, racially, and economically. It runs past extreme wealth, middle-class strivers, to extreme poverty marking out despair on faces of various hues. The businesses along the way also change to reflect the makeup—check cashing places, and liquor stores in the poverty stricken areas with billboards overhead painting portraits of the good life, if you buy what those stores offer. More upscale stores in the middle-class areas … Starbucks, fine dining, banks, stores beyond the scope and scale of "Everything for 99 Cents." And finally, in the wealthiest areas, where there is a manicured, grassy area with flowers dividing the lines of California Avenue—there are no stores immediately along the avenue, just large and gated homes. The wealthy guarded their area, and certainly wouldn't allow businesses or services that would draw the wrong crowd.

The man with the belabored movement had been sent far from this wealthy area, with its signs of more than enough spilling onto lawns in the form of fountains, circular driveways, and "armed guard response" home security signs. Ford sent him to a shelter—For Haven Sake—on the other end of town, in the middle of poverty. The small building housing the shelter was a marker of hope, a glimmer of "maybe" on an otherwise bleak landscape. No real green space, massive bars on windows, faded paint, and loud city sounds. And the priest was comfortable with him going after work—whatever he did for a living—because as the city grew dark he'd really see its desperation, signs of its despair hidden during daylight.

This was a darker section of the city, few whites ventured this way. They would play on that.

There were alleys, and lots that resembled untamed wilderness. Any of these could serve as a proper location for the ritual of penance. All provided enough distance from the street, and enough cover to prevent Ford and Michael from being disturbed. Both knew enough about this area to know people kept to themselves and didn't get involved in things not affecting them personally. That was a strategy for survival. They would only need to get that body to one of those areas.

Ford and Michael waited three weeks. Others during that time drew Ford's interests, but this man's sin stayed on his mind in a way that made it clear he needed extreme penance. Or, was it the sounds that man's body made as it negotiated the sanctuary? Ford couldn't shake those sounds. The others were set aside, given prayers of absolution, penance, and then they moved on.

Michael and Ford worked out a plan, one that drew on the man's desire for forgiveness and the work of the people in that area. Ford positioned himself in one of the untamed lots, the one near a parked car—a late model luxury sedan that you'd see in a glossy ad—that had to belong to this man. It screamed I don't belong here. The owner was out of place and the car showed it.

Michael parked behind the man's vehicle. It didn't really matter if the molester saw their car. Michael would stay in position between the two cars until he saw a white man leaving the shelter—he assumed their guy would be the only white who'd risk being over there so late. Once the man was spotted, Michael would pretend to be injured and in need of assistance. He'd ask the man for aid, say that his young daughter was in the thick growth in the lot and was also hurt. He'd moved her—it was important the other victim be young, less chance the man would say "no." He'd moved her there to protect her from further attack until he could get some assistance. It wasn't likely the man would refuse to help Michael—a white male, well dressed, clearly of middle-class standing. Michael would explain that his GPS system misled them. "You know how the routes change in a city always under construction." And they had been attacked. The guys ran off but not before injuring him and his daughter. Michael would hold his side as if in great pain.

They gambled the man would follow Michael into the thicket where Ford would be waiting. If he refused to volunteer assistance, Michael would use the hammer hidden in his waistband resting on the small of his back.

The man approached slowly, and Michael faked alarm and begged for his assistance. The man followed Michael into the lot. Hidden from street view, Ford jumped out at the man. The man gasped, grabbed his chest, and fell to the ground. Heart attack.

They hadn't planned for this, although sounds he made as he approached the confessional combined with his physical appearance spoke to health conditions. They had startled the man; he had no reason to think he'd be attacked in the lot. The man was too absorbed by Michael's plight, too interested in seeing Michael's daughter to give consideration to what might happen in the lot.

Lying there, he didn't look quite human to Ford. The soft light of the moon faded the edges of the body, and Ford could almost imagine him some blob of stuff oozing out of the earth.

He reached down, without any medical training, touched the man's neck and his wrist looking for a pulse. None. The eyes were open, stirring at Ford, and frozen in a look of penetrating fear. The man seemed to peer through and beyond the priest. The mouth was open as well, formed to scream but no sound came out. The left arm was crushed behind his body. Was his last act an effort to brace himself? The right arm lay across his body bent at the elbow, and the right-hand still rested on his chest as if trying to grab and massage his heart—to pound and press it into working. There was a wet spot on the front of his khakis that looked in the dark liked blood, but Ford knew it was the activity of his bladder at the moment of shock. The left leg was straight and locked in place, with the sole of his well-worn wingtip facing the priest. The right leg was bent at an odd angle. Ford looked at the large belly, covered by a wrinkled dress shirt, and for a moment thought he saw it move.

The priest hovering over the body, and Michael standing nearby looking toward the street had to make a decision. Should they move the body to the car? But why do that ... to make it appear he'd had a heart attack in the car? Was that too much planning on the fly? They agreed the body should not be moved. After all, once it was discovered authorities would assume he was threatened by thieves and died in the process of being robbed. Wearing their gloves to prevent leaving prints, they removed the wallet, and scattered its contents in order to suggest the thieves ran off. Why he was in that neighborhood at that time of night—the autopsy would indicate time of death—would center on the shelter. Because it is so close to the crime scene, police would certainly ask its employees about the victim. And they would be able to identify him.

This wasn't how they planned the ritual. The man was to be beaten, and mutilated in such a way as to make him feel pain and force him to reflect on the suffering he'd caused. But the sinner's heart couldn't withstand the process. It stopped too soon.

Had proper penance been offered when the man died of a heart attack? Did penance require pain directly related to payment for the sin, as opposed to pain being a consequence of genetics, poor diet, and lack of exercise? Had he been able, even in death, to escape the demands of penance? Ford and Michael thought about this, and talked about it on the way back to their respective homes.

Ford was more upset by the death by heart attack than Michael. For Michael, death after the confessional was death. The priest thought there should be more to it than the mere fact of life ended. He wasn't certain if this was a result of his disposition toward ceremony, toward ritual as marker of transformations—christenings, first communions, communion ... confessions. Eventually the priest came to a conclusion similar to Michael's, but one with more theological nuance. Although they worked out rituals for penance, an element of mystery remained. Even this heart attack is death for life. They must be careful not to confuse their will, their desire to be instruments of God's will with God's will. Not to confuse their desire to act on God's behalf with the penance God requires.

As morning approached, and this conclusion settled into his spirit, shaping his perspective on his ministry, Ford slept a little.

The days went by and Ford thought about that large man dead in the lot on California Avenue. Did the dogs eat at the corpse? Did other animals make a meal of the fingers, the eyes, and other parts of the body? If not found soon, would the sun and the increasing heat of the season cause the body to swell, decompose, and ooze?

Weeks passed and Ford went through his routine. Memories of that man were just beginning to fade, replaced by other thoughts about his ministry. It was around that time he heard the report.

A badly decomposed body was found on California Avenue—it was part of the morning news that seemed to always revolve around tragedy in that section of town. The body couldn't be identified easily by sight, but dental records indicated it was Mr. James Morke. Married to Margerie Townston Morke, he was the father of four children, and the grandfather to several others. He was a long time employee of the public school system and most recently served as principal of one of the area high schools. Mr. Morke, the reporter then said, was an upstanding and well-regarded member of St. George Church. Morke's demise produced sadness for his wife … his children … and family friends and fellow employees of the school system. For the priest, such feelings for Morke pointed to the blindness of people, a discomfort with confronting wrongdoing. "Cover up sin with smiles and empty words," Ford said as he stood to his feet, "God requires us to probe life's dark corners."

He hadn't said it on California Avenue, in the overgrown lot, but he knew he had to. He'd thought this through and had clarity. Ford had to say it, to have a sense of completion, to finalize the task, "I absolve you."

Ford turned off the television.

Because Morke was a longstanding member of the church, he expected a visit from his wife and children. They would want to arrange the funeral—closed casket—and would want prayers for his soul and comfort for theirs. As expected, they showed up with tear stained faces and black clothing for the occasion. They slouched as he welcomed them in, and they sighed as they took their seats on the couch. Knowing what he knew, Ford listened with as much interest as he could muster.

He'd gotten better at controlling his facial expressions so as not to reveal through his eyes and mouth what he knew from the confessional. No looking away at key moments of the conversation; no tensing of the lips; no squinting; no signs of anything other than a priest listening to the sounds of misery voiced by parishioners.

Ford also noticed he seemed more drawn those times he looked in the mirror. His body showed the signs of his work. But wasn't that to be expected? He was serving the Lord—body and soul—and flesh would necessarily show the signs of that type of deep discipleship. Extreme penance takes its toll on the penitent and disciple. At those times, looking in the mirror, he would smile a faint smile at the Ford on the other said of the mirror. To worry about his own welfare would distract from his ministry. He couldn't do that, and didn't need to do it. Faith caused him to assume God would take care of God's disciples; nothing could harm him before God was done with him.

The priest spent much of the morning with the family, letting them work through their pain and grief. They sat in the office until Margaret shyly knocked and quietly told Father Ford it was time to conduct mass. The priest said a prayer with the family and brought the meeting to an end.

CHAPTER TWENTY-SEVEN

Ford felt himself walking differently, and observing things differently with increased sensitivity to surroundings and encounters. At such times, when he was aware of these changes in himself, he'd think again of Thoreau and determine to live deliberately for the glory of God— mindful of body and soul and the links deeds forge between the two.

The confessional was the centering moment for him, the space in the world where heaven touched earth, and where he had most clarity and felt closest to his God and the work required of him. Ford came to crave the confessional, to mark out the day in terms of his sitting in the box of contrition. The smell of the confessional, the sounds that marked it off, the feel of the wood, the touch of the screen, and the slightly visible breeze when the curtain moved—these were the sensations for which he longed.

He was beginning to believe he'd learned the "type" who'd come to the confessional, and on some days the priest thought he could tell something about the sin by the sounds he heard—the way bodies slid across the wood, repositioned, and knocked against the confessional walls. He felt himself growing spirituality.

Despite the changes he saw and felt, Ford didn't want to think too highly of himself. He was the instrument, the fleshy tool for penance. Ford understood there was distinction between God and humanity. That distinction did not allow humans to know the mind of God, but it did not prevent humans from being sensitive to the movement of the Spirit and acting accordingly. John the Baptist did. Mary Magdalene did, when she was the first to announce the risen Lord. Paul, Ford thought to himself, also did after being knocked off the horse and devoted to spreading the Gospel. The saints of the Church, like St. George, were also sensitive to the Spirit. He, James Ford, was sensitive as well.

Ford felt certain Michael was also having similar thoughts—understanding his particular role in God's plan for penance and reconciliation. But he wouldn't ask. He'd simply be prayerful about it, and mindful of their work together.

He and Michael—the two disciples—went through their days. Work. Mass. Meetings. Confessions, and phone calls about sinners.

Chapter Twenty-eight

This confession hadn't started in the traditional way—no "forgive me father" as the starting point, as the mark of contrition. But he didn't worry. He just listened.

"Father, I've been a member of this parish for eighty-two years … since my family moved to this neighborhood when I was three years old." The voice paused for emphasis. "I've lived in the same house, not four blocks from this church for all of those eighty-two years. And the place has changed!"

The voice was a little loud and clearly agitated. But, the age of the penitent, and the disillusionment expressed in the voice, caught his attention and he allowed her to continue, with just one caution. "Please," he said softly, "you will need to keep your voice down."

"I'm so sorry, Father Ford. I just get worked up when I think about all that has happened around me. You know, my house is the last house from the old neighborhood. Now all these things they call townhouses, condos, new apartment buildings with gymnasiums and stores below them." The voice trembled, and Ford knew falling tears now marked the face on the other side of the screen.

"I've been here a long time, and I've tried to adjust as well as an old lady can. It's hard. These new people don't understand me. They don't understand what this neighborhood used to be; how it has changed over the years; how many people raised families and worked hard, and called this place home—not just an investment to show off money. Now it's different Father … so very different." Her voice trailed off …

"What is your sin?" He wanted her to speak her mind, but he also

134

needed to push the conversation forward.

"Oh, yes. I'm sorry. I know better than this … Forgive me father for I have sinned. It's been four days since my last confession."

Ford was beginning to remember this voice. He'd heard it before, quite often actually, but it had a different texture and tone today, and that threw him a bit.

"Yes … what is your sin?"

"Murder …"

Silence.

Ford was stunned. "Murder?" Did he hear the voice right? How could that old woman be guilty of murder? He repeated her confession, "Murder?"

"Yes, Father, murder."

She'd assumed an experienced priest had heard it all, nothing would surprise him. But then again, how often would a priest hear an eighty-two-year-old woman confess murder? She'd have to provide more information, a bit of context for the sin.

"My neighbors, Father Ford, the Mortons from Scarsdale. They moved into the huge modern looking something next to my home maybe five years ago now. Horrible people, Father, horrible!"

She remembered his request that she keep her voice down, so she paused, adjusted herself in the seat, and continued. "The husband is a bad man, an attorney working for a large law firm. He gets charges against big companies dropped. They pollute lakes and rivers, and people are sick and dying. Didn't he commit a mortal sin by helping to destroy the environment? … Have you heard about these companies on the news?

"Yes, I have." As he spoke the priest wished he'd had an opportunity to assign penance to that attorney.

"It's atrocious, Father. Such a crime." She began to cry again. It took a few minutes for her to gather herself, but Ford was patient.

"And you know what he did after winning some of those big cases, Father? You know what he did? Well, he bought a new car—one of those expensive sports cars. Must have cost a small fortune!"

Quiet down and tell the story—she remembered the instructions.

"He walks around smiling a sickeningly egotistical smile. And the wife is no better. She's a doctor, but not for people like me ... or you. She's one of those special doctors that only works for a small group of people who can afford to pay lots of money. What's that called, Father?"

Ford spoke quickly hoping to provide an answer to the question and get her to move through the rest of the story, "a concierge doctor."

"That's right, Father ... a concierge doctor. My goodness. What's happening to this world? I was sick one day Father, had one of my episodes."

She didn't elaborate on the nature of the episode, and the priest didn't press the issue. He wanted to hear about the murder she confessed.

"And I made my way over to their house. It was evening and she was home. I didn't think I would make it to the house, but I did. I knocked, and knocked again. I had to sit down. She came to the door, looked at me, and asked what the problem was. I told her I was having an episode and needed her help." More tears, and a pause. "You know what she said? YOU know what she SAID, Father?" Another pause. "She told me she couldn't help me because she didn't want to take a chance on being sued. Sued, Father. Me?"

Again, a break in the story, and Ford waited.

"But she said she'd call an ambulance. How was I supposed to pay for that Father? I'm on a fixed income!" Reminding her to keep her voice down would be useless at this point, so he let her talk.

"The two children, Father, are no better than their terrible parents. They are disrespectful and rude. That's not how children should be. My children weren't like that. They are dead now, and, oh ...huh ... do I miss them. I'm alone, Father. But they were never like that. They were respectful ..."

He imagined her smiling when she thought of her children—feeling pleased to have had them, and proud of the people they'd become.

"These kids are mean to their parents and no better when they address me. I've asked them to keep their music down and they've called me an 'old hag.' The parents did nothing about that. It's like they're afraid of those kids. Who are the parents there, Father. Who?!"

Ford adjusted his legs. His right leg was falling asleep. He stretched his back, interrupted and spoke, "Please put the pieces together."

"Sorry, Father. I'm an old woman, please be patient. I'll get to it." She adjusted her position, and Ford could hear something that sounded like a metal frame shift. Perhaps a walker, he thought.

"Then, Father, they got a couple of dogs. I don't know why, seems like they're barely home. But they got a couple of dogs. And those dogs bark all the time. Boy, do they bark! And so loud, and they don't do anything about it. That was the last straw for me, Father. I felt like everything was taken away from me—my neighborhood changed, and the Mortons were stealing my dignity. That's all I had left! It was like I was invisible to them, nobody they needed to hear or respect."

Ford remained silent, taking in all this information, imagining how it must feel to be that woman.

"So, Father, while the parents and kids were gone, I cooked up a special treat for the dogs. I put some rat poison in some food and fed it to the dogs. That took care of the dogs, Father. No more barking. No more dog droppings on my lawn."

"Is that the murder? You killed two dogs?" Ford was surprised to hear a faint laugh from the other side of the screen.

"No, Father. That's not it. That was just the beginning." She wanted to make certain Ford understood what she was saying, the implications of her comment needed to be clear. So she asked, "Do you understand Father?"

The priest wasn't going to solve a mystery. This is the confessional and so he responded, "No." One word that said "keep going."

"They found the dogs dead in the backyard. It was a mess. Vomit and dog droppings showed their struggle to live. The Mortons didn't suspect anything. I heard them talking to the people who came to remove the animals. They said the dogs could have gotten a hold of anything. The house was built on old soil, they were told, and that soil could contain a lot of different things that would poison a dog. They weren't going to pay the money needed to exam the dogs and secure a cause of death. The dogs didn't matter that much." The voice was lighter, with less misery expressed, and with an odd joy shaping the words.

"I realized that it wasn't the dogs that I needed to get rid off. The people were the real problem. They represented the death of the neighborhood I'd grown up in and that I loved. They wouldn't leave. So, I would get rid of them."

The priest wondered how this old woman could do that. He had a different sense of the elderly based on what he saw during the week and on Sundays, and as he walked the neighborhood most days. But, he thought, "How many of them hold dark secrets?"

"I couldn't shoot them or burn the house. I'm an old woman and couldn't do the labor necessary to burn the house. I'm old but I still didn't want to get caught and spend my last days—could literally be days—in prison. So, I thought … if the poison worked on the animals without suspicion, maybe poison for the family?"

She recounted from the news stories that the husband's legal cases gained him a good number of enemies. He didn't take them seriously, but one of them could easily be angry enough to kill the family. Not just the husband; but, the whole family as a way of getting the justice they didn't get during one of the court cases. Lots of suspects would lessen the likelihood the finger would be pointed at her—a little old lady murdering people? Who would believe it?

She had a plan. They'd had disagreements in the past—nothing that went too public, but there was tension. She'd try to make amends by bringing them some baked goods. And the baked goods would contain poison. Knock on their door, apologize, and offer them the cookies as an "I'm sorry. Can we start over?"

She gathered her baking supplies. Mixed the dough, added the chocolate chips and rat poison, shaped the cookies, buttered the pan, and put the cookies on the pan. Oven. Done. She let the cookies cool, and then placed them on one of her best plates. Ready.

Putting on a smile to cover her deep hatred for them, she got her cane—couldn't use the walker and carry the package—and left the house with the cookies in tow. Down her driveway. Down the sidewalk. Up the steps, and onto the porch.

"I'm slow moving, Father. But I was confident no one saw, or at least no one paid attention to what they saw—just an old lady moving down the street. I didn't matter enough for anyone to take note of me.

I rang the doorbell. The son answered the door, and motioned me in. He was on his phone and couldn't stop that conversation long enough to say a word to me. Actually, I was surprised he invited me in. Maybe I didn't matter enough for him to really be offended by our exchanges in the past?"

Ford repositioned himself in the box, but didn't say a word.

"He pointed to a room down the hall. I looked back as I made my way to the room. He waved and I assumed he wanted me to turn right. The boy never took the phone away from his ear and he never stopped talking. I could hear a television as I walked into the room. It was big, bigger than my downstairs, and it was on the wall. I cleared my throat to get attention." She cleared her throat for effect.

"The attorney and doctor where in there and they seemed surprised to see me. Can't blame them. It was a surprise. I said that I was sorry to interrupt, but that I wanted to come over and apologize for all the misunderstandings—that I was being unreasonable and needed to say I was sorry."

Ford couldn't see her face, but he assumed she was also acting out the smile.

"'Ah, well …' who'd think the attorney would be without words. 'Excuse my husband,' the doctor said. 'Thank you for coming over. We should be the ones coming to your house.'" As she finished saying this the daughter came out of the kitchen, saw the old woman and her parents, and startled.

"Not to worry. I wanted to bring you some cookies. They're chocolate cookies. I hope you enjoy them. The husband reached for them, but the daughter was faster, and without saying a word, she grabbed the plate, unwrapped it, took a few cookies, and handed the plate back to her father." She paused. Ford could hear her take a deep breath before continuing.

"The doctor, attorney, daughter and the son who eventually made his way to the room, shook my hand, and thanked me again. My pleasure, I said, and smiled a big smile."

Ford had nothing to say.

"I left, and went back home to wait."

"Did you feel any regret? Any remorse?" Ford thought she might feel some contrition—some shame, or some other emotion that meant she recognized she'd taken life.

"They had a beautiful home, Father, built on the misery of others. The son in what had to be expensive jeans and shirt made to look old and beaten up. Father ... who pays money to look destitute?! The daughter was dressed the same. What sense does that make? I don't know much about jewelry, but I know the attorney had on a gold Rolex watch. The doctor was all made up, with lots of diamonds. They had so much and got it through the pain and suffering of others. That family was everything wrong with my neighborhood! Everything wrong! No respect, no consideration!!" He'd asked the question that sparked it, and he'd have to ride out the anger.

"Remorse? No! They deserved it, Father."

It couldn't end with this, Ford wanted to know more. What happened to the bodies? Did the police think of her as a suspect because of the cookies? "What did you do after delivering the cookies and then going home?"

"I waited. No fear—just relief. A few days later, I went back to the house early morning. I wanted to get in and remove everything associated with the cookies. I'd collect the plate, and I knew from television about fingerprints; but I'd worn my gloves so that wasn't a problem, and I had them on again when I went back. I was able to get in the house because I had a key they'd given me the first year they were in the house, before our problems. The family was going on vacation and they asked me to put the mail in the house. They're so busy, so all over the place, they didn't remember to get the key back. And I didn't return it. Not certain why I didn't give it back, but I didn't ... Anyway, I took the plate and the covering, looked to make certain there was nothing around that might make me a suspect, and I left."

Ford had to know. He had to ask, "What about the bodies?"

"They were a gruesome sight. And the smell ... I won't go into details. But I'll say, you could see the pain frozen on their faces. The bodies were fixed in postures that screamed agony. The poison must have caused them to become disoriented, unable to gather enough energy and insight to call 911 for help. There'd been no ambulance. I would have heard the sirens."

She said the police came by when the children hadn't reported for school in a couple of days; the attorney hadn't been in the office working on important cases; and the doctor hadn't responded to request from her special clientele. They asked her some questions: did she see anything? Hear anything? No.

It was reported on the news. Everyone was disturbed and troubled by the unexplained death of every member of this family—Edward Morton, 58; Joan Morton, 50; Nicholas Morton, 17; Susan Morton, 15. It had been determined by the police investigation that it was murder. Leads where followed, interviews conducted, but no arrests where made.

"Have you come in contrition?"

"I'm here Father. In the confessional, telling you what I did. I thought I'd bring this to God."

"Have you come in contrition?" He asked again. What the old woman said didn't answer the question as he needed it answered— "yes" or "no."

"I suppose you want a short and sweet answer but I can't. Is murder wrong? In most cases I guess. Do I regret what I did? Well ..." There was a pause that startled Ford.

"Well ... I'm not certain of that. I'm old. My neighborhood isn't me anymore. The people and things that anchored me in that place are gone. I'm alone. I don't have much and they were taking from me the little I had—my dignity. In a way, Father, you could say they were killing me. They were attempting to kill me slowly, not with a knife or gun, but through disrespect. My self-worth was being stolen from me with every disrespectful comment, by every refusal to be neighborly, through every dismissive look." She'd given this some thought, and was confident in her answer. "So, I might want to think about this as self-defense—defending myself from destruction by removing the real killers. Dignity is the way we know we are alive and matter when all signs suggest otherwise. It's the spark of life, a bit of God's image that wasn't taken from us when we were forced out the Garden of Eden. It wasn't destroyed by that original sin committed by Adam. I killed the people who were trying to kill me ..."

Then silence.

There was just the sound of breathing, hard breathing, and bodies uncomfortable and moving within the confines of the box.

She broke the silence with a question, "Is that difficult to understand, Father? It might not be in line with your theology or such; but it's true. To not respond to them, to protect myself from disrespect, would have been something like suicide. And that's a sin, right?"

She was awaiting Ford's response, hoping that he would understand, ask her to make prayers of absolution, and then leave her with some penance to perform.

Outside his role as priest, as disciple, to the degree he could create some space he wanted to sympathize. He also knew the sense of loss when neighborhoods are destroyed, when those who should care about people are only concerned with material gain. The priest knew this firsthand. That part of him agreed with the old woman. However, there was a stronger pull, a more lasting sense of how things should happen. It was this inner self that won the day, and guided his response to the murderer. What he and Michael did was consistent with the will of God. They killed not for selfish reasons, not to advance themselves. They killed to advance the Kingdom of God, to punish sinners in a way the Church could not muster without them. This woman killed only for her benefit, and without any attention to the true nature of sin and penance.

"Rationalizing it doesn't change anything … what you committed was a mortal sin."

As he said this, he thought again about her defense: they were killing her by taking away the last thing that kept her alive in a place that was foreign and lonely. They were killing her by robbing her of her dignity, rendering her insignificant, wiping out her presence through their lifestyle and their destruction of the old neighborhood. To not preserve self, to maintain her dignity, would be the equivalent of suicide. And that would be the sin. Who was to judge the value of human dignity? Was it to be defended even with murder? Was it really that spark of life distinguishing us? And what did she mean by Adam's sin in the Garden of Eden? Was she suggesting a different read of the story because the Church tends to blame Eve—"The woman gave to me and I did eat." Was this old woman with no training saying Adam was really the guilty party, and for what reason? Cowardliness? Was his sin unwillingness to own his actions, and to claim dignity? Would there have been a different response had he taken responsibility for his actions and by that to claim his personhood and his significance in the world? Even that claiming wouldn't have resulted in him staying in the Garden. There was still an act of disobedience—a break with God's will. He and Eve would still have been thrown out and our current condition would remain the same. Adam would have owned his actions and acknowledged his significance, but he would have still been punished. And why would it be any different for the descendants of Adam and Eve? Mortal sin is mortal sin. No desire—however noble in and of itself—wipes out the meaning and consequences of sin.

"The blue haired baker of death," Ford thought, "was guilty. Her age and her excuses be damned."

The priest was firm. Age didn't make a difference. She killed with forethought and malice, and for deeply selfish reasons. Self-defense? Ridiculous.

"You must make penance. You should consider making this right in terms of human law as well, but I won't compel you to do so."

Feeling a bit defeated and misunderstood, she responded to this judgment. "Father, perhaps when you are my age you will understand. But you are my priest, this is my church, and I will honor what you tell me to do to revive my spiritual life and redeem my soul."

Ford couldn't send an eighty-two-year-old woman out to perform service in some institution. But against his first mind—the human inclination—he knew this required extreme penance. Where and how?

"What must I do, Father?"

The priest had to give a response, "You must pray for their souls." In and of itself that wasn't enough—not a fitting start to what was necessary for her redemption. How could he and Michael set up an appropriate situation? As he was thinking of what to say, he heard a noise. It wasn't the typical movement of a body to get comfortable, or the bump against the walls of the confessional. This was more violent and lacked the controlled motion that usually informed movement in the box. It sounded like something large sliding and hitting the floor.

He hesitated, then he stood, moved quickly to the opening and looked out to the right and to the left. Looking down he saw a walker turned over, part of it sticking out of the confessional, the outline of the lower half of a body—black orthopedic shoes, wrinkled stockings on legs with large blue veins showing years, and a black skirt that was long but twisted above the knees because of how the body slid. He pushed his way in, began to help the old woman up. He could smell her age, and could see the years had taken a toll on her. That weary body, bent, and twisted by the years had paid a pound of flesh for that dignity.

Ford recognized her face. He'd seen it at most masses. Blue hair—he'd been right about that—an aged face with so many deep lifelines, lipstick put on by shaking hands and simple but elegant earrings—probably an heirloom she treasured as a memory of better days. On her black jacket matching the skirt was a brooch, a small golden brooch in the shape of a circle. Jammed against the wall of that small space was an oxygen tank. She hadn't mentioned it. Maybe some of the sounds he'd heard earlier—the metallic ringing and the hard breathing—are accounted for by that tank?

"Are you okay? What happened? ... Are you ok?"

She was uncomfortable, embarrassed, and shocked. But the old woman adjusted herself, took in a deep breath from the tank, and spoke. "I'm sorry, Father. I must have lost my balance somehow. I thought we were done, you said to "pray for their souls." I thought that was my penance, so I was trying to stand up ..."

"But ... are you alright?"

"I"—struggling for a deep breath—"think I am. Just let me sit for a moment. I'll be okay to walk home in a few minutes. Just give me a little time, Father."

He helped her to the seat, and she rested. He stood there looking down at the tank as she worked to compose herself. That's when he noticed the valve. It hit him. "This has to be handled differently, and I'll need to use this opportunity. Can't wait for Michael."

He was getting nervous because he knew he didn't have much time. She'd feel well enough to stand and head home. But he had to act first. He'd seen these tanks before and he knew he could adjust the valve so that it would affect the oxygen supply. He could fix it so that by the time she reached home, four blocks away, and went inside, she would run out of oxygen. After the fall and the walk, the old woman would be too weak to secure another tank. She'd collapse again, and die.

Ford distracted her, and while she wasn't paying attention he adjusted the valve. It wasn't difficult and it didn't take much time.

A few minutes later, after a casual exchange having nothing to do with her sin, she stood and asked for clarity, "Father is prayer for their souls my penance?"

"Yes," Ford replied, bending to touch her gently on her shoulder. She felt comforted and somewhat understood, or at least heard.

"But there's more. I also want you to think about life. Every moment during your walk home, think about life and what you would miss most if it were to come to an end."

She was confused by this request. She'd been going to confession for a long time, but had never received penance like this. But he was the priest and she would honor his role in the process. "Yes, Father. I will do that."

He helped her to the door, and reminded her of her obligations. As she moved down the ramp, the old woman looked back and smiled. Father Ford waved, and said in a faint voice, "I absolve you."

That Sunday he announced very sad news to the parish. Mrs. Wilma Smith, eighty-two years of age, long-time member of this community and this parish was found dead in her home. The funeral would take place at the church on Tuesday. She didn't have family. She'd outlived everyone. The day her body was laid to rest, a few members of the church, and Father Ford, were present.

Michael had been in church and heard the announcement, but he didn't know the full story. Ford would have to tell him.

The following Sunday Ford maintained his usual practice of greeting the parishioners as they left the church building. Michael and his wife, who didn't attend regularly, were last in line to say hello. Ford shook her hand, and thanked her for attending.

"It's always wonderful to see you." As their hands separated she replied, "Thank you for your inspiring sermon."

The priest had spoken on the need for charity as a marker of

Christian commitment. He'd developed the topic around recent struggles in Washington, DC over national debt and high levels of unemployment. It wasn't inspired and he hadn't put much thought or time into it, but at least one person found it useful. Or, she might have said that just to be pleasant, to have something to say in response to his "wonderful to see you." It really didn't matter either way. He needed to speak with Michael, and he didn't give much thought to his sermons anyway.

Having been greeted by the priest and after giving her response, Michael's wife moved on. Before getting out of earshot she turned and said, "I'm stopping by Starbucks, and I'll meet you at the car." She turned again, and started walking.

"Okay, don't be long," was Michael's reply. He wasn't certain she heard, but the look on Ford's face said they needed to talk, so he didn't worry about the logistics of his wife going to Starbucks and getting to the car.

"I won't hold you long, but we need to meet. Let's say the Thai restaurant a few blocks away—Thai Heaven—tomorrow, 12?" Michael was a bit nervous. They tried to avoid meeting unless it involved extreme penance. Instead they typically talked by phone.

"Okay. I'll be coming from the office, so I may be a few minutes late." Ford nodded and Michael, forgetting what his wife said about the car, began walking in the direction of Starbucks.

CHAPTER TWENTY-NINE

Ford sat at a booth in the middle of the restaurant. While he needed to be guarded, he didn't want it to seem as if he and Michael were hiding. They couldn't afford any rumors, any assumptions—but maybe he was being paranoid. Would a priest and a computer geek be of real interest to people eating lunch before going back to work and their own lives?

12:05. Michael was late.

"That's right …" Ford relaxed as much as he could, "he said he might be late."

The priest told the waiter the other person was on the way and so water would do for now. Waiting, he took a sip of the water as he thought about how he would have this discussion with Michael. How would Michael react? More water. Would Michael react at all? Ford picked up the glass again. This time, as he set the glass back on the table, right on top of the circular watermark, Michael walked through the door.

The priest couldn't get a sense of Michael's mood. They'd learned to control their expressions. It was an important part of their ministry. But just one slip would have been helpful today. But no luck, Michael could have been sad, mad, happy—anything—and Ford wouldn't know.

"Hello Michael. Day going okay?"

The priest heard the words come out of his mouth and realized the question probably sounded as stupid to Michael as it did to him. Why was he so nervous? He and Michael needed to do the will of God, and he was convinced he had with respect to Wilma Smith.

"Everything is fine."

Michael didn't want to prolong the niceties; he'd assume that the priest was okay. No need to ask. He'd just seen him the day before and nothing about him looked any different. Ford must have called the meeting for a reason, and Michael was interested in getting to the point. He was a bit anxious, a bit nervous, and curious.

He took a seat hoping the priest would get the idea—without being offended—and move into the reason they needed to meet. Ford did get it, so he launched into it. No sugar coating. He sat up, folded his hands on the table, and began to share the details.

"Mrs. Wilma Smith …"

"Yes," I remember," Michael interrupted. He wanted Ford to move the conversation along and he thought stopping the moment of reflection would help.

Ford paused, looked Michael in the eyes, and continued. "It wasn't natural causes. That's what the police and medical examiner think. Her death was really for spiritual causes. Extreme penance, Michael."

"What?!" Michael raised his voice and jumped forward, grabbing the table—white knuckles against the red wood. But then he remembered where he was and what was at stake. He looked around to make certain he hadn't received too much attention. People looked but turned back to their food. Michael calmed down.

"What do you mean? When … how … Why?" All sorts of possibilities crowded Michael's mind.

Ford explained that she'd come to the confessional and told him that she'd murdered her neighbors—two adults, two children … and two dogs. He recounted what she said about saving her life—keeping her dignity—by removing the threat. Ford told him that she said not to do so, to save her dignity, would be suicide, which is an unforgivable sin.

"Contrition?" Michael was stunned and could only get out that one word. Based on her age it was difficult for him to deal with the idea she was a killer.

"No."

"Not at all? No signs of contrition?"

"No. I asked several times, and no. She believed she was justified."

Michael wanted to be able to read his expression, get a sense of whether or not he felt sympathy for the woman, whether or not it was difficult for him to exact extreme penance alone and to tell about it. Ford was stone faced, so Michael probed for answers.

"Why did you act alone? Isn't this *our* ministry?"

Michael was content in the role of John the Baptist—making clear the path for the priest, but he couldn't help remembering that he'd been the instrument God used to get Ford on this path of service in the first place. And now, Ford acted alone? Was Ford disconnecting from him? Should he understand this as the priest saying he no longer needed him, that he could do God's will without him? Had he reached the end of his stewardship, his discipleship? He wanted to avoid reacting out of ego, out of a sense of his own importance. Michael wanted to remain humble before the Lord, but he had to know.

"I have a problem with this. Nothing else could be done for penance for an eighty-two-year-old woman with limited days?" Michael thought this, but knew it made no sense to say it. So instead he said, "I will trust you and believe you are correct. Anyway what's done can't be undone. It's with God." But Michael still had questions he couldn't hold in, "But why did you do this alone? Am I not a part of this ministry?"

Ford felt both guilty and offended by those two questions. This would require some careful wording and nothing spoken in hast. Ego had to be controlled. Ford smiled in an effort to ease Michael before speaking.

The priest leaned forward, looked across the table, and spoke. "There was no time, Michael. There would not be another chance like it. Can you think of a way we might have handled it if I'd waited? We hadn't encountered mortal sin in such an aged and limited body before. It pushed against the limits of my thinking. But just where humans reach their limit, God steps in and opens another way. It was our manna from heaven in a way … not exactly, but in a way. It was something we needed, but something we couldn't arrange ourselves. Send her somewhere? Go to her home? Nothing like that would have worked. She was known in the church. She'd been in the neighborhood for a very long time. Our options would have been nonexistent without this unexpected development."

Michael was finding it hard to object. Ford saw a change in Michael's body language. He was a bit more at ease, so the priest made his last statement. "God let her ailment become the source of her penance," Ford paused. "I didn't plan to act alone. There was an opportunity … a ram in the bush, so to speak.

Where were the holes in the argument? Was there something pointing to Ford as self-centered and wanting to remove Michael from this work?

"Okay … I guess you are right." He couldn't think of a way around it. Whether or not he believed deep in himself that it was a mortal sin requiring extreme penance wasn't the issue. That was now up to God to ferret out in God's ultimate wisdom and compassion. The question hiding behind his response didn't revolve around sinners and their God, but concerned his relationship to the priest and the trajectory of that connection.

Michael repeated himself, "I guess you're right, Father."

They'd never really worried about names, and this wasn't the first time Michael called him Father. This time it struck his ear differently, as if there was another intent behind it. Should he be concerned?

"Stay focused, don't stray." Ford knew the importance of these words, and this wouldn't be the last time he would rehearse them in his mind.

Michael and Ford ordered food—"Push the Spice" with chicken for Michael, and "Putt You" with shrimp for the priest.

There was some small talk, nothing about their mission and Mrs. Wilma Smith or any of the others. They paid the bill, and departed— Ford to the right and Michael to the left.

As Michael turned to see Ford walking away, he couldn't help but wonder if Ford's turning right spoke to a position on the right hand of God. Was it symbolic of the priest's closeness to God? "Stop it, Michael. That's enough of those thoughts," he told himself.

Ford looked back to see Michael at a distance getting in his car. And he wondered, in spite of what was said in the restaurant, if all between them and between them and God was well. "Yes. Oh, yes. In spite of any doubt that might surface, yes," Ford thought as he smiled to himself and walked the rest of the way to St. George.

CHAPTER THIRTY

Michael overheard people on the job talking about him. Thinking he didn't hear them, they commented on his demeanor as of late.

"Michael seems unusually withdrawn. I mean ... he was never the big social type, but he's even more quiet and to himself the past couple of months."

Even when he didn't hear them speaking near the water cooler or on the way to lunch or the elevator, their careful approach gave them away. "Hey Michael," pause, sullen look and continue, "you doing okay? How's your wife? Big plans for the weekend?"

All these questions were meant to gauge his mental state, to make certain he was balanced and didn't pose a threat to himself and, in particular, to them.

They didn't know and couldn't know about his ministry. Sure, they knew he went to church—some of them went to various churches as well. But that was the extent of it. He felt blessed to be called to the work, but performing the will of God takes a toll on one's body and mind—despite any assumption that God would take care of God's disciples. Michael's wife noticed the changes in him—his walk changed, less expression on his face, deeper lines around his eyes, and some weight loss. She begged him to go to the doctor to make certain he was healthy. He went. Nothing. Nothing physically wrong. Oddly enough, the doctor asked if he was feeling okay emotionally, spiritually.

Trying to maintain such a strong sensitivity to God's plans for reconciliation pulls at the limits of the human's constitution. At times Michael found himself wondering what cost he'd pay ultimately for the sake of the faith, and his commitment to being God's force against mortal sin.

Unlike Michael, there weren't many around on a daily basis to observe the impact of Ford's true ministry on his mind and body. But Margaret did ask him somewhat regularly if he was okay.

"Father, is everything okay?"

"I'm fine, Margaret."

"… Do you need anything Father Ford?"

"I'm fine, Margaret."

"You will try to rest won't you? Should I cancel your appointments so you can have some time to yourself?" She had the ability to rearrange everything except mass and the confessional.

Margaret noticed what Ford saw when he looked at himself in the mirror. Change. He and Michael were resolved. "To God be the glory, in all ways God's will be done. Amen." In separate contexts of life and when tied together by the demand for penance, something along these lines was the mantra they desperately tried to maintain.

Ford and Michael moved through the tasks and conversations of life with as much energy as they could manage, and that wasn't always much. They dressed for each day, moved through it completing the required assignments and meeting expectations as best they could considering their thoughts were really on much more compelling concerns. They'd eat their meals—maybe watch a little television in their separate living spaces, all in anticipation of their greater work.

Four people guilty of mortal sins needed special consideration, and that need had been addressed. They had no sense of how many more would be brought to them, but they would stay alert, ready, willing … able.

CHAPTER THIRTY-ONE

The voice was familiar. He'd heard it before. As the man spoke, the priest made an effort to place it.

"Forgive me Father for I have sinned."

Perhaps he'd heard it in the confessional? People came more than once, and some voices he'd remember and be able to place from one confessional meeting to the next. Maybe it was during a meeting in his office, about a christening, or something? Ford asked the questions, and sat alert trying to come up with an answer.

"It has been six months since my last confession."

"Okay," Ford thought to himself. "It wasn't in the confessional." But from where did he know this voice?

"Father, I was in a counseling session you ran with me and my wife."

The voice paused and Ford could hear the body shift, a kind of effort to alleviate mental discomfort with physical movement.

"Oh ... should I have not said that? Does it make a problem?"

The priest remembered him now—a somewhat young man, maybe early thirties. Thin, a head full of black hair styled in that style Ford didn't understand—looked like he'd just gotten out of bed—jeans, but not those really tight jeans and a button down shirt with the sleeves rolled up. No visible tattoos, no piercings, but that hair. His wife was about the same age, blonde hair cut short and plastered to her head, just a little makeup, a blue sundress. He remembered them being nervous and wanting to talk about a specific problem in their relationship. He wondered if this confession had something to do with it.

Ford couldn't remember the details—he hadn't been that interested in the angst of this thirty-something couple. He did recall it wasn't about adultery, but had something to do with his work.

"It's not a big problem," Ford reassured him. "Anonymity is assured, even with that bit of information. What you say here is privileged. I won't say anything about it." Except to Michael, if necessary. But Ford left this last part out.

"Okay, Father, thanks."

"How have you sinned?"

The young man didn't expect the priest to move into the particulars so quickly. He kind of remembered that the priest would ask that question, but he thought he remembered it taking more time—with them working up to it. Then again, it was a different priest. "Ah, well, Father, I work for Your Food Groceries. I'm the city manager. Your Food Groceries also owns Your Market. Those stores, Your Market, are … well, the low-end stores, located in less prosperous communities. And Your Food Groceries is the upscale, all organic shop."

"Does your sin have to do with your job?" Ford wanted to move the conversation along. He assumed the answer to the question, but he thought posing it would help the young man.

"Yes, Father. It does, but can I just tell you a little more about the stores? It will help."

"Of course, go ahead. Sorry to have interrupted." Should he have said that? Ford thought about it as he waited to hear more. Did apologizing hamper the confessional process by redirecting authority? Was he, as priest in charge, within his rights to push for a clear stating of the sin? These questions were just a distraction, and Ford needed to focus and be present as the young man spoke.

"My job is a new arrangement, city manager. I joined the company out of college and worked my way up. We moved here because of my wife's work. She's a … well, ah … never mind that."

Ford thought the sudden stop when talking about his wife's job was odd, but he wouldn't press; and it was clear the confessor had nothing he cared to add.

"I moved up and now I have this new job. I'm responsible for all the ready-to-eat food stations, all the steam table foods we prepare at Your Food Groceries, and a few other sections, but mainly the prepared foods. And I'm responsible for the same products at Your Market, but because we do fewer prepared items at Your Markets, I'm also responsible for much more of what's on the store shelves."

The priest wanted to break in to get more detail about his job, but he resisted and let the city manager for these markets talk.

"We use different ingredients at the two places, stock different key items, different price points, and different clientele. Organic and high quality at Your Food Groceries and not so high quality and not so selective at Your Market."

The young man heard Ford shifting in his seat, moving to get comfortable, and he assumed the priest was shifting because of the drawn-out telling of his sin. He decided to pick up the pace.

"There are two problems related to my job, two reasons I've come to confess."

He took a deep breath, and Ford could hear both that breath and nervous energy being released.

"We have an obligation to keep a really high profit margin on our prepared foods. It's not just my stores, but also its true for all the markets in the national chain. Really high profit margins, Father. There have been corporate complaints about managers like me having a difficult time meeting expectations, even though we worked hard and try to provide items customers say they want. I spend money on local ads to bring people into Your Food Groceries, have special events, classes, giveaways ... huh, I tried everything I could think of trying. But nothing seemed to work."

The young man must have been reflecting on all the hard work, all the effort to meet corporate expectations, because there was a break in his story telling. He caught himself, and continued.

"With profits slipping nationally, all the city managers had to attend a meeting at the corporate headquarters. Executives, scientists, and experts from the horticulture division and stockbreeders were present. All these guys are part of the corporation. Everything that can be produced in-house is produced that way." Was he providing too much detail, trying to remove his responsibility for what had taken place? He'd have to press on.

"Well, anyway … we were told that those three groups had been working for a good number of years to develop select produce and meat that would cause a craving for those items. It was finally ready, but it was only scheduled for use in produce and meats related to prepared food stations, not the general items for take home. It was a nontraceable drug injected into the produce and meat that altered brain chemistry and made our products 'must have foodstuffs.'"

"Is that it?"

Ford didn't put anything past corporate interests, but even this seemed too much. His question wasn't meant to be naive; he was just trying to wrap his mind around the young man's story. There was no time limit to a confession, but Ford wanted to get to the point. He second-guessed his rough response, although he said nothing else.

"Ah … no Father. I apologize for taking so long, but I am getting to the problem now."

Ford did nothing to ease the building tension.

"There were side effects for the land, the animals, and the customers. They'd handled this issue with the FDA, and kept things moving. But early tests demonstrated grave health concerns within six to eight months of ingestion."

The young man said he and some of the others asked questions about these "grave health concerns," but they didn't get answers. The corporate attorneys stepped in and said things that didn't come across as being said in English.

"Because of some of the questions raised, the executives agreed to allow city managers to determine if they would use produce and meat injected with this substance. We were told that for at least the next two years not all produce and not all meat would be injected; they would phase enhanced products in slowly. So, we could use treated products or not. But, and they were clear on this, profit margins had to meet projections given by the corporate office."

Ford was told that the meeting ended after that; the city managers were sent back to their individual locations, and given three weeks to think about it. At the end of the three weeks, they were to call and indicate their preference. He wanted to avoid using enhanced products, but the store's profits were dropping and he didn't want to lose his job.

"Father, I didn't want to, but ... but I had to."

Ford spoke up, "You *had* to?

The young man was embarrassed by the question; it made him think—access accountability.

"Yes, Father. I called and told them I would use the enhanced products in my Your Food Groceries. I kept hearing in my head what we'd been told about the side effects, but I tried to fight that. I just hoped they weren't really all that bad, and I hoped they'd find a way to at some point enhance the products without the side effects. Scientists do that. They find ways to make things better and less harmful, right?"

Ford didn't respond to the question. He wouldn't provide comfort; he'd demand more information. "So, how long did it take to change over?"

"It was pretty quick, Father. I thought they'd want me to sell out what I already had. But they came in one day after hours, worked all night and transitioned my stores to the new products. I was the only one there with them at each store. My employees don't know about it. City managers were told not to tell, and if they did they would be fired and their future employment options destroyed. They even made us sign something."

The city manager went back to his initial train of thought, and tried to anticipate what the priest might ask or want to know.

"You couldn't really see a difference in the stuff. The things we used to make our prepared items didn't look or smell any different. But that stuff sold! At all my stores the profit margin was great. We couldn't keep enough of the prepared foods, long lines, called in orders. We were making money; corporate was happy, everything seemed fine until those times I'd think about the side effects and wonder what they were and if the people I saw were suffering."

He didn't want the priest to think he was happy, so he stopped for a moment and went back to his somber tone.

"We raised the prices and people didn't care. Whatever the scientists had developed worked. I can't think of any other reason people would be willing to pay $12.00 for a container of mashed potatoes they could make at home for $1.50. Can you?"

He let the priest take in the impact of the chemical, and then kept talking. "It was the same with all the prepared items, every item, Father."

"What is your sin?" The young man didn't expect the question. He thought it was obvious from his story. "Isn't it clear Father?"

"Contrition involves you acknowledging and naming your sin." This made sense to the city manager. He was a bit embarrassed. He should have remembered that; should have known it.

"I'm sorry, Father. I have knowingly destroyed the lives of so many people by using the enhanced food."

He'd have to let go of any illusion that the side effects would be minor. The executives and scientists would have said that if they were minor or superficial.

"I put professional self-advancement, my own desires and wants, above the health and welfare of others. I've destroyed life, slowly killing people and charging them large sums of money for the privilege of dying."

"Do you and your family eat these prepared foods?" The young man assumed this question was coming.

"Ah, no, Father. We don't even shop there for prepared foods. I tell people we live in the neighborhood but can't afford the convenience of that food. Friends and coworkers buy the argument, and it helps that my wife and I like to cook. And I tell them we don't shop at Your Markets because they aren't in our neighborhood. It has been a source of some stuff in my marriage, though Father."

Ford wondered where he was going with this. The young man hadn't said much about his wife, not even her line of work.

"I've been so opposed to the prepared foods in my home that my wife has gotten a bit suspicious. She wonders why I won't bring them home and what that might mean about them or my stores in general. She's not asked point-blank questions, but meal times are tense times at my house. We thought counseling sessions with you might help, but there was so much I couldn't say."

"What about your friends, other people with whom you are close?"

The young man thought for a moment, "My friends who can afford it do shop there for prepared food … and I don't say anything."

He thought about what might be happening to them, how the foods might be destroying their bodies and killing them slowly. Each time they got together for a movie, a meal (he'd always volunteer to cook), or anything, he wondered what his store's food was doing to them. But he said nothing to those he claimed to care about— no warnings, not a single comment of concern for their health, just knowing looks and the occasional awkward smile or weird remark about cooking.

"I'm killing them too, and not just them but the land where the vegetables and fruits are grown, the animals … everything is damaged," was his last comment on it and it was accompanied with a shift on the seat and a sigh.

"You mentioned two issues, what is the second sin?"

He thought about it, and started with a comment for context. "Like I said, I'm responsible for prepared foods, that's not all; but most of my attention is given to the prepared foods."

"I remember that." Ford was still thinking about Your Food Groceries. Do members of his parish buy the prepared foods?

"I didn't mention it before, but executives, scientists, and the others at the headquarters meeting also said that they were adding a different chemical to prepared foods at Your Market. The CEO took the floor and began to talk about the political and social policies of the founders of the chain of stores—right wing, racists … you get the point. Well, he said that they were deeply concerned about the takeover of the country by Hispanics and blacks. Their birth rates had long surpassed that of whites, and as a result whites were losing the country they built. I couldn't believe what I was hearing."

This story caught Ford, and his thoughts about the prepared foods at Your Food Groceries were stopped cold.

"The CEO went on and on with this racist stuff."

He didn't want Ford to think he was a racist; he wanted to say something that would distinguish him from *them*. He knew it was a stupid move: claim murder but not racism. That didn't stop him from trying to show the difference.

"Father, I didn't know this about the company; it just seemed like a good job with good benefits. This racist garbage wasn't in any of the employee literature, and no one I'd met who worked for the store had talked in these terms."

He wanted to make certain the priest believed him. He'd already confessed something pretty bad and didn't see much reason the priest would believe he was concerned about "those" people.

"We were told that for years the corporation had quietly supported a range of organizations and outfits that had a similar concern but different means of addressing it. Anticipating what some of us might be thinking, he reminded us of the paperwork we all signed when taking the job. That paperwork, written in legalize, implicated us in this social and political shit … oh, sorry Father; I shouldn't have used that language. It made us look like we support the agenda and had an active role in carrying it out. The money we gave to support community service projects was actually supporting these racist efforts. We were stuck … I was stuck."

Ford didn't interrupt. He had to hear the rest of this story. He controlled his movements so that he wouldn't distract the young man.

"It was only to be used in the Your Market shops because they were in predominately black and Hispanic areas. They would slowly introduce the chemical to these stores until every food item manufactured and controlled by the corporation contained it. We'd have a sense of how the chemical was being introduced because the main office would tell city managers to put particular items on sale— really low prices and deeper discounts if payment was made with food stamps or government checks. Corporate thought these low prices would bring people in. We were also to do promotional events, increase the number of TV commercials in local markets—anything to increase consumption of the enhanced products."

Ford made a sound; he didn't mean to. It was an unconscious response to what he heard. He didn't want the young man to stop, to change his story in response. So Ford spoke, "I apologize for that. It meant nothing, please continue."

"Okay, Father … the scientists explained that this chemical would not harm animals or the earth and would not destroy fully the health of blacks and Hispanics—side effects would vary, maybe muscle loss, impaired vision over time but what was of most importance to the corporation was that the chemical would prevent those shopping at Your Markets from having children. One of the scientists told us that the chemical would begin to have an effect on the body within six months, and the next census with significantly reduced birth rates for blacks and Hispanics would be the sign of success."

He shifted on the seat to relieve some of the pressure on his back, and then he continued. "One of the city managers seemed too eager. He asked if there would be a way to make certain governmental and community organizations didn't become suspicious and noted that the reduced birth rates were geographically arranged around our stores. The head of marketing for the corporation said that they would control for that by providing a large sum of money for media campaigns pointing to different possibilities—'sick' homes, environmental racism, any and everything not associated with the stores. The corporation would match this with 'good will promotions' in particular markets involving physical checkups, highlighting an attack on high blood pressure and heart disease. All this should take attention away from the food as the source of the declining birth rates."

The young man finished telling his story, straightened up, and waited."

Ford asked, "What is your sin?" He knew the answer, but the young man had to name his second sin.

"I took away the possibility of life. My actions denied the value of certain of God's people."

"Why did you do it? Greed? Hatred? Indifference?"

Ford thought these questions might go a bit too far, push too much. But by the time he thought to restrict himself, the words had been said. He repeated, "Why?"

Silence.

Chapter Thirty-two

The young man's story was nothing like anything Ford had ever heard before; it was a conspiracy theory writ large, one you would expect to watch on TV—not hear in a confessional booth.

The city manager, the young man with the odd hair, and the others like him were killing and preventing people from honoring the command of God to produce life. And this was all heightened by his willingness to acquiesce to racism. There were two things here for the priest—an acceptance of racism that belittled and damaged the humanity of people, people who were children of God, and his active participation in the destruction of life. The inability to have children, in this case, was not a matter of genetics, not an accident at work or at play, or anything like that. It was an act of sin—the knowing destruction of life's potential. These two, taken together, were a mortal sin that must receive extreme penance.

How to arrange this? Ford was at a loss and that's why he hadn't assigned penance before the young man left the confessional. The priest simply told him that this was a significant mortal sin, one requiring something great from him in order to secure reconciliation with God. As his chemicals damaged the bodies of those around him, his sin was destroying his spiritual life. Ford told him this delay in penance was a bit unusual—but so was his sin—and he wanted him to come back to the confessional in two days, at the same time, to undertake penance. The young man agreed.

Ford called Michael that evening, "There is a sinner in need of penance."

To make certain both were clear that this was a shared ministry, they met physically to discuss the penance—a different approach for an unusual mortal sin. This was going to push them beyond the previous rituals of penance.

Back at the coffee shop, the one where they'd met before, near the front of the room, they sat and talked in hushed tones. They leaned in but not so much as to make people wonder about the conversation. Michael had a look on his face that wasn't the typical stoic look cultivated for this ministry. Ford could read concern around Michael's mouth and in his eyes.

"Everything okay, Michael?"

"No worries," Michael spoke quickly and changed the subject. "I've not been able to get something out of my head. It's the idea that mortal sin has something to do with not treating one's neighbor as oneself. You know better than I, but it seems to me that it can take a variety of forms … even what the city manager did with the food."

Ford had usually been the one to make these connections—to weave theology, doctrine, and the confessional together with application. Now it was Michael, but this didn't bother the priest.

"Say more," was Ford's reply.

"Maybe the proper penance should involve him feeling the pain he has caused his neighbor, and in that way restore the balance between the needs and wants of the self and the other."

Michael was aware he wasn't using grand theological terms, but he thought the idea was consistent with their calling, and could be accomplished.

"What exactly do you have in mind?" Ford asked this because he needed to have Michael connect the idea of loving the neighbor to penance performed.

Michael met the challenge, and shared an idea. "Well, this is a horrible, mortal sin, and it requires extreme penance. No doubt about that. But the damage he has caused will take time to manifest. We can assume it won't be pleasant and will be painful as their bodies' change and die due to the chemicals. And those who are denied children because of the chemicals will experience a different type of pain. He needs to experience pain, the same gradual sense of loss. You said he was coming back to the confessional to secure his assignment for penance. Why not tell him that his penance involves prayer but also sessions with you—over lunch—to discuss how he might expose the corporation. He would be served prepared food from one of his stores, and you would eat your normal fare. I will bring you the food for him, and your food can be prepared however it is normally prepared. Over time, his body would experience the decline and pain he is causing others."

The city manager had mentioned differing metabolic rates and genetics could alter the time frame needed before symptoms emerged. And, as he put it, the medical conditions could vary; but the details on that he didn't know. The scientists didn't share them, and to Ford and Michael such details didn't matter. They had time.

Ford nodded in agreement, but didn't say anything.

"You said he and his wife are fairly young, probably around the time of life they would begin thinking about a family. He has a secure job. His sin would also destroy him in that regard as well. He'd see the consequences of his action, his sin, on himself and someone he loves."

The young man showed up as he was supposed to. Ford told him the nature of his penance, and the young man agreed.

The church wasn't too far from one of his stores and so getting there would be easy. "Should I bring lunch, Father?"

He couldn't see Ford's face, but the priest nodded and said, "No, that won't be necessary. The meal will be prepared for us. Can we say Mondays, Wednesdays, and Fridays, at noon?"

"For how long, Father?"

Ford and Michael hadn't really thought in terms of a time frame, so he responded by saying, "For as long as necessary."

The young man was comfortable with that. He'd committed a significant sin, and needed time to work through it and make amends.

"Okay, Father Ford. By the way, my name is Herman. Seeing as we will be eating lunch together, I thought you should know my name. I didn't want to assume you remembered it because of the counseling session. That was some time ago, and I can imagine you are pretty busy, meeting lots of people."

The priest didn't remember the name. "Okay, Herman, I will see you on Friday. Come to the church office, and you will be directed to the dining room."

After the young man left, Ford went to the church office and told Margaret of his ongoing lunch meetings with Herman. She knew to expect him and to send him to the dining room.

This would be the first time Ford used the formal dining room; he always took his meals in the kitchen. However, it seemed right to him that this penance be done within a more formal setting to reflect its serious nature.

Michael brought the meals on his way back to work from lunch. They weren't certain how long it would take and they wanted to be careful with money. The meals were expensive, but Michael made the adjustment by reducing his Sunday offerings. It seemed a reasonable shift—either way he was giving to the work of the Lord.

Ford and Herman met as planned, talked about a variety of topics related to the corporation and Herman's work, and they ate. At times it crossed his mind that the meals looked familiar; but he was with Father Ford, the man of God, who was helping him redeem himself, so he let those thoughts pass without much probing.

Ford monitored Herman's appearance and reported his findings to Michael. Over time, he seemed to be growing frail, his face became drawn and gray, and his body bent more than a young man body's should be bent … Although his wife pleaded, Herman wouldn't go to the doctor about it. He'd tell her he was just working hard and not eating right, but perhaps deep inside he had other thoughts about his condition. If he did, he didn't share them—not even with Father Ford. Herman simply showed up, talked, and ate. He found it increasingly difficult to gather the strength to get to work and to make it to lunch, but he did both. One was his professional responsibility and the other his spiritual need.

Herman began to take on the look of death.

"It would only be a matter of time, and not much time," Ford thought to himself each day he saw Herman.

He and Michael were surprised he didn't go to the doctor, not that it would have made a difference at this stage.

"Perhaps," Michael said on one occasion, "Herman not going

to the doctor was like God hardening the heart of Pharaoh in the Hebrew Bible preventing him from freeing the Children of Israel … Maybe God has touched Herman and has removed the desire to see the doctor in order to make certain God's will and God's power are made manifest in his situation?"

Months passed, and then one Friday Herman didn't show. The next Monday he didn't show. That Wednesday Ford received a call in the office.

"Father Ford," Margaret called him using the intercom function on the phone.

"Yes, Margaret," Ford had the receiver in his right hand.

"There is someone on line wanting to speak with you. She says it is urgent." The priest asked that the call be put through.

"Hello, this is Father Ford." He heard someone on the other end trying to fight back tears.

"Yes, Father Ford," it was hard to make out the words through the sobbing and the sniffing, "I am Herman's wife, Emily. Herman told me about your lunch meetings. He wouldn't tell me why you met … ah … just that he was working through something with your help. I assumed it was about our relationship—sessions beyond the one we had with you." She tried to compose herself.

"Hello, Emily, what can I do for you? It sounds like you might be in need of some assistance."

Sensing why she might be calling, he waited for her reply. He was filled with spiritual contentment because he assumed the call was about Herman's penance. Ford was confident Emily would say something that would confirm for him God's power to exact justice.

"Father, it's Herman. He's not doing well. It seems his health has been declining for some time now, but I couldn't get him to go to the doctor. Finally it became too much and I made him go." She couldn't fight the tears.

"I know this is difficult, Emily, but please try to tell me what's wrong. Take your time, take a deep breath, but please try to let me know so that I can assist as best I can." This seemed to help some. Emily managed to get the words out.

"Father, Herman is very sick. It's cancer, stage four liver cancer,

Father …"

"Stage four?" Ford repeated, but not because of shock. He knew a call about Herman would come at some point.

"I don't know what I'm going to do without him, Father. We've had our problems, but I love him."

It had been hard up to this point, but talking became almost impossible for her. So, Ford decided to visit her at their home, to give up on the idea of a phone conversation.

"Emily, are you at home? Would you like me to stop by to talk?" Ford only heard sobbing, uncontrolled sobbing on the other end of the line.

"Emily, what is your address? Emily … I know this is hard for you and I want to be of assistance, where do you live?"

It seemed a long time between his question and her response, but finally he heard through the crying, "84205A Hennepin Avenue, unit 304."

Ford didn't want to waste time walking, so he got in the car he barely used and traveled the fifteen minutes to the address she'd given.

It was an older building—he thought it had been a hotel at one point—in the general area of the church that had been turned into condos with all the amenities—hard wood, and high ceilings. Ford parked the car, climbed the stairs to the front door of the building, and rang the bell for unit 304—Herman and Emily Jackson.

He was buzzed in and got on the elevator to the third floor.

Emily greeted him at the door, eyes puffy from crying, hair undone and no longer plastered to her head, clothing showing signs that there are more pressing issues than looking good. She hugged him needing to feel the reassurance a human body can provide, she released her grip and led him through the apartment to their bedroom.

The apartment was what he imagined "thirtysomethings" would want in that part of town. Mid-century modern furniture and accessories, signed lithographs, elaborate rugs. The bedroom continued this aesthetic. Ford didn't have any of these items, didn't really know their value; but he'd read enough magazines and watched enough HGTV to have a sense of their importance for particular populations.

In the bedroom, on a king-size bed, he saw Herman. He was

covered, only his gray face, sunken eyes, and tortured lips exposed. Ford could hear his belabored breathing from across the room. Emily explained that because he was stage four, the doctors thought it best to let him stay at home—to exit this life around those he loved, in familiar surroundings.

"He doesn't say very much; he sleeps almost all day and night, but he started asking for you. So I called."

Emily stayed by the door leading back to the living room.

Ford moved close to the bed and took the chair to the right, the one facing Herman, probably the one used by Emily and hospice workers. The priest touched Herman on the shoulder and Herman opened his eyes, and tried to smile. The pain and the sorrow were visible in his fading blue eyes.

"Hello Herman, Emily called and I came as quickly as I could."

Herman tried to adjust himself, but he didn't have the strength. "Thank you, Father." The young man was barely audible.

Ford leaned closer.

"I've tried, Father ..." Tears flowed slowly down his cheeks.

Ford smiled at him, knowing the end was coming.

"I hurt so many ... I tried to make penance as you told me."

Herman gave a violent cough that shook his whole body, and threw him around. Ford thought the cough might break him in half and expose his heart.

"Did I do it ... did I?"

Pained breathing, and tears continued as the priest bent close to Herman's ear. As Herman closed his eyes Ford whispered, "I absolve you."

The funeral for Herman Jackson, 32, was held four days after Ford's visit.

CHAPTER THIRTY-THREE

In the back of their minds there was always an understanding that this would be hard work. It would be the type of ministry that pulled at one's heart, mind, and body. That is the nature of transformative missions. They understood they weren't the first to encounter this challenge—frail humanity seeking to hold together and perform a divinely commissioned ministry—and they wouldn't be the last. But even so, there was something about Herman that weighed on Ford and Michael. He haunted them for different reasons; memories of that extreme penance plagued each with the same intensity.

They talked about this situation as best they could, and turned to stories of the saints and other disciples—not that they thought of themselves as being of the same caliber, nor did they believe their work rivaled that of the best of the biblical figures. It was more an aspiration to find models for their devotion and to ease their minds.

Together, they talked of the lessons they might learn from the Hebrew Bible prophets—those who proclaimed a harsh message about sin and death, and absorbed in their own bodies the consequences of that ministry. When working through these issues apart from each other, Michael continued to think of John the Baptist, and Ford thought of Paul and other apostles. Flesh and blood is what we have, they would often say to each other, but can it always, properly reflect the glory of God? They would work to make it so.

Chapter Thirty-four

St. George Church was a relative young congregation in comparison to many other Catholic churches in the city, but not in relationship to the growing nondenominational churches preaching what detractors called the "prosperity gospel." These prosperity churches related material success with spiritual growth. From the perspective of preachers using that take on the gospel, there was a direct relationship between biblical literacy, adherence to biblical principles, and spiritual growth/material success. Father Ford, and those before him, didn't preach that gospel, but the church still held its own and gained a respectable percentage of the middle-class residents of the neighborhood.

Because it was a relatively young church, three funerals in a short period of time caught the attention of the Bishop. He came for a visit, "to talk with Ford and catch up on his work at St. George Church," as the Bishop put it. He was not a conversationalist and, as far as Ford was concerned, wasn't much of a religious leader either.

Why was he coming to St. George rather than calling Ford to his office?

Margaret arranged the meeting, and told Ford about it only a day before it was to take place. She meant nothing by the late notice, and Ford didn't mention it because it wasn't something he wanted clouding his thoughts.

The priest knew the meeting couldn't be avoided. After all the Bishop was being reasonable wanting to check in with a priest in a new parish that has experienced an unusual number of deaths. Ford, however, needed to make certain he didn't give the Bishop a reason to think him a problem. He didn't need the Bishop or any other church authority monitoring him too closely. The priest could be asked about his theology as presented in his sermons and other activities. The Bishop could use this as an opportunity to ask about his ministry. Ford needed to make certain the Bishop did not probe too deeply into the question of his commitments.

The day arrived and the Bishop showed up at the office early, just minutes before mass. Ford tried not to react, but instead smiled, invited the Bishop to participate in the mass, and to perhaps offer the homily.

Father Rodrigo Alexander.

This was the Bishop's given name. Ford never gave the Bishop's name much thought until now, when the Bishop was in his space, his parish, poised to threaten his ministry. Something about the circumstances brought the name to mind … Rodrigo Alexander.

Perhaps the name was a cruel joke on the part of his un-churched father? Why would any parent name a child after one of the most infamous Popes—Rodrigo Lanzol Borgia—in the Roman Catholic Church's history? It wasn't common for priests and others to call the Bishop by his given name because of its history. He was sensitive about it, and he was flustered by the invitation to give the homily. He told Ford he'd much prefer to hear the priest preach.

Ford was careful during his homily not to give the Bishop reason to suspect anything, to be critical of anything said.

They took lunch in the dining room, and moved back to Ford's office for a conversation. With Ford on the couch and the Bishop in one of the comfortable chairs, the conversation started.

"How are you getting along at St. George, James?" The Bishop hadn't called him James in a very long time, not since Ford first moved to St. Barbara and that was more than a few years ago.

"I'm doing well, Bishop. Thank you for asking. How are you?"

The pleasantries went on for a few minutes, both being very guarded. Ford smiled, but thought to himself, "Enough of this. We can't do this all day. Let's get to the point."

The Bishop did have say over his authority as a priest, so he couldn't show disrespect; he could only make such bold statements in his internal conversations. A lack of regard for the Bishop was safe in the guarded spaces of his thoughts.

There was an uncomfortable silence, an emptiness palpable for both of them, so the Bishop spoke to ease the discomfort. "James, are things going well for you here? Are you … are you happy here?

This was more honesty then Ford expected. He assumed the Bishop would remain covert.

"Bishop, I follow the will of God and the instructions of my Church …" What he didn't say was the will of God, of course, could easily trump the demands of his Church; and, he would always side with the will of God as it struck his heart even when it meant shifting the teachings and theology of the Church.

The Bishop could hint at discord, but based on what—a few funerals? God's grace and mercy were shields for him and Michael, and their work was protected by the sanctity of the confessional—all authorities recognized that. Ha! They were safe, and free to continue their work. Only God could redirect them, and that made him happy.

The Bishop wanted to make certain Ford understood the context for his question, that he appreciated the nature of the conversation.

"Ford," the Bishop changed up—the more familiar approach seemed to have little effect on the priest in that it didn't soften him up—"I simply want to check in with the priests in my charge, to make certain their ministries are progressing and to assure them I am always available for conversation and counsel."

The Bishop smiled a strained smile, folded his arms, and continued, "The departure of Father Connor could have easily created a certain range of … ah, well, let us say concerns and challenges for you. I wouldn't be a responsible shepherd if I didn't acknowledge that. I didn't have time nor opportunity to bring this up earlier, but the recent tragedies made this conversation all the more pressing."

The priest had a feeling there was more to it. "Bishop," Ford wanted to test his theory, "is this about the media attention regarding Morke?"

The Bishop was visibly uncomfortable with Ford's question. His face reddened a bit, he fidgeted in his seat and then spoke. "You must understand Ford … ah, James … the church is in a delicate situation. There is much at stake and we want the public to understand the great efforts we are making to be all God would have us be as His representative on Earth."

Ford was right, the Bishop was saying as much without actually saying it—so the priest pushed … respectfully of course. "Is the media attention your concern? Are you worried I'm saying something in mass, in meetings, on the street that would damage the Church's position and interests?"

The Bishop went from being uncomfortable to being annoyed, and it was visible as he spoke, "You are pushing Ford but, okay, I will give you an answer that can go no further than this room. In some very real ways your ministry depends on your ability to trust and guard THE Church."

Ford thought about the Bishop's words, observed the somewhat threatening tone but comforted himself with the assurance his ministry did not rest ultimately on the good favor of the Bishop. He might at times, in moments showing his humanity, wonder about the Bishop's ability to alter his ministry. But these were not deep concerns, not worries that really shook him. He was beholden to the demands of his God, not the whim of the Bishop. Still, Ford wanted to probe further, "I'm not certain what you mean Bishop."

"Okay, Ford. I will make this as plain as I can … listen carefully, we don't need the media attention. It could easily raise questions that would damage the interests of the Church."

"Bishop, do you mean the business interests of the Church, like the St. Barbara deal? The media attention may compromise others like it?" The St. Barbara question was resolved, still Ford believed it set a precedent the Church wanted to preserve to its advantage.

He stood and looked at Ford with anger in his eyes. Raising his voice, hovering, and pointing at Ford, he made his final comment on the subject, "I believe you understand me Ford. Be mindful of the needs of your Church!"

The Bishop paused and assumed his full height, "and you will remember that you are in my diocese and I have authority to teach the faith *and* rule the church. You may not understand all that takes places or the meaning behind it. Be that as it may. Much of it isn't your concern anyway." This last statement was meant to humble Ford.

"The Church-wide decisions, as you know, rest with the princes of the Church. You, my priest, are not counted amongst that number." The Bishop's final remark was meant to hurt.

The Bishop paused, and gave Ford a stern look he'd never seen on the Bishop's face before that day.

Just to make certain the priest understood what was being said, the Bishop summed it up with a mean-spirited observation. "These matters you have the nerve to critique are—how is it put?—beyond your pay grade," he said with a smirk. "Know where you are in the order of things. There is nothing you can do alone. You have promised respect and obedience to your Bishop. Do remember that!" The Bishop turned to leave.

The priest had never seen the Bishop like this. Even so, from Ford's perspective, the tense conversation was worth it. Ford understood that, as a priest, he owed respect and obedience—but to God first and then only to those who do the will of the Lord.

On the other hand, the priest realized, it would be a mistake to get cocky, to be ego driven and lose the protection offered by God. He'd need to sooth the Bishop's hurt feelings and assure him that he had no intentions of harming the Church's financial or spiritual interests. He would not harm the spiritual interests of the Church because his ministry cut to a dimension of the human-God relationship more fundamental and more meaningful than the spirituality cherished by THE Church. And the money, well, he had little concern for it anyway.

Before the Bishop was out of the office, Ford called to him.

"Bishop, I didn't mean to offend. I just wanted clarity so as to avoid doing harm. I respect what the Church is." Ford smiled, more of a silly grin really, and it took a good deal of effort on his part to maintain what it was meant to represent as he continued to ease the Bishop's mind. "I am a priest who wants to be devoted to the will of God, and who wants to follow the authority of the Church."

This seemed to calm down the Bishop. He and Ford would never be the best of friends, confidants, but there was nothing about the workings of the Church's hierarchy as it effected Ford that required such a strong bond.

The Bishop nodded his approval, left the office, and headed back to the comfort of his home. He'd spend time handling the media attention at St. George. It was about funerals and the like, it would be short-lived he told himself. This priest, Father Ford, should not be a major source of grief for him. He couldn't afford much trouble from that priest; his professional growth in the Church demanded Ford fall in line. The Cardinal, and others of authority, assured him that if all went well in his diocese the Church would not forget his devotion and service. The Bishop could see himself in the garb of a Prince of the Church.

Ford stayed in his office thinking about the conversation with the Bishop. He'd done all he could, and the rest was for God. This thought was comforting, and the Bishop's stress only served to renew the priest. At that moment, the words of St. Augustine came to him, "the violence which assails good men to test them, to cleanse and purify them, effects in the wicked their condemnation, ruin, and annihilation."

CHAPTER THIRTY-FIVE

Ford debated whether to tell Michael about the meeting with the Bishop. Would it provide useful information, fix his resolve, or create doubt?

Wanting to avoid any misunderstandings, any difficulties, and to alert Michael to how the Church understood the recent media attention, Ford decided to share the conversation. The phone would do for this conversation, and so Ford called Michael using his disposable mobile phone.

He'd only met the Bishop once, Ford's first Sunday at St. George Church, when he introduced the priest. Still, Michael didn't like the Bishop. Nothing about him seemed genuine. To the contrary, the Bishop seemed a businessman draped in a robe, and not bothered with the true mission of the Church to establish in some and restore in others a right relationship with God. So, the Bishop's concerns about St. George and Father Ford by extension didn't surprise Michael. He, the Bishop, presented the worst aspects of the Church, the use of authority in the name of God for demonic—life fighting life—purposes. The Bishop's smile as he shook hands after church was that of a wolf before consuming prey—a hunter of humankind! He and Ford, as the scriptures proclaim, "wrestle not against flesh and blood but against powers and principalities ..." The sin sick soul, those far away from the will and glory of God, come in a variety of shapes and forms.

Chapter Thirty-six

"Forgive me, Father Ford, for I have sinned."

"It has been a long time since my last confession ..." That voice didn't belong to anyone he'd recently encountered at St. George Church. This person was known to him, but from a different phase of his work, from a different location.

"St. Barbara Church," Ford thought as he waited for the voice to confess a sin.

"... It's probably been longer than it should have been, Father. I should have come sooner." The voice stopped for a moment. "I'm not a member of this parish. Does that matter?" There was a pause, not to create space for the priest to speak, rather to collect thoughts. "I know you, so I'm hoping it's okay for me to be here."

Ford wanted to place a name and face with that voice.

"What is your sin?" Maybe as they talked he'd figure it out.

"Father Ford, I don't want to just blurt something out. I need to explain. Can I explain? It might help." Joan thought Father Ford would remember her if she could say more. But then again, he might not. Either way, if for no other reason than her own need to confess, she wanted to tell the whole thing.

"Yes, please say more." Why wouldn't he let her tell as much as she cared to tell? He'd let others do that.

"I was a student, a college student—the first person in my family to go to college. My parents were so proud of me, and I was feeling really good about myself. Things were going well. But my second year I ran out of money. Couldn't get more loans, no more financial aid. So

I had to drop out and come back home."

Joan! It was Joan, little Joan, Ford was certain of it now. He was glad to have contact with her, but was troubled that it was in the confessional.

The priest had a difficult time sitting still, the hope this was a minor issue kept him from settling down.

"Well, I really wanted to get back to school. I couldn't stay in the old neighborhood. Most of my friends … ah … they weren't doing so well. I didn't want to get trapped. I wanted a good future. No community college, nothing local, I wanted to get back to the school I had picked."

This story brought back powerful memories of life in the old neighborhood, and Ford listened intensely. He couldn't help himself.

"My family doesn't have money, and the small jobs I could get in the neighborhood didn't give me much to save up because I needed to help my family. No living for free in that house."

He feared what she would say next. Prostitution? Theft? Drugs?

"I needed to make a lot of money and fast. I thought if I could make enough, I could go back for the spring semester maybe … or, at least enroll for the next fall."

Anticipation was wearing him down. He blurted out, "What did you do? What is your sin?"

Joan wasn't ready, but Ford had pushed her. "Okay," she thought, "I'll just spit it out." Ford took a deep breath and steadied himself.

"I started selling drugs … typical, right Father? To be expected from someone from my 'hood, right? I know it might be wrong, but do most people sell drugs for the reason I do? I want to be an attorney to change things, and you need to bend the rules sometime to make things right!" She hadn't planned on this justification. It just came out—being defensive came natural to her. "I don't make drug addicts, and I don't use myself. I just sell to people who are already hooked. They come to me. I don't go to them."

Joan knew she was rationalizing. Regardless of her motives she was helping people destroy themselves. Who knew what these people did in order to get the money to buy from her?

Ford was hurt by this news. He'd wanted so much more for Joan.

"How did you start? Who got you started?"

Father Ford knew how the trade worked in her neighborhood. How someone gets involved wasn't a mystery; staying out of the trade was the difficulty.

"Getting a start isn't hard Father. There are a whole lot of people who will give you an opportunity to work for them. I got fronted some money to buy an initial supply and got an area assigned to me. It's not like in the movies. It's pretty easy to get setup; but do we really need to have that conversation … You looking to make a little extra money Father Ford?"

Joan laughed the way he was used to her laughing, which lightened the moment and caused the priest to think. The sarcasm was refreshing. It didn't really matter how Joan got involved in the business. What she was doing constituted a crime and a sin, but Ford hoped there wasn't more to it—nothing that would mean extreme penance.

"The money was pretty good, and I kept telling myself just a little more. If I can save a little more I'll be good. I can go back to school, and each summer I could make enough money for the year. I was able to give my parents money. And when they asked, I'd just say I got a good job downtown. They needed the money so they didn't ask many questions. I also got my own place, just a studio apartment. I need the space because it was too hard to hide the stuff in my parent's apartment." Joan giggled, the type of giggle when reaction to a private thought spills over. "I must admit I liked having my own space. It wasn't much, but it was mine."

The voice trailed off, and the mood changed. Ford could hear the type of breathing that would soon produce tears, and as they fell Joan continued to talk.

"My younger brother and sister would come over. They liked my place, and I'd let them eat whatever they wanted. So they had a great time." There was a pause as she fought back tears. The sniffing sound was piercing.

From his side of the confessional, Ford could feel her body shake violently—"Take your time. There's no rush."

"Uhhh …" Ford was steadying himself for what would come next. The children got into her supply and, thinking it candy or something, had ingested the drugs and were now barely holding onto life.

Joan jumped in and cleared up the confusion embedded in the sound he made. "No, Father. It's not what you think. I'm smarter than that. I didn't poison my brother and sister. They're fine. I sometimes get choked up when I think about them. I want it to be easier for them."

The priest was relieved, but now had no sense of what her sin might be, beyond dealing drugs.

"I have enough money, and I'm back in school. It took much longer than I anticipated, but I leave for Williamstown soon … It's all good."

Was this just a social visit, one that would have been better placed in his office? That couldn't be it. Joan was familiar with the confessional because she'd been a part of the Catholic Church all of her life. The confessional was about sin, about contrition, penance, and reconciliation and Joan had been taught that from an early age. She must have anticipated Ford would be thinking this.

"I'm not wasting your time, Father Ford. I do have something to confess." And, I'm getting to it.

"What is your sin?" From the way Joan moved he could tell he was in for quite a story.

"Do you remember my uncle? The one who raped me when I was little?" She paused, and it made Ford more uncomfortable than he'd been in some time.

"I remember you coming to see me in the hospital. You brought me coloring books and a stuffed animal. By the way, I still have it. When I got out of the hospital, I would come to your office and we would talk. You said I could talk about anything on my mind, and I would … except for that. You remember, don't you?"

It was a memory Ford would like to forget, but the failures of his Church and the sins of its members kept it fresh in his mind. "I remember, Joan." Perhaps it was this memory—of Joan blooded and bruised in the emergency room—that made so visceral his feelings toward Father Connor and Morke.

"My name, thanks Father. It's better to be called by your name, to be thought of as a person. Although you can't be seen through the screen, you're still somebody with a name." Joan was right; Ford knew it, but there was something about using her name that changed the air, and that altered the space of the confessional.

"He went to prison for what he did to me, but he was to get out soon. Can you believe it? After what he did to me he was going to be freed?"

Ford was surprised by how calm she was in saying this; her voice was level, no signs of stress, no tears—not like when she spoke about her sister and brother.

"I've looked things up online and in books, things about the charges rapists face. Prison may be tough, but does it compare to the pain he caused me?"

"I understand, Joan. The years have passed, but it must be difficult. I can appreciate that."

"Sure you can, Father—from a safe distance. I appreciate all you've done for me, but you can't really understand because you've not gone through what I've gone through." Of course she was correct; but he was a priest—a professional and spiritual man who was supposed to empathize with suffering humanity.

Joan stopped, she wanted to say something to make him hurt. It was a natural reaction, one of the ways she'd learned to cope.

"Or have you? All those stories about priests and young boys … Or, do you think it's better to receive than to give?"

Joan regretted those words as they were coming out her mouth, but they were out and she couldn't take them back.

"I'm sorry. You didn't deserve that."

Ford didn't want to make things worse by speaking because he couldn't trust what he might say. He decided to sit silently and wait for Joan to continue.

"I'm sorry Father."

There was no response from Ford—no acknowledgement of her apology. This silence didn't bother Joan.

"Okay, I didn't hear you leave, so you're still here. I'll keep going. I couldn't let him get out. Serving some time wasn't enough to make up for what he did. What does the Bible say, 'an eye for an eye, and a tooth for a tooth?'"

"What did you do?" It was almost as if Joan didn't hear the question.

She just continued with her story as if Ford hadn't interrupted her, hadn't broken in with his words.

"You never know what will happen from day to day. You can be making good money selling, and the next day you get caught and you're sentenced to jail time. For my supplier it was the three strikes rule that got him. Caught with cocaine in his car—the stupid guy ran a red light!—he was going to prison for a long time. Just so happens he was sent to the same prison where my uncle was serving time. My uncle had survived in prison by being in protective custody. Nobody likes the guy who rapes a little girl."

Joan paused to let Ford absorb her words and the imagery associated with them. She wanted him to see her uncle, and to see her.

"I decided knowing someone else in the system was my chance to pay my uncle back for what he'd done to me. So, I made certain my supplier had enough credit to buy things on the inside, and I made certain he continued to have some drugs to sell on the inside."

Ford could sense her pride, and could hear in her voice appreciation for her quick thinking and her planning. All he could muster, though, was intrigue—a desire to hear the rest.

"It's surprising how quickly you can get to someone if you are motivated, Father. Within a matter of a few weeks, my supplier and his friends had gotten to my uncle. They took turns …" Ford knew what she meant.

"My uncle spent the next few months with a broken nose, damaged right eye, broken ribs … and stitches."

After that last word Joan laughed a laugh that frightened Ford.

"But that wasn't enough. The more I thought about it, the more I realized he'd recover, and he'd make it out of prison, and he'd be back in the neighborhood. And I have a little sister … I can't let anything happen to her while I'm away at school. She'd only be safe if he were dead."

"Here we go," Ford thought to himself, "this is it." Hearing Joan talk struck a blow—a hard strike against any lingering thought that his former ministry had any merit. This young girl had suffered in his church, and was now about to confess murder.

"I put word out that I wanted him dead, and my supplier—in

exchange for what he needed to make prison life doable—agreed to handle it. I told him only one condition: I want him to be in pain, to die slowly, and to know that I had it done."

Ford could think of nothing productive to say.

"My family got word that my uncle had been found dead, in protective custody, with his throat slit and his penis cut off. It was found across the cell, and apparently it had been used like a pen to write a message on the well—'*bonis nocet quisqus malis perpercit.*'" Joan had chosen those words, learned in her first year of college in an introduction to the law course, and had written them down for her supplier so they would be spelled correctly—"Whoever spares the bad injures the good."

Of course the priest was shocked and dismayed, but he couldn't help but appreciate the creativity and irony in her words.

"There were no witnesses and no suspects. Even the guards had little information to offer. Their silence is for sale, if you know the price."

"You had your uncle killed …"

"He deserved to die," Joan replied without remorse and without Ford having any reason to believe there was contrition.

"Joan, what you've done is a mortal sin."

"Call it what you want, Father. Use whatever kind of language you want; but he got what he deserved. The police and courts didn't work for me. My family hadn't protected me. And the Church didn't protect me." Then Joan went for the jugular vein: "Where were *you*, Father Ford? Coloring books and toys don't make up for the fact that you and your Church let this happen to me."

She stopped talking, and Ford found the silence hard to handle. Too many memories taking control while he waited for her words— any words to fill the void and stop him from having to think about her uncle and her young body.

"Sure, you visited me in the hospital, but YOU should have kept me from being there in the first place! Isn't the Church supposed to protect its people? What do you get for being faithful? You get shit!"

The Church had failed in a variety of ways, and Ford knew this. That's the reason he was so angry with the Bishop; the reason St.

Barbara Church had to be purified through fire, and mortal sin had to be punished.

"You say you are the shepherd of the flock assigned by God to nurture Christians in the faith, but you didn't do a damn thing to help me. Pray for me and give me toys when I'm in the hospital ripped apart and in pain? That's all you got?!"

Ford sat and accepted the accusation. It was clear her life in the city had given her experience hard to name, but her year in college had given her words and ideas that cut like a knife.

"I remember when you said that Jesus loved the children, had a special place for them. I still remember that scripture, 'and Jesus said, suffer the children to come unto me for of such is the Kingdom of Heaven.' The key word is *suffer*! Understand Father Ford you and your Church promise rewards that are there for the taking if you simply follow a set pattern and believe fixed things. You make these promises, but where's the proof? Life continues as hard as ever—more misery and no real signs of heaven or even mercy. The Church's ethics are all wrong, Father. There are no guaranteed outcomes. Humans are too messy, to fickle for that. But the Church doesn't say that, maybe it isn't good for business?"

Ford wondered if he and the Bishop had this in common—business above people. He didn't want to believe it to be the case, but Joan made him think.

"If you think about it, the best we can do is struggle, try to do something that will preserve our integrity, and that will scream to the world that our embodied lives matter. You may find it hard to pull all this together, Father. Not me."

Her words hit him hard; he thought he was better than that depiction. Ford believed himself to be concerned and more committed than this.

"Joan, have you come prepared for an act of contrition?" Ford waited for a response, but it wasn't what he hoped to hear.

"Sorry for what? For having a beast put to sleep? That isn't a sin in my book. If anything I am sorry I had to do what YOU could not do. Shouldn't you thank me?"

Joan giggled, a different giggle this time, and paused to give the priest an opportunity to think about it before continuing, "but if I have offended God by taking justice into my own hands, I regret it. I guess I don't want God to be angry because I did your work for you. I wouldn't want to be punished for that, and I wouldn't want my family to suffer because of that. But regret the actual death of my uncle, no way!"

Ford hadn't ever encountered a session like this. Not even the little old lady who killed her neighbors had this effect on him.

Others had talked tough, and danced around their sin; but all of them, all those requiring extreme penance had given some indication of contrition required for reconciliation. Joan was different. Ford didn't want this session to end without perfect contrition. While penance would require her life, that was better than continued spiritual death and what it would mean to go through physical life without reconciliation.

"This is a serious matter, Joan. It is a mortal sin. You are doing damage to your spiritual life and your soul. Reconciliation with God requires perfect contrition. Be prayerful, Joan. Think about what you are doing and the consequences of your actions."

"I understand, but you are asking me to do and feel what seems wrong. Shouldn't I value this life I have and the body I've been given. Aren't we made in the image of God? What did you call it that time? *Imago Dei*? Did I get that right?"

"Yes, *Imago Dei*. But that comes with responsibilities and obligations."

"Yes. But I think it's an obligation to respect and honor my body as the temple of God. You called it that before Father, when you were talking to my mother outside my hospital room. I remember those words—temple of God. Well, that's what I did."

The theological debate between Ford and Joan continued, and the trained priest was finding it almost impossible to best this child.

"You are denying God's grace, and you are denying the real meaning of God within us. Yes, we are to respect the body and treat it like a temple housing the soul and our connection to the divine. But you are placing your body above the demands of God on that body. Like Christ, sometimes suffering is the way in which God focuses us.

It can serve a purpose."

He couldn't believe he was saying that to a young woman who'd survived rape. The words were out there and he could do nothing but regret his poor choice of words. He'd try again.

"Keep in mind that our bodies are imperfect vessels for the spirit of God, and their wants and desires, their needs and their comfort can't be the way we determine what God would want for us. It is only with discipline and prayer that we can get a sense of what God wants for us while we live in these bodies. We are prone to sin, Joan, and we must struggle against that and seek to correct it by means of the sacrament of penance." Ford thought this comment was better, but it still didn't put him at ease.

"That all sounds good, Father, and you have been at this a long time, I know. But it's my body that was in pain." Joan turned his high regard for her against him, and used it to point out a contradiction in the Church—hypocrisy.

"Why does your Church hate my body so much that it wouldn't try to protect it, but would ask me to sacrifice it? Nothing about this Church looks like my body! Almost everything said in services disrespects my body. It's like I walk into the church and become invisible, and the only way I can have any say or matter at all is by pain. You come up with ways to say that pain is good; you try to erase my body. But perhaps pain and suffering are signs of something wrong. Even with Jesus, maybe the pain of the cross was a sign of humans' *fucking*," she emphasized the word—*fucking*—"something up." Have you every thought about that? Maybe we should try to get rid of pain and suffering rather than calling it something holy. How about that, Father? How about thinking about suffering as the problem? How about preaching against suffering rather than all this shit about sin?"

Ford didn't want to believe Joan, at least he wanted to understand himself as somehow outside the critique. Joan wasn't done with him just yet.

"Father, people like you talk like people are helpless, that Adam and Eve messed things up for everyone and we spend our lives trying to get back to our starting point. Well, what about this, what about people being lazy, following the easy example rather than doing the hard work to protect them, and to grow like God wants them to grow? You assume God wants what you say God wants. But how does the Church know? Aren't we all just humans—even priests ... even the Pope? Maybe the Church says what it says because it's good for the Church and not because it's good for people? Seems to me the Church makes a great deal of money and gains a great deal of spiritual credibility by keeping people on their knees, and by making them assume they can't get anything done unless they deny themselves."

Joan stopped talking. Ford feared she wasn't done, and she wasn't finished. Joan was just getting started. Now a more direct attack on Ford.

"Everybody doesn't suffer like that, Father. Where's *your* cross?"

"Cross," the word echoed in Ford's head. "I have a cross heavier than you can imagine," he thought to himself. Joan made his ministry weigh heavy on him, and the priest didn't like that feeling.

"Listen Father," Joan said for effect, "I've toyed with attending a lot of churches since I've been old enough to get around on my own—Baptist churches, Methodist, nondenominational, even Pentecostal churches—but I think the Catholic Church is probably the worst when it comes to this suffering thing and bodies. Suffering bodies all over Catholic churches. All the churches I visited had stained glass windows with Jesus on a Cross and people seeming to enjoy his pain. But the Catholic Church doesn't stop with that, we are overachievers on the suffering front—the Stations of the Cross, crucifixes round every neck, the list goes on. Here's a suggestion Father Ford, we might change the name of the church to 'Sufferings Are Us.'"

Joan laughed and the box shook. The priest wanted to join in—something amusing about her comment—but he knew he couldn't. She couldn't let it end with laughter, and she couldn't let Ford think she said all this from outside the Church. Joan wouldn't allow her critique to be dismissed.

"Don't get me wrong, Father. I'm Catholic ... I, I'm Catholic. But that doesn't mean I can't comment on our baggage, does it?"

"Of course," Ford thought, "something about my ministry entails this very thing." Out loud he heard himself say, "That's correct; but what about reverence?"

Joan ignored Ford and continued pushing him, and testing him. And now she was ready to hit him with the biggest challenge of all to his faith. "Say, since we're—or at least I am, and you are courteous enough to listen—being irreverent, and taking some theological risk, let's push the envelope … maybe there isn't a God anywhere." She stopped for effect, before wrapping up the thought, "What if God is something we've created to ease our minds, to give us something to blame or praise for the developments in our lives? Either way, if there's no God and there could easily be reason to think there isn't—just look around—we are shortchanging ourselves. We are throwing rocks and hiding our hands, Father. And when called on it, we point to the invisible force that makes us do it. Don't get me wrong. I'm hedging my bets just in case."

No, he didn't expect this from Joan, but in an odd way, he felt proud of her because she saw and named all the crap. He just didn't like being associated with it.

"Well, you and the Church can take some responsibility for it. You read more than I do, and know more theology than I do. One thing's for certain, I've lived more than you. And that counts for something that books, and all you've learned through others, can't beat down."

Ford took her words in without using any of his own. He waited for her to say something else and she didn't disappoint. Her thoughts were sharp and demanding, pushing Ford out of his comfort zone, and forcing him to see the religious world through a different set of assumptions and a different life grammar.

"Father Ford," Joan slowed her speech in a way meant to force the priest to follow along without missing anything, "do you know Bob Marley, the reggae artist?"

"Yes, I've heard of him and I've heard some of his music."

"Then maybe you know this line. I can't remember the title, but maybe you've heard these words. They may not be exact, but you'll get the idea—'you can fool some people some of the time, but you can't fool all the people all of the time.' … Ring a bell?"

"I remember them."

"Good. Here's the point …you can't fool me again, Father Ford."

Ford was being taught and challenged in new and unlikely ways.

He was both troubled and intrigued.

Joan hadn't forgotten Ford's promptings to think about her sin. She'd said what she wanted to say about his theology, and she was ready to think about sin—just not the way Ford wanted her to think about it.

"If I had enough money would I even need to worry about this? Or, could I buy my way out of this?"

Without him saying a word, Joan knew this question would bother Ford. She remembered enough about him to know it would insult his integrity.

The indulgence issue was just an aside, a verbal assault to make the priest aware of the idiosyncrasies of his Church, should he want to get self-righteous about his employer. And atheism, well, that's something she gave serious thought to—enough serious thought to recognize Father Ford and the Church were ill equipped to address disbelief. Their whole enterprise was dependent on God, and so, even if not real, God had to remain in place. She understood on some level the nature of that move, and respected it for what it was. She'd read enough her first year in college, and something about that take on life made sense to her. She might be able to do something with it later on. When she thought about what she had accomplished, the way she spoke up for her embodied importance, a song came to mind, one her mother played for her when she was young: "Mama may have, Papa may have, but God bless the child that's got her own ..." Something about the song haunted her and tensed her body, but there was also a strange comfort in it, even during her most troubled times.

The priest cleared his throat as if he were preparing to speak ... but instead he kept his thoughts to himself.

"Indulgences, Joan? Really?" was his first thought. Then he turned to himself. Maybe his relationship to the Church, in spite of what he said about his new ministry, pulled him out of the world and made it difficult to appreciate the life experiences, the roughness of the world, informing how people experienced themselves and their religion.

Joan broke the silence. "Watch what you say, Father Ford. Remember, I'm gonna be a lawyer, and I'd hate to have to sue you for breech of contract." Joan let out a hearty laugh, so energetic that the priest both heard and felt it.

Should he confess the shortcomings of this Church and its theology to Joan? Who was really in charge of this confession?

Joan raised questions for him that were troubling, that cut him to his theological core. He'd had his battles before, and in some ways the pull of his ministry kept him on his theological toes—always trying to be diligent. But this was different. It had nothing to do with Joan's background, but it was her willingness to question and to do so from the vantage point of her body that struck him. He thought he and Michael were conducting themselves in this way, but maybe Joan was pointing out a deficiency.

One thing was for certain—the priest wouldn't entertain the atheism question. He had no space in his sense of ministry for that, despite the kind of evidence Joan presented to the contrary.

Joan wanted to get back to the point: perfect contrition wasn't so perfect if it required denial of her body as something important enough to protect.

"You want contrition, Father Ford? You want contrition from me? How about this—I'm sorry you didn't help me. I'm sorry your Church let me down and tried to convince me that it wasn't such a bad thing? Is that enough as an act of contrition? Does that get me a few prayers to say, a couple 'Hail Mary's' to recite? Will that get me absolved and make me right with God?"

Joan was satisfied with the point she'd made, and felt she could back off a bit. "I don't mean to disrespect you, Father. I'm just trying to get as close to what you want as I can without losing myself in the process."

Ford didn't say anything.

Joan tired of waiting. The priest heard her leaving.

Should he ask her to sit back down and talk more? If he did, would it be for his benefit or her penance? He wasn't certain. The two seemed blurred.

This was hard. He thought being a disciple would be hard, that it might mean having to take an uncomfortable position related to people held dear. But he didn't imagine it would involve someone like Joan. He'd worked to try to get perfect contrition from her—if nothing else death would have spiritual and physical significance. As he knew and believed sometimes reconciliation requires that level of sacrifice. If at all possible, he would prefer a different path for Joan. In thinking this, Ford found new symbolic value in the internal struggle Jesus had—if possible, please take this cup from me was his prayer before the betrayal that led to his crucifixion. He didn't imagine himself Christ, just one of Christ's disciples. Still, in trying to be Christ-like, the priest believed he felt some of this same turmoil, a desire for another path—but all the while knowing there is only one way.

For now, he sat there thinking about what Joan had done, what she'd said to him, and he tried to feel his body and discover if he might be able to know what she meant.

CHAPTER THIRTY-SEVEN

He knew there was something troubling Ford. He'd called him, but he hadn't used the phrasing Michael had come to expect—"There is a sinner in need of penance"—instead he heard Ford on the line say, "We are needed ..."

Michael thought he could be reading into the words. This change might be nothing more than an insignificant and unintentional shift in language, or it could mean some sort of complication. Either way, Michael had a feeling that the conversation stemming from Ford's call wouldn't be easy. He'd steady himself and prepare as best he could for whatever lay ahead.

Michael sat waiting for Ford to say something that would explain away the worry he felt. The priest needed to reassure him that there was nothing going on, nothing going wrong. He'd finished his cup of coffee and thought about another when Ford finally spoke.

"Do you remember Joan ... Joan Chavez Douglass? She was a part of the St. Barbara Church."

Michael shrugged his shoulders letting Ford know that he didn't recognize the name. The priest rubbed his forehead and then his right eye before looking at Michael and finishing his thought—"She came to the confessional two days ago."

That couldn't be the full story; there's no reason Ford would bring them together just to say someone had been to the confessional.

"What else? There's more to the story, isn't there?"

Ford didn't really want to go on rehearsing what had happened during that hour or so in the confessional with Joan. She'd shaken him up, and forced him to confront demons that lurked behind his many convictions.

"Joan committed a mortal sin by selling drugs and having her uncle killed." Context was needed, so Ford added to the story.

"She sold drugs to pay for her schooling, and had her uncle murdered in prison for revenge, and to protect her young sister from this man who had raped Joan. He was scheduled for release," Ford paused, assuming, like he the day before, it would take a little time for Michael to absorb this information.

"Joan acknowledges all this, but even when pressed there is nothing in her conversation resembling perfect conviction that seemed to surface at least in rough ways for all the others. It threw me for a loop. Not the mortal sin, we've encountered some monsters, but the way she explained it pushed me. She raised questions about who was at fault for the sexual violence she suffered: where was God, the Church in all that, and where was I as her priest?"

Michael sat up straight, as if moving his body would help him process what Ford was saying about Joan.

"Why didn't we do more than make her feel bad and sinful for having a body someone would desire? She brought into question the Church's ability to safeguard the people who gave it their allegiance, and that perhaps rather than being punished she should be thanked for appreciating both body and spirit."

Ford had given Michael a snapshot of Joan's argument, at least the portion that implicated them, but that last portion needed some additional attention.

"You and I, we've done this work on the assurance that we are doing something to the body for a greater good; but do we ever stop to wonder about that body—to understand how it is in the world? Should we consider the bodies damaged souls occupy, or would that reduce the spiritual significance of our work?"

Ford stopped talking, leaned forward, and pierced Michael with a look. There were so many questions generated by his encounter with Joan, and he could only hope Michael valued their substance.

"How do we know we are actually doing God's will? How do we get undeniable affirmation of that in ways that don't simply involve a stating of our wants and desire for ourselves and our relationship with God?"

Michael reflected on their experiences together as Ford spoke. He had his concerns—mostly the pangs associated with growing in one's ministry, the type of momentary questions that mark out growth of spiritual muscles. Had they missed something?

Centuries of wrongheaded thinking had made necessary this battle with the look of bodies in churches. Usually these things lurked on a subconscious level, but every now and then, something or someone forced them to the surface. Joan would have shaken him as well; and Michael knew this. Here's a young woman without formal theological training, from a neighborhood that poses a whole set of challenges, she confesses sins but in the process brings into question the full structure and meaning of the Church and its rules.

Michael would ask the question Ford must have been thinking in the confessional and now at their table. He began slowly, "Father Ford," the occasion seemed to require a bit more formality, "is it possible that conditions of life impact accountability? Does social, political, or economic privilege impact the nature of contrition as they shape our encounters with the world and with those things in it?"

"You don't think extreme penance is required in this case, Michael?" She committed a mortal sin. Joan had admitted as much, and shouldn't that require the same penance felt by the others? He'd wrestled with this very thing in the confessional, with her sitting on the other side of the wood wall.

"Maybe God has a preference for the poor and despised?" Michael was hinting at a brand of theology dismissed by the majority Church, and this didn't escape Ford.

"You mean a 'preferential option for the oppressed'? That's liberation theology, Michael."

The priest wondered how much Michael knew about this brand of theology. Whatever the case, Ford hadn't really used explicit categories from it. This theology argued proper relationship to God required work to destroy classism and economic destruction. This conversation in Latin America caught the attention and ire of the Church.

"You know, Michael, liberation theology is not embraced by

the Church. It's a marginal theological position. Some would say it contradicts the teachings of the Church, and replaces spiritual growth with fleeting material concerns."

Ford wasn't confident he wanted this conversation to end, but he needed to provide that disclaimer. The priest wasn't certain how he felt about what he'd said. More important, however, was Michael's response to it.

"Ford," Michael stopped for a moment because he wanted to be sure his wording was correct, as correct as it could be, "have we really been that concerned with the strict teachings of the Church? Isn't our ministry a correction of Church practice—a deeper commitment to penance and a more firm focus on spiritual life in relationship to the acts of bodies?"

Ford had to understand, to really see their relationship to the Church.

"I know Joan has raised some questions about this. I know … but maybe God is presenting us with an opportunity through Joan? Isn't that possible?" Michael was hitting his stride, and he was shocked by what he was saying to the priest.

"It could be the case that God does have a special place in His heart for those whose bodies have been despised and abused. Why wouldn't God be more concerned with justice for them than penance from them? Those we've dealt with before Joan all had a certain degree of privilege, and it was fairly easy—perhaps too easy. But now, with Joan, it's different and possibly God requires something different from us."

Ford, against all his training, was comfortable with Michael's commitments. He, at the very least, wanted to think about it some more—and talk with Michael about it some more. The priest did wonder, however, why he hadn't thought of it first. Why he wasn't trying to read this situation through the lens of a new theology. He'd read liberation theology—granted, early in his training as a cautionary tale—and believed he'd understood its principles, whether he agreed or not was a different issue. He'd press the point.

"I've told you about my conversation with Joan in the confessional. You know what she's acknowledged. Do you think Joan's mortal sin requires extreme penance? What about Smith? She claimed a similar

196 · ANTHONY B. PINN

defense when she said that the family was killing her by taking away her dignity. Should she not have faced extreme penance?"

Always aware Ford was the formally trained one, Michael didn't want to overstep his theological boundaries, so he spoke with care.

Leaning back in his chair as if to create some space between himself and Ford, he placed his hands on his lap and opened his mouth, "Smith said she fought for her dignity, but not really. She killed to preserve a certain way of life, to take back her neighborhood. Even Smith, in spite of all she said, acted with a certain degree of privilege unavailable to Joan. Taking drugs is a mortal sin, and also selling them, I suppose. But causing injustice and poverty is also a mortal sin for the Church. So, Joan was first sinned against, and her behavior was conditioned by that fact. Maybe her action against that sin is not mortal sin ... And maybe the killing of her uncle and the protecting of her young sister is her penance? Death is for life still, but not her death."

As Michael had leaned back to make his point, Ford moved forward in his seat with a question: "Who are we to make that judgment?" Neither had anticipated there would be a time they'd question the scope of the ministry, but whether or not they were ready for it that conversation was happening—initiated by Joan.

"Ford, haven't we made *that* judgment in every case? You, inspired by God, listen to confessions and only in some cases contact me— 'There is a sinner in need of penance.' I'm sure you don't hear a booming voice from heaven saying that's the one! More like a knowing that you know based on an inner stirring, right?"

"Yes ..."

Ford had no objection to what Michael was saying. He would have liked to say he was wrong, but he couldn't.

"Is there really any way to remove completely the human from spiritual considerations and practices? Why would God require that? How could God require that and still appreciate the bodies He made?" Michael was done for the moment feeling that he'd said enough, perhaps too much.

"Michael, are you saying no penance for Joan? That we have finished our work with Joan?"

There had been five before Joan, but only Joan pushed them.

Michael didn't want his point lost. And so he spoke again. "Not at all. I'm saying we need to entertain the possibility that she has already made her penance, and that anything else on our part would be to sin against God and Joan." Michael had another thought. He paused before continuing, "perhaps there are times when God works directly with the sinner to achieve the necessary end, with us playing a more passive role as a bridge between the two? Maybe this is one of those instances?" Michael wasn't done, "perhaps we've been too narrow in thinking about death and how it comes?"

There was silence after Michael spoke, and Ford didn't move to fill the void with words. They weren't bothered by the looks from those around them in the shop, and didn't give much mental space to what they might be assuming about the two men sitting in silence. The stakes were too high for petty considerations. They sat and thought, recognizing that this was a pivotal point in their life as disciples. It could be that God was trying to teach them a new lesson about their ministry, and in the process was teaching them something about themselves.

Ford and Michael felt somewhat in doubt concerning what God was calling them to do with respect to Joan. Ultimately, these matters were for God to determine, and the challenge for them was to prepare themselves as best they could to follow God's leading.

Theological language and the strictures of doctrines and creeds could never fully explain the human's relationship to the will of God. And so, even for the disciple, recognition of this requires openness to uncertainty as the possibility of God. It would be for Ford and Michael the thorn in their flesh that reminded them of their limits, the troubled nature of bodies moving through this world to the tune we call life. It was the look of the impossible possibility of our hope for spiritual wholeness, a nurtured soul, both in a body appreciated and despised.

They continued to sit there rehearsing and taking in everything they'd discussed, but now the silence was broken by Ford, who repeated Michael's words in a sort of affirmation of their importance. "As difficult as it may appear, it could be God's desire that 'we entertain the possibility that she has already made her penance, and that anything else on our part would be to sin against God and Joan.'"

To this Michael said, "Amen."

As they got up from the table, Michael to head back to work and the priest to his office for scheduled meetings, Ford stopped to ask a question. "Are we humanists now?"

Michael looked at him not knowing if he were being serious or if Ford had in mind nothing more than to lighten the moment, responded, "at least more human."

Chapter Thirty-eight

"At least more human," those words stayed with Michael and Ford for a long time. Only four words, but they seemed to cover with power what they were feeling and that with which they wrestled.

For Michael the words highlighted his calling lived out with Ford, but they also reminded him of other obligations. He'd try to be a better husband, give more time and attention to his wife—a type of indifference had settled in. He still loved her, and he was confident most days that she loved him as well, but the evidence of that love wasn't as visible and consistent as it had been early in their relationship. There were no young children demanding their time, no babies to blame for this distance between them.

Truth be told, Michael and Susan recognized they were too familiar with each other, and approached their relationship with an assumption there would always be time to say, "I'm sorry," and to get it right. There was a time when they'd both tried hard to say things to make the other smile. Now their cleverness found a home in words meant to jab, subtle putdowns that were meant to express the hard stuff of their relationship without full confrontation. Michael used to touch her just to feel her skin against his, and in that way feel that he'd found the person who made him whole. He'd come close to smell her neck and hair because it was the smell of comfort. And she'd smile and stroke his chin, kiss him on the cheek, and know she was loved. Now touching her was something on the "to do list," and the real joy for him came in being able to cross it off the list. Have sex with my wife … done. It was like crossing something off the grocery sheet, or completing a project at work.

Michael had every reason to believe it was the same for her. But now he was more mindful—"at least more human"—and he'd try to bring this to his relationship with the woman who'd taken his name—Susan Thomas. This new sense of self as it is lived out in connection with people loved. Work had eaten much of his time over the years, and advancement had meaning for him—along with its uniform of wingtip shoes and suits. This was changing. His ministry and his relationship with his wife would sustain him. God's will was to be found in the nurturing of both, as best he could and for as long as he could.

Ford also experienced himself differently. He didn't have a wife, had never *known* a woman. How could he when he committed—actually committed—to the priesthood so young? That was the thing about the priesthood for Ford, although he rarely expressed it, young men commit to following Christ and to leading the faithful without knowledge of the world tugging at them. He had no full sense of how bodies gave and received pleasure and, as a result, he missed out on knowing a major motivation for so much that took place in life and in the history of his religion and Church. Without that gut knowledge, he always felt a dimension of human meaning, and a motivation or longing that shaped movement through the world, was closed off to him. The priest could provide absolution for sins connected to the longings of the body. In that respect, the confessional was a good space for him—even when not involving extreme penance. Bodies could be heard but not seen. He, if he wanted, could deny bodies and instead control them by telling himself they were ultimately unimportant.

Since this new ministry the confessional was alive with bodies that demanded attention. It was even more so in his office. Ford had to provide counseling to couples about activities of the body he'd never experienced outside what he'd viewed in movies or came across in books—including the Bible—but he didn't know the longing when it is satisfied. "As the Bible says, a husband must cling to his wife," the priest had started many conversations with those words. Or, "sex within the committed relationship of marriage is the only acceptable way of giving one's body to another. Remember what the scriptures say, 'it is better to marry than to burn.'" That statement, said with a stern look, was also in regular rotation. Couples and individuals never raised questions concerning his firsthand knowledge and whether or not he was really in a position to provide this counseling. They didn't say anything because they were trying to be *good* Catholics, still he could often see the questions in their eyes and in their body language. The priest was always relieved that the questions were never verbalized.

He'd read Saint Augustine's wrestling with his physical desires as barrier to relationship with God, in *The Confessions*. The priest had made an effort to learn a negative lesson from that saint of the church—to recognize the dangers of being controlled by one's desires and also the dilemma of those desires and wants being a part of our human makeup. Particularly when he was a younger priest he'd tried to discipline his body into submission like Saint Francis, who had done so by throwing his body into physical pain and lack.

"God is enough. Relationship with God is sufficient for me!" He'd say this late in the evening, early in the morning, and in that way quiet himself. Ford thought he'd won the battle—that his body learned those lessons. Most days he tried not to think about it.

This new sense of being human pushed Ford's shortcomings to the forefront and made it difficult not to recognize them. There would always be at least this one way in which his body was dead to him, and unresponsive to the gift of sex. Here was a contradiction, but perhaps only within human capacities, not within God's plans for human redemption. He could never know if celibacy was a gift from God to those who devote themselves to the Church, or, was it really about the economic and political influence of the Church?

Ford would pray, and seek to control the body he was beginning to sense in different ways.

"Lord, have mercy on this your servant. Strengthen and guide me as I seek to do your will. Thy will, not mine. Your way, not mine. Your justice, not mine. Mercy, and reconciliation only through God."

Even as Ford prayed this prayer, and did so with increasing regularity, he still remembered the question he'd asked Michael and Michael's response … "at least more human." Perhaps, Ford reasoned, weakness is what makes him human. It is not a problem, but rather an opportunity—cracks in human arrogance big enough for God to manifest God's presence and accomplish what humans can't achieve.

CHAPTER THIRTY-NINE

Ford and Michael never discussed the revelation each had concerning life, both the pleasures and inadequacies of life. Some things, each thought, are best handled alone. They did talk, but when those conversations were not about penance they involved the theological and spiritual challenges posed by their ministry.

Their ministry continued without interruption and without suspicion. Moments had arisen when they wondered if they would be questioned in a serious manner. For Michael this was always by extension in that there was little reason to engage him on such matters; as far as everyone was concerned he was just a member of the parish. He wasn't anyone special as far as they were concerned; although in some ways certain members of the parish found him oddly quiet. He seemed to be around the church and around the priest more than anyone else. Perhaps he was just that deeply devout? Maybe he had lots of spiritual needs to address? They saw his wife but only on some occasions. She clearly wasn't as spiritually minded as Michael, so maybe he was in counseling with the priest about his marriage? Or, for those who didn't question the strength of his marriage, they thought Michael and Susan were still in the stage of life where children would be considered, and maybe he was in counseling in order to address questions regarding children? These sorts of questions, however, were easily and quickly dismissed, and replaced by their own concerns and interests only some of which they cared to share with the parish priest.

When Michael greeted members of the parish, he often sensed their questions. Why wouldn't they wonder about him?

He thought about what their questions might be, but he didn't worry. "People talk," he'd think to himself as he smiled and said hello before and after services, "but they don't know what they're talking about. They just like running their mouths. I don't have time for that," he had a ministry, he was a disciple, and he'd remind them of this without saying a word—just a knowing smile and firm handshake.

For the priest, there was more direct engagement. Family members coming to the office, looking for some comfort and asking questions that usually could be sidestepped.

"I know you are in pain, and please know we are praying for you and your family. I am here to talk with you as you need," he'd say with concern in his eyes.

"Father, did he ever come to confession, ever come to see you about anything … maybe say something or do something that might be a clue?"

Maintaining a look of concern and compassion, he'd respond, "If he didn't speak to you about going to confession or about a counseling session, there's nothing I can say to confirm or deny that he has been in touch with me. I know this is difficult and it is not meant to increase your pain, but so much of the ministry of this Church can only take place if anonymity is maintained … I hope you can understand."

They were never satisfied with this, but they respected the authority of the priesthood and didn't press further.

Ford assumed they left these meetings thinking more times than not that it was best to simply try to hold the good memories of that person's life and leave the rest. For those who left confused and frustrated, he'd be there if they returned in an effort to find some type of something they could call peace of mind. If nothing else, maybe they would learn lessons from the situation, fortify their spiritual lives, safeguard their souls, and avoid the need for extreme penance in their own lives.

Ford received the occasional visit from a police detective, always respectful in dealing with him, and never seriously questioning him. It could be about a burglary: "Father, did you see any one suspicious?" Or, a hit and run—"Father does anyone in your congregation have this or that type of car?" On a couple of occasions the calls had to do with death—"Father, you probably don't know anything about this case but I have to ask … was so and so a member of this church? Did you have any dealings with them?" He'd always respond politely, but without much information to share.

The Bishop showed up now and then, and at times brought other priests and officials with him, "just to learn more about the work being done in this very important parish." Ford's dislike for the Bishop remained, and neither he nor the Bishop had forgotten that angry exchange they'd had some time ago. A clear head was key, so the priest knew he couldn't allow those memories to cloud his judgment and jeopardize his ministry. He'd be civil toward the Bishop and behave in the presence of those who often accompanied him on his visits with enough respect to avoid additional contact.

When not thinking about his strategy with the Bishop he noticed that Margaret was asking questions concerning why he was willing to adjust every aspect of his schedule but his time in the confessional. That had to remain fixed.

"Father Ford, we can adjust the confessional schedule to make time for some of the other church business you've mentioned. No one will mind. You've been so generous with your time," she'd say with a confused look on her face.

Everything did seem a bit formulaic, routinized—fixed. Even the wait staff at their coffee shop would anticipate their orders. "Coffee, cream, two sugars … right? And, for you, a no foam soy latte, right?" At the restaurants it was the same thing. "Father, same booth? It's waiting for you. The chicken or the beef today?" They tried to avoid meeting in person too regularly, but even when they were spotted it could be easily explained away.

None of this familiarity, the limited degrees of separation between the confessional and the sinners, visits from the Bishop, nor their routine observed by others worried Ford or Michael enough to matter.

Even if someone had raised hard questions about particular confessees, Ford could easily deflect them. It was a violent city, he would have responded, and so and so is an unfortunate victim of that fact. More likely, however, when news got out about the dead or missing person's activities and professional connections—as media needed to do in order to maintain an audience and attract sponsors—people felt no need to approach the church with questions. Immediate family members and close friends, after the sadness of funeral arrangements or in conjunction with efforts to secure the whereabouts of the missing, would spend so much time trying to fight the negative attention on their loved ones found online, in papers, and at times on TV that the media and civil authorities became the targets of their bitter questions and rage. No one thought to wonder about the priest, not the person whose ordination spoke to an obligation to guide and nurture the spiritual welfare of those claiming the faith.

Even if they had thought about the priest, he and Michael rested in the certainty they were doing the will of God, and "no tool formed against them by the enemy would prosper." Nothing could harm them as long as they were doing God's bidding.

The priesthood was made for such complex ministries, but only those most sensitive to the leading of the Lord, only those most committed to the depth of the Gospel and its imposed obligations, and only those willing to act out the fullness of the Church's true theology, could maintain the priestly functions of deeper discipleship to which God was actually calling.

Those after Herman Jackson covered a variety of mortal sins and were dealt with in ways consistent with the damage they'd done.

Once extreme penance—always determined through the leading of the Lord—was enacted, the sinners didn't cross their minds in a meaningful fashion. Thoughts about them didn't involve regret or remorse. Both would be more comfortable describing it as righteous anger. Joan, of course, weighed on them heavily, and in a way that wasn't about anger or remorse. Joan challenged them and forced them to make certain they were listening closely to the voice of God. Whereas the others reinforced their sense of ministry in a way that expressed the continuity between their deeds and God's will, Joan's time in the confessional challenged this sense of continuity. She forced them to acknowledge in uncomfortable ways the infinite and qualitative distinction, as one theologian put it, between God and humans. This is a distinction maintained even in the case of the most committed of disciples—"less of me and more of Thee."

Deaths and missing bodies—now totaled 10.

CHAPTER FORTY

Ford heard the person approach the confessional. The sound was pointed, and as far as he could tell he was hearing a woman walking in heels. Ford wasn't certain, but he thought the sound from shoes was accompanied by a "swoosh" that he imagined was made by a fitted dress against stockings.

"Click … swoosh … click."

He'd heard similar sounds as women walked into his office. He imagined the woman making these sounds was of a certain regal stature, and concerned with her appearance—intentional in her movements. Maybe she was wearing blue, or maybe red, something that called attention to her good taste, but not so much attention as to make her uncomfortable or nervous? The priest thought about her hair, makeup, and jewelry—yet nothing too particular really came to mind. He just assumed her hair was probably pulled back away from her face, light makeup and maybe pearls around her neck.

"Click … swoosh … click."

The sounds continued until they were replaced by her entering the confessional and sitting down. The priest could hear her breathing. It was soft, and he imagined the breath was sweet and warm. He imagined there might be light perspiration around her hairline, maybe catching some of the fine hair and creating delicate swirls near her temples. Ford was embarrassed by his thoughts.

"Why am I having these thoughts, and why about this woman I can't even see?" Quickly shifting his body, he stopped himself, focused, and waited for the opening line.

There was a slight sigh, as if she were burdened to even think what might come of her words. Then the voice.

"Forgive me Father for I have sinned. It has been so long since my last confession."

"What is your sin?" Ford was eager to hear the voice again. There was something odd that made him uncomfortable but also captured him.

"It's complicated, and I'm not certain where to begin ..."

"At the beginning is a good place," Ford said cutting her off and feeling rather clever—also just a bit unprofessional. Did she notice? Did it mean anything to her? Was he flirting with this woman he didn't see and would most likely not see unless it was for the purpose of extreme penance?

After a bit of nervous laughter at the priest's attempted humor, the voice continued, "I am an assistant professor at the university, Father. I've been there four years, and I am to put together my tenure file the end of next year."

She paused before completing this thought just to make certain the priest had enough context to get what she would tell him.

"That's the process, Father, that will determine whether I am able to keep my job."

Ford knew something about this, but he didn't feel the need to interrupt. For some reason he didn't want to embarrass her, so he let her continue. He listened as she explained.

"We have to present evidence of outstanding achievement in research, teaching, and service to the university. Many people apply for tenure; but at my institution less than 30 percent of all assistant professors will achieve tenure and a good many of those who do are in the social sciences and natural sciences, not in the humanities where I teach—I am a historian concentrating on twentieth-century military conflicts involving the United States."

There was a pause, allowing both to think about what was being said—and then she continued, "The last two assistant professors in my department who applied for tenure were denied ... I'm nervous Father."

Ford cleared his throat and she worried that he was bored, or maybe she was providing too much detail. She had to get it all out. She had to tell him everything so that he would understand what she'd done and why. So, she continued her story.

"I've worked hard, Father. I have a PhD from a good program. I have received national fellowships, grants from the school, and I graduated with honors."

It was clear she was proud of herself, and he suspected she wanted him to be impressed—if not sympathetic.

"I was so happy to receive this job; it was my first choice—a dream job, really. Everyone in my field of study applied for the job, and I got it! My family was so proud of me. My parents are professors and they were so happy to see me starting my career in such a good job. My sister was so happy for me, and my friends threw me a party."

She smiled and shifted in her seat remembering the good time she'd had at that farewell party—all the good food, good music, drinks and gifts. She still had some of those gifts, like the Mont Blanc she used to grade papers and sign important documents. That black Mont Blanc pen meant the world to her because her friends chipped in to buy it. And she still used the briefcase—Louis Vuitton classic—her parents gave her with such a pleased look on their faces.

"I was determined to make the most of this opportunity. I studied the department and the school. I memorized the school's mission statement, the president's vision statement, and took part in as many university-wide conversations concerning the future of the school as I possibly could. The school was my world; my life revolved around my hours on the campus."

Ford sat listening, trying to connect his image of this woman with what she said about her career. Did she wear these shoes and outfit on campus—"click … swoosh … click"?

Did she wear dressings, suits, jeans, and sweaters? Did she always wear her hair pulled back to look professional? Was makeup part of her morning routine every day? What did others on her campus and neighborhood think about her and her style?

Why these questions?

She still worried the priest was bored or annoyed, but she had to risk it in order to get her point across. It was important she gave a full sense of why she did what she did. For some reason, on her way over to the church, she'd convinced herself that proper information would make a difference. It did in her profession. She'd have to chance it and continue.

"Better to ask forgiveness than permission," she thought to herself. "Ask for forgiveness … wow! Isn't that why I'm here?" Maybe it was just nerves. "I'll get it together … just keep talking." She crossed her legs, pushed her shoulder against the wood, crossed her arms, and continued with the story of her job.

"I thought hard and long about the proper steps to make in order to be successful. I dressed the part."

Ford had the answer to some of his questions about her look, her style, why the sounds her moving body made.

"Knowing that I couldn't negotiate the university alone, I secured three very important mentors to help me understand how the university worked and how to avoid many of the major problems that sink careers. I poured myself into my classes. My first two years, it wasn't unusual for me to be in my office until 9 or 10 o'clock in the evening working on lectures, pulling together PowerPoint presentations, and thinking of clever assignments that would keep my students engaged. I worked hard to be a good teacher and I believed …"

Ford was struck by her choice of words, "believed, not believe?"

"I believed that being recognized by my students as a good teacher was part of what I needed to do to keep my job and to stand out in the department. I even went so far as to check RateMyProfessors.com just to see where I might be falling short. Well, at my institution, it's really a popularity contest … Ah … I, I mean students don't always make a distinction between good teaching and good performance. So I tried to do both—to meet all the needs and expectations. Doing this drained me, but I thought it would be worth it in the long run."

She looked at the wall as if she might be able to see through it and read the priest's face to gauge his impression of her.

Ford didn't feel her staring at him, and he didn't speak. He just thought about the question he kept asking himself—"Why am I so concerned about this person?"

This worried Ford. He couldn't let anything take him away from his discipleship. "O, keep listening," he urged—and he tried to follow along.

"More important than teaching, Father, is publishing. Everything about the PhD program focuses on learning to conduct research and how to write books. My department has a list of approved publishers—university presses for the most part, presses like Oxford, Cambridge, Duke, North Carolina. Do you get the idea?"

Ford understood something about the publishing world from his days in university and seminary.

"And my department expects a published book and at least a proposal for another book in place by the time the tenure file is submitted for consideration. My mentors helped me think about this, and everybody—my mentors and everyone else I asked—said the same thing: rewrite and publish your dissertation. 'It's the rough draft of your first book. Take advantage of that' is something I heard over and over again. I took their word for it. Getting that dissertation transformed into a book and published has been my mission."

She paused and Ford wondered why; he was getting used to the sound of her voice. He wouldn't wait for her, he'd encourage her, "Please, continue."

"This is where it gets difficult. Because the chair of my department has responsibility for determining whether someone can put their case forward for tenure, I thought I should involve him in my efforts to revise and publish my dissertation. I thought I was making progress, and why not assume the chair of the department, the person who chaired the job committee that hired me, would be helpful?"

This seemed reasonable to Ford. It wasn't a world he was familiar with in any deep way, but he'd wait to hear more.

"He was a senior member of the faculty, a full professor with thirty-some years of experience, and a good number of books to his credit. His feedback was critical."

As she spoke about the importance of this person, Ford couldn't help but think about his Bishop, the religious leader who was supposed to be so helpful with the spiritual development of those in the diocese. If her chair was anything like his Bishop, he had a sense of where this conversation was going. He was on the edge of his seat, waiting to hear the problems caused by the leader of her department.

"The chair is a Vietnam veteran—exchanging army gear for khakis, a button-down shirt, and a blue blazer—and took a special interest in my work because of the war theme. Every conversation with me or anyone else somehow tied to his experiences in war—the sounds, the smells, the tastes, and feel of war and the way all of this produced a type of energy and passion he brings to his work. 'Research involves risk. There's got to be energy, investment of yourself in it. Nothing disinterested will shape the field!' He said this so often; I'd hear it every time the topic of research came up. Don't get me wrong, Father; of course we should put ourselves into what we do. Our work should be invested with a piece of us."

Ford smiled and looked at the wood separating them as if she could see his smile and would appreciate his agreement. He sat there thinking how right she is, how much he and Michael invested of themselves in their ministry—body and soul committed to discipleship. But of course she couldn't see his smile, so his "huh" would have to do.

This gesture on the priest's part had its desired affect, and she continued with a feeling the priest understood her situation and was sympathetic—as much as he could be—all things considered.

"I have some articles, but that's not enough. I need a book. I'm trying to get that done in time. My chair would read drafts of the chapters, and each time he'd tell me that 'its factually solid but it lacks passion; it lacks commitment and energy. You don't feel what you are describing. It's missing a piece of you, the author. Until you can find a way to feel and experience the frustration, the agony, the misery you are describing—until you have a sense of what it's like to lose and cause loss you won't have a compelling manuscript and you won't have a published book. A lot is riding on this.' It was driving me crazy. I was working so hard, visiting all the necessary archives, and spending a lot of money and time working on this manuscript. And each piece I showed him got the same response."

Her voice began to shake with anger and fear, "This is getting critical. I don't have a book contract and I'm running out of time. Friends say I should just submit it to presses without his approval, but I've already involved him in the process, and who knows whether or not those presses will contact him to review it."

She paused, and adjusted her position on the seat before continuing, "There's a bigger concern in that he also said once it's ready he'd like it to go in a series he edits for Cambridge University Press. I feel trapped. I don't know what to do. Some days I'm so frustrated with him that I want him dead. Sometimes, Father, I find myself asking God to kill him."

She gasped, realizing what she'd said, and wanted to correct it before the priest could react.

"Oh, ah, please understand I don't really mean it—just my frustration speaking. I might say it quickly in a moment of particular panic and frustration, but it's nothing I actually want. That's not my sin, Father. I didn't kill my boss."

Ford couldn't resist asking, "What *is* your sin?"

"I'm sorry Father," she was apologetic but insistent, "I will get to it. I just need a bit more time. Is that okay?"

How could he refuse? "Please take your time."

"Thank you for your patience. It's just … well … this is very important to me and I want to make certain that I am being clear. Getting this off my chest … I need to tell someone what has happened, and Father I need to tell someone who can help me think about this in terms of my spiritual life. I just want to make certain I say it all."

"Yes, of course, I understand." Ford pushed his back again the wooden wall, wanting to be comfortable, assuming he might be in there for a while.

The professor continued her tale, outlining how discouraging the chair's remarks were. He'd talk in terms of his personal experience, and how that time in the absurd world of war informed his award-winning books. One particularly challenging afternoon, over a cup of coffee at the campus coffee house, he asked if she had pain from which to draw.

"Has your life really been so perfect, so free from stress, that you have nothing from which to draw? Is the misery you describe in chapter two, for example, that foreign to you? I know you haven't served in the military, but surely you have felt something from which you can pull."

He said this, looked at her, ran his fingers through his hair, sighed, and stood to his feet. "Surely there's something … anything at all." She heard him whine as he walked toward the door and back to his office.

"That stuck with me, Father. But there wasn't anything about my life up to that point that involved what I thought he meant by misery. I had to work hard, but my parents sheltered my sister and me. There were no horror stories, no really embarrassing skeletons in my closet."

Ford wasn't convinced. He believed he knew too much about human nature—as a priest and then disciple he had encountered too much—to be convinced. Even if she had not acted out, human nature is soiled with misery and nastiness. The professor might have suppressed these base desires and wants, and locked away the urges that wouldn't garner the admiration and respect of family, friends, and colleagues. They were there nonetheless.

He determined to just wait it out, listen for the clues, because the sin was there to be named. The priest believed he'd heard pretty much every excuse, every attempt to talk around issues, to paint sinners as saints, or at least as not so bad as some others. But human nature is flawed, and the only question is the type of sin expressing this flawed nature. Even Jesus was tempted in every way as are humans … but without sin. That isn't a feat we can duplicate. Isn't that why we have confessionals?

The priest knew there was potential in her—in everyone—for precisely what the chair demanded. The question was when and how that would be manifest in this seemingly tame and controlled professor.

"I was losing weight and not as careful about my appearance, and this started to concern my friends. My classes were still going well, and I did my share of committee work at the university, but my body was suffering the effects. And Father, how I looked matched how I felt. About three months ago, one of my friends stopped by on a Saturday to get me out the house. He was determined we would go to the Museum of Modern Art and lunch. All my friends know how much I love modern art, particularly the work of artists like Duchamp, Pollack, Warhol, Jean-Michel Basquiat. Odd selections, right Father?"

It occurred to her that he might not be familiar with them. But it didn't matter; she'd continue her thought because it wasn't really about them, but about her reaction to art.

"Their art and lives don't seem to fit the description of myself, right? They are creative, and I like to consider myself somewhat creative. Yet, the motivations and inner turmoil generating that creativity isn't there for me as it was for them. Strange, right?"

Ford didn't find it so odd, knowing more about them than she suspected he knew. He'd taken Art Humanities as a student, and he had been to a museum of contemporary art or two. These artists were just in touch with the tragic nature of life in a way she didn't want to acknowledge, but that wasn't a huge difference to overcome. Human nature is the same.

"Not so strange at all," he responded. "Artistic taste run in the directions they run."

"Well, I love them, and normally take every opportunity to see exhibits of their work. This particular weekend was the last few days of the work of some performance and conceptual artists I didn't know. My friend said he wouldn't take 'no' for an answer, and I couldn't think of a way to get him out of my apartment without agreeing to go. So, I got ready and we headed to lunch, then the museum."

There was deep breathing by both the professor and Ford. One eager to know what happened next, and the other anxious to tell.

"The art shocked me, troubled me, but I found it interesting, Father. It was the work of a few local artists who were influenced by performance artists like Marina Abramovic and Kira O'Reilly.

Are you familiar with them, Father?" She thought she should ask, not wanting to again assume anything about the priest's viewing habits—as she had about the other artists.

"I've heard of them," was all he said, so she continued.

"I didn't know much about Abramovic and O'Reilly beforehand, but that evening, after getting back home, I did a little online research to get a better sense of who they are, what they do, and why."

What came next was a natural tendency of a professor. She lectured the priest on these artists. "Abramovic and O'Reilly explore the ways in which pain and manipulation of the body allow interrogation of the limits of the body. These artists we saw that afternoon did that through cutting themselves with a series of knives and having the process filmed. One of the artists was on a stage surrounded by the audience and the other was below the floorboards with a similar set of knives and he mirrored the artists on stage by cutting himself on the opposite arm for example, or leg. According to the posted information, the purpose was to demonstrate the links between the visible body and the unconscious represented by the artist below the stage. The idea, Father, is to test the limits of the body, to unpack and expose the way the manipulation of the body is felt and perceived. The fact that both artists were standing in what seemed awkward and perhaps painful positions was meant to increase the viewer's awareness of the ways in which pain is communicated and how it informs our thought and behavior. The body becomes both the means for understanding sensation and also the product of sensation. The body becomes fully aware of itself and known by others."

The professor realized she was doing the typically academic thing—diluting conversation with abstract ideas about things that are actually concrete and known to our senses. She was uncomfortably aware that she was running the risk of overwhelming her conversation with jargon. She'd try to correct for this as best an academic could. "I'm sorry Father, for all the abstractions."

The priest sensed her concerns and wanted to avoid her closing down the conversation, and so he needed to provide some comfort in order to get her to admit her sin. Mustering in his voice as much calmness and empathy as he could manage, Ford said, "It's okay. I imagine the performance was difficult to see and even more challenging to describe."

The professor was encouraged by his reply, and continued with her description of what she'd seen. "I'd never encountered art before that involved such pain, and blood. It flowed down arms and legs. I could tell that the hurt was instant but also necessary. Everybody has cut a finger or something, and the natural tendency is to jerk the finger back. But with this performance art, with each cut you could almost see the artist push into the pain—to absorb and embrace it like it is necessary for saying something important. We couldn't see the other artist, but the knife had a small microphone attached and we could hear the slicing sounds, and almost hear the rip of the skin as it pulled away from the blade. I couldn't see the blood but with that sound you knew it had to be flowing down legs and arms ... it was intense. Intense."

She paused and jerked a bit as if remembering what she saw also pushed the knife through her body.

She wasn't finished with her description. "After the initial cutting was finished, the artists came together, hugged, and exchanged knives. I thought that was the end, but it wasn't. They started cutting each other, superficial cuts, but with growing intensity. That went on for a few minutes with blood oozing, covering more of their bodies, and the floor. For me it went on too long, but I couldn't stop looking. I couldn't turn away."

Ford imagined the blood, but he replaced the artists in his imagination with the soldiers putting their knives into Jesus as he hung on the cross. And he thought of his cutting the trafficker ...

"They stopped cutting each other and then left the stage. They came into the audience, each with a smaller knife. They both tried to hand the knives to members of the audience, but everyone was reluctant to accept a knife. People would turn away trying not to touch the knife and not to be touched by a bloody, naked, body. For others that wasn't enough; they left with looks of trauma and disgust on their faces. We stayed, but simply moved out of reach. After numerous attempts, the two artists left the gallery floor."

Ford was thrown by what the professor described. But then as she talked he remembered Christians through the ages expressing their closeness to God by disciplining their bodies—by mirroring on their own bodies the passion of Christ. Was this a secular version of the same effort to understand and relate to our bodies, to see and feel the intensity of life through the practice of pain? What was the real distance between penance and what these artists tried to achieve through suffering? Did people just naturally attempt to understand themselves through manipulation of their bodies?

Ford thought these thoughts, but he wanted to believe there was a difference—a significant break between what the professor described and penance in that only the latter addressed the relationship between body and soul through spiritual life corrected. Penance—extreme penance—involved the will of God to perfect the soul through contrition and sacrifice of the body. It was a controlling of the body for the sake of the soul. Could these artists she described say the same?

He and Michael weren't like these artists because they were disciples of Christ who did this work, harnessed pain, through an explicit surrender to God—not for its effect on an audience but in quiet for the redemption of one. "And, unlike all the others, they had accepted the knives in order to do God's will to those bodies. That's the difference that makes all the difference," Ford thought to himself.

She thought about it—the way in which bodily discomfort energized exchange between people and heightened awareness, and spoke with an energy that a body free of pain could not. Her memories of the bodies, the blood, the energy were vivid. She was desperate to make progress on her book and needed to understand what her chair had in mind, and what those performance artists taught her might just provide the answer.

The professor came to understand that evening the chair's requirement. She would develop some passion, and she would lace her words with knowledge of misery through her own version of performance art. Life had been mild for her, but she would have to introduce pain and feed off that pain to communicate the story of war.

She would need to experience what she sought to describe. It wouldn't be possible to write with blood, but she could certainly be inspired by the feel of her flesh cut and her blood flowing down her arm, like the performance artists.

She'd cut herself. She'd stand naked in her bathroom, cut her arms, and translate the experience to the book on her computer. Her body would provide a vocabulary and grammar for creating her prose. It would be consumed publicly in her book that captured the shedding of blood as the feel of war.

"How to cover the scars?" This question came to her, and the answer seemed obvious. Her clothing style would help with this— her long sleeve dresses, pants, pencil skirts, and long sleeve shirts and sweaters covering from view the inspiration marking her body. People were used to how she dressed so there would be no suspicion, and she wasn't in a relationship so there was no one to see her unclothed body—no one to wonder what the mutilation meant, no one in her private space to question her … no one attempting to stop her for her own good. She would give everything to her work.

"I'd cut myself in order to understand the pain I was trying to describe in my book. It wasn't the pain of war, but it was pain in the body. I tend to do my best work in the mornings, so that Monday I stood in my bathroom, my nightclothes on the floor at my feet and a new knife in my hand."

She'd purchased a knife from an upscale shop. Nervous when she talked to a sales person about it, she didn't pay much attention to the name: Henckels? Wüsthof? Doesn't really matter. More important than the name, she'd been told, is the construction of the blade. Not a stamped one because the sales clerk said those weren't great. And the professor wanted great as she imagined it going through her skin. It cost her several hundred dollars. She thought of it as an investment in her future. The knife had a nicely honed edge to cut sharp, and to do a cleaner job in a nervous hand. The tip of the knife for piercing items sparkled when the overhead pocket light hit it. Until the knife was cleaned, the black handle would hide any blood that leaked down her arm to her hand.

"I held out my left arm in front of me. I'm right-handed and thought that the right hand the best hand to cut with."

She paused and Ford imagined what he thought must have been delicate arms; nothing about her voice suggest anything but a delicate, petite body.

"My natural inclination was to look away, but I fought it and looked down at my arm. I'm not very large, so my arm is thin and I workout so the veins are prominent. I hadn't paid much attention to the look of my forearms before, the freckles dotting the upper forearm, the cut of the muscles sharp and exposed with little fat to hide their look when flexed, its shape from the elbow to the hand—looking something like a …" Nothing came to my mind.

"I took a deep breath and could feel the tension throughout my body, the shaking in my legs and the taste of adrenaline in my mouth. Adrenaline—increased heart rate … the cuts will bleed a lot."

The priest was anxious to hear what came next. "Was this her sin?" he asked himself.

Ford looked at the dark and jagged grain of the wood surrounding him and the professor, and he wondered if the scars from the cuts look anything like the wood grain.

"I wanted to cut and avoid the veins, but then I thought that kind of care would take away from the experience of pain I needed for my work. But then I thought the pain of the cutting was enough, and the direction of the cut was of less importance. I held my breath, looked at my arm and pushed the tip into the arm right below the elbow. There was a sharp pain, but it was somewhat dulled by the surprise that I'd actually carried this out."

Ford listened and wanting to catch all her words, he leaned forward.

"Before losing nerve, and fearful I might pass out, I held the knife firm and pushed it about two inches down my arm. The space it created was quickly filled with blood that spilt over the cut and down my arm. I didn't want to go so deep as to have to go to the hospital, but deep enough for it to have meaning. The pain, Father—it was real and it felt like nothing I'd experienced. I'd been cut before using a knife in the kitchen, but an intentional cut has a different feel to it. You take all the pain in and every sensation lingers because you aren't distracted by the surprise of the cut. There is no shock, just the feeling of metal against flesh. I know it might sound odd, but it intensified my senses."

Ford thought about blood, blood he and Michael encountered in doing their work for God's glory. He'd caused the shedding of blood, but now he imagined how what she described felt on flesh.

"I wrapped my arm in a towel and ran to the computer and starting writing. The words and the experience of my body combined in a different way. The pain and blood gave me a different way of crafting thoughts. I'm not certain if this makes sense, Father. But it was different, and I wasn't the only one to notice."

She paused for a moment, taking in air in a way that signaled satisfaction and then she continued the story.

"The chapter I worked on that day, all day, I showed to the chair of my department and I'll never forget what he said after reading it. He called that same evening—'Now that's it! That's the stuff! I don't know what you did, but it isn't safe and dull like the other draft. This has life.'"

The priest imagined a big smile on her face, relief in her eyes, as she heard these words about her work.

"I thought my problem was solved. I'd be able to write the book, get the chair's endorsement that would get me the right publisher, that would get me a book people would notice, that would get me tenure. I used the memory of the pain and the look of the wound to rework the second chapter. But as the memory of the pain and the look of my arm no longer provided the connection to pain I needed, I went back into the bathroom and cut my right arm in the same way ... with the same results. The chair had the same reaction."

The priest began to wonder how and when the story would end. Was this her sin, mutilation of the body? "Patience," he thought to himself. There was a change in her tone and he assumed her posture as well. "Okay, here we go."

"It stopped working, and that third chapter," pause and sigh, "the chair had the same problem with it, but more frustration because he'd liked so much the revised first two chapters. So I cut my legs in the same way, above the knee so that the marks wouldn't be noticeable when I wore dresses. That worked for a while, but that stopped as well. Then my stomach, and again that worked for a while, although not long enough to get through the rest of the manuscript revised. I was frantic. I needed to finish the book, and my pain wasn't enough any more."

Ford sat kind of numb, wondering what would happen next. He couldn't see her. Maybe she removed fingers or toes next in order to experience the kind of pain that would allow her to write? It sounded ridiculous to him, but maybe.

"I had never been in trouble with the law, not even so much as a speeding ticket, so the idea of committing a crime in order to meet this need wasn't something I wanted to entertain. I'd heard about young men who paid the homeless to fight. Could I pay the homeless to experience this pain for me? That just seemed so wrong. Life has got to be difficult enough without someone intensifying the pain of their tragic circumstances for a book project. I couldn't do that, but I needed to find a way to meet this need, my job, my sense of who I am in the world, was at stake."

Even if this weren't a matter of ministry, Ford would want to know how this story ends. It sounded to him like the stuff of television drama, maybe an episode of *NCIS*. He liked that show. He'd tune in for something like this, but instead the storyline was developing on the other side of the confessional. "Where is she going with this?" Ford wondered. He wanted to remind her that this is a place to confess sin, to begin a conversation with "I have sinned." Maybe he would need to.

An anxious tone and bit of a shiver in her voice brought him back. He leaned to the side and listened.

"The solution came to me in my seminar on war substitutes. We were talking about the ability of the wealthy, people of means, to secure others to do their military service for them. In some of our examples it was explicit, but then we talked about the ways in which rich Americans in the twentieth century were able to avoid military service without substantial penalty. After about an hour of this conversation, one of the students broke in and said, 'if you have the right thing to offer in exchange, you can pretty much get a person to do just about anything.'"

A New Testament question crossed Ford's mind as he heard the student's observation, "What would it profit a man to gain the whole world and lose his soul?"

"It was a simple statement, Father. Yet, it stood out for me. Could I get what I needed in exchange for giving a student what he or she needed? My chair always talked in terms of knowing the pain we describe, and putting something of ourselves in our writing; but couldn't that also mean knowing something about the inflicting of pain and misery? He mentioned that too. Isn't war about more than feeling pain; isn't it about causing enough pain and suffering to win the day? And while it was bizarre on a variety of fronts, this might just work for me. The faculty handbook—something I'd read cover to cover— didn't explicitly address this type of situation, but I couldn't imagine it wasn't something that would get me pulled into the Dean's Office for a serious conversation should it be discovered. Why couldn't it be kept a secret? Rumors wouldn't be enough to expose me. I thought about the several faculty members who were rumored to have relationships with students and who also kept their jobs. I was working through all this in my mind after class, during my office hours for student meetings."

The voice faded a bit, but then regained strength.

"I'd figured it out in my mind, but could I really do this? Who would I approach and how? What would I offer, good grades? How could I even consider this? I'd always thought myself a stand-up person, good morals and ethics, dedicated to fair play. And now that my sense of who I am as a professional ... really as a person, was being threatened, I found myself willing to trade on another's pain."

The professor described to the priest the internal struggle with this experiment. She talked about what she feared this would mean about her moral and ethical outlook and her capacity for charity and generosity. Sitting there she explained that ultimately the preservation of her way of life took precedence over the temporary pain she would inflict on another. Situational ethics, and everyone gained something they needed ...

Thinking about it this way, she felt as if her arrangement would allow everyone to win: students get good grades and she produces a book that allows her to keep her job.

"I decided I could use my office hours to find students. Around the due date for papers and right before exams students who are doing poorly flood my office desperate to figure out what they can do to improve their grades. I'd need to be careful and avoid students who might cause trouble. The student, or students—I needed to be prepared to find more than one just in case—would have to be somewhat isolated socially. I'd look for students who dressed in a way that would allow the cuts to be covered until they healed. To have a student go from typically wearing clothes that didn't cover the arms and legs, to long sleeve shirts and pants might raise questions and I didn't need these students exposing what was taking place because someone questioned their change in appearance."

The professor was providing a lot of information, and she'd reached a critical point in the story, so she stopped for a moment to let the priest catch up with her, then she continued.

"One Thursday afternoon I found the right student. Let's call him JJ, a sophomore without many friends, somewhat antisocial really. JJ is

from a large city, a rough place, and he'd grown up middle class but
with a lot of exposure to the gritty element of his city. On campus he
wasn't involved in many activities, didn't say much in class, and tended
to sit in the back off to a side. And he always wore this old jacket
that covered his arms and jeans. He came to the office because he
wasn't doing well in the course. In fact, he was on the verge of failing
unless some miracle increased his grade. I couldn't come right out and
ask—'Say, JJ, you interested in being cut for an A?' So, I made up a
story and tried to sell it as part of a larger experiment I was conducting
for a book project. I would assure him that the school approved it
and that there was no need to mention it because secrecy was part of
the experiment. If necessary, I could always just threaten to have him
kicked out of school because of his grades. Come to find out, he was
on probation and a low grade in my class would mean removal from
the school. People would believe a professor over a student."

Ford thought—yes, just as they'd believe a priest.

"JJ explained his situation and asked if he could do extra credit,
or rewrite his papers in order to improve his grade. I told him those
two options weren't available to him, but I had another possibility. I
explained that as part of a book project I was working on, I'd gotten
permission from the school to hold an experiment. The project
looked at the effect of inflicted pain on perceptions of war held by
the nonmilitary. In order to draw him in, I told him that I was only
selecting a couple of students out of all those taking my classes, and
that those students in exchange for their participation would receive
an 'A' in the class and a strong letter of recommendation should they
need one for any reason during their time on campus. However, the
students involved couldn't mention their participation and if they did
they would be suspended. In his case, his original grade would stand
and he would be removed from the school. He had three days—I
needed to start writing again soon—to make a decision. But before I
could get that sentence out, JJ agreed to participate. He didn't really
care about the terms. All he needed to hear was the students will get an
'A.' His only question, 'What does it involve professor, and where do I
need to be?' I had to think about the location, not my home of course,
but would the campus be the right place? Against my initial resistance,

I told him he was to meet me at my home in three days, at 6:00 p.m. I gave him the address, thanked him for participating, stood, and saw him out the office."

The priest didn't move. He was having some difficulty connecting what he imagined of this woman and what she was describing. But, then again, he remembered based on the other confessions he'd heard that all humans are capable of atrocities, their look means nothing because this potential is the consequence of their fallen state. They, by the mere fact that they are human, are prone to sin. This is what scripture teaches, and he was committed to the truth of the biblical witness. He hunkered down and listened.

JJ showed up on time, looking nervous, but a bit relieved because he saw an "A" in his future. "How hard can this be?" She could almost hear him saying to himself as she came to the door and showed him in. Dressed in jeans and a sweatshirt from the school, the professor led JJ to the kitchen, and sat him at the table. She'd covered the table with plastic and placed two knives on the table.

"What are those for?" JJ asked. His body stiffened, and she could hear nervousness in his voice.

"What's going on?! I thought you said some type of experiment for your book? What's with the knives, professor? What are you doing?!"

JJ was frightened. He wanted to knock her out the way and run— run anywhere as long as it was away from her. This was a side of his professor he'd never seen before and all he could think about was the newspaper headline: "Student found dead in ally, throat cut, and college professor the main suspect!!!" He felt close to death and had to move.

"I gotta get out of here. What are you doing?!"

Before he could get far, the professor caught his arm, and gently moved him away from the kitchen door into the chair at the table. She had to calm him down, and make him commit. The professor picked up the knives and put them on the countertop away from JJ, and turned toward him smiling.

"Relax, relax, JJ. You've taken courses with me; we've talked, you know you're safe. Don't worry—you'll go home tonight in the same condition in which you arrived."

The professor touched him lightly on the shoulder and let her hand stay there for affect.

"Remember … this is for your grade. You need this 'A' don't you? I'm trying to help you stay in school." She turned up the lights in the kitchen hoping seeing the whole room and how ordinary it is would calm him.

"Yes, but …"

The professor cut him off, no need to let him finish that thought; it would only increase his fear and his fight or flight impulse.

"Well, you will get the grade if you cooperate. Don't worry, I'm not a killer. This isn't some slasher movie. Please, keep your seat. You'll be okay, I promise."

This eased his mind some, but even if it hadn't, JJ knew he couldn't afford to leave. He was still nervous, but "she promised he'd be okay," he thought to himself, and took a deep breath. He looked her in the eyes. He couldn't make out what he saw in them, but he was stuck. She was a teacher, and couldn't lie to him. JJ sat back in the chair.

The professor asked JJ to take off his long sleeve shirt, and leave on his undershirt. He did as instructed. His arms were large, no hair, but looked like those of an older man—someone who'd worked construction. The biceps showed hard work—in the gym or through physical labor she couldn't tell. But they'd gotten some attention. His forearms were also strong and the muscles sculpted. The veins were large, bluish, and close to the surface. The shape of his arms reminded her of the arms on the famous statue of David she'd seen a few years back during a vacation. His arms trembled a bit, like her arms had.

"Trust me, JJ. Trust me. I wouldn't do anything that would cause you permanent harm. Trust me. Believe me … this is part of the experiment. It's for a good cause and you are helping me out a great deal."

JJ liked the idea of helping a professor. It made him feel important.

"Really, I'm helping you?" He thought, "If I'm helping her, she won't do anything really bad. At the end of the day, she may not think I matter much, but she's sure to think she and her work matter." If she didn't kill him—and she said she wouldn't—and didn't hurt him bad—it would be worth it. They'd each get something out of the deal.

He'd have to take a chance.

The professor smiled at him, turned to the countertop, and took the two knives in her hands. These were the knives she used on herself—clean, and no longer new. She wanted to make certain he saw the knives, watched as they caught the light, and saw the dark and elegant handles. In war, people have a sense of the weapons used against them; have a sense of what those weapons were capable of doing. As part of their training they study their weapons and the weapons of the enemy. JJ had to have the same experience because it could only enhance the effect she needed. His awareness, combined with the pain, would give her the sensation and experience, and she would translate that into words for her book.

As she brought the knives close, JJ looked at them as she anticipated he would. To him they looked expensive, not like the knives at home. They looked like they could be dangerous, but they were also beautiful. The black handles were elegant to him, like pieces of a precious stone, and their shape reminded him of the contours of his favorite cloud formation. As a child he'd spent a lot of time alone, in his backyard looking at clouds. He was trying to capture that feeling again sitting in the chair in his professor's kitchen. Doing so would help him, would distract him—he hoped. Thinking of those summer evenings in his backyard, he spoke just below her ability to hear him, "It'll be fine … it's cool."

She slowly and with care placed the knives back on the table, arranging them with tips facing him and pointed at his eyes. The professor hoped the knives positioned this way would threaten him, and that this would intensify his emotions.

"Arms on the table please directly in front of your body, palms up." JJ complied with her request—"Trust her … trust, her."

The professor moved to the other side of the brown, wooden table for four. She sat across from him, looked him in the eyes, smiled an odd smile JJ didn't remember ever seeing before—"Is she enjoying this—maybe a little too much?"

Picking up the knives, she positioned them over his arms, tips down. "Is this some sort of game, maybe a type of game like that one people play with guns?" He wanted to say this out loud, although he didn't. The pounding of his heart and the sweat that was beginning to drip down his face and his back distracted him.

He wanted to move his arms, to run out the kitchen, out the door and to the safety of his dorm room. But he needed the grade and being in a position to help his professor made him feel significant like he'd never felt before. He'd stay there. He'd sit still, and trust.

Tips down, pointed at the middle of his forearms, she lowered the knives, and touched his skin.

JJ jerked, but worked to stay in his seat—"Shit … oh, shit. Okay, trust her. She's the teacher."

The knives pierced the skin.

"Ah! Oh, my God!!!" He began to tremble, tears forming, but there was too much holding him in that chair for him to move.

The knife went deeper, but not too deep. The professor spent time before this evening practicing on a rib-eye steak—the cuts on JJ had to be right. The trembling moved down his body, what was just barely visible became violent. The professor moved the knife down his arm maybe two inches, but not too far to cause suspicion should the cuts be seen. Tears formed a trail down his cheeks similar to the trail of blood leaking down his forearms. Pulling the knives away from his body, the professor smiled at JJ and assured him that it would be okay, that he was an important part of her work, and … he would get his "A."

JJ took the towels the professor handed him, wiped his arms and looked at the cuts. "They aren't deep cuts, JJ. They will heal without stitches. But you will need to keep your arms covered as they heal."

"Okayyy …" JJ was compliant, short in his response, but peculiarly content.

She asked if he wanted something to drink, if he were feeling okay. "Yes … I'm fine, I, umm, I think …"

After gently toweling off his arms, he took the gauze; wrapped his arms; and put tape over the gauze to secure it. He stood to his feet, a little woozy, grabbed his sweater, and put it on. JJ looked at the professor, tried to smile and walked out the kitchen to the door.

"Thank you, JJ. I will see you in class." This seemed an ineffectual thing to say after what had taken place, but it's what came to mind.

"Okay, professor." JJ walked out the door and she closed it behind him.

"Father, it seems unnatural to me, but I enjoyed cutting JJ. It felt like I was absorbing his pain and fear, and in me it became confidence, energy, clarity of thought. Afraid I might lose some of this feeling, I went to my desk and turned on my computer. The words flowed, and they seemed to paint a picture so vibrant, so compelling, and representative of what my chair had in mind. In a matter of hours I'd revised a chapter and when he read it his reaction was the same as for chapters written with my blood. I was able to complete the revisions of a couple of chapters based on JJ's blood and pain.

Ford was curious and had to ask, "And JJ, what happened to JJ?"

She expected this question, and had planned a careful answer. "He attended class, and initially seemed awkward around me. I tried to ease any tension, but this was new to me as well, and I was responsible for the awkwardness. My cuts were healed, and JJ being younger I assume his healed without a problem. He did come to my office once and asked me what would happen if he told what I'd done."

She let out a soft giggle as she shifted and thought about the student's weak attempt at blackmail.

"I reminded him that he would fail because I would change his grade, and college would be over for him. I lied and added that nothing would happen to me. Everyone would believe a respected teacher before they'd believe a student on probation, desperate to remain in school. That was the first and last time JJ brought up *that* question."

Feeling she'd given a sufficient account of JJ's whereabouts, she moved back to the story.

"As I said, JJ got me through a few chapters, but I had two left when it became clear what happened with my cuts and writing was happening. I couldn't ask JJ to be cut again. That's obvious, but I needed someone else. There was nothing about what I was doing that followed school regulations concerning research; nothing about it that could be reported to the committee responsible for monitoring research; and nothing about this experiment that maintained the requirement to safeguard the welfare of human participants. I turned a person into an object."

She thought about what she said, debated with herself, and then continued. "Okay, fine. But, I had to finish the book and I didn't have much time, if I was going to get it to a publisher and have it in print in time for my tenure review. I wanted to be consistent with my setup just in case JJ said something to another student. It wasn't likely but I wanted to be prepared. So, as soon as I found another student, I'd say the same thing—experiment for a book project, an 'A' for participating."

Ford moved, looked at his arms, and took a breath. He saw blood, but was it his, or the blood of one of the confessees splattered on him? He caught himself. It was all an illusion—a response to the professor's story.

"It didn't take as long as I thought it might—so many students barely getting by and eager for the easy way out. This time it was a female co-ed. Let's say, Francis. She's a junior history major who has taken a good number of my classes, but she's never really stood out. It should have been pretty obvious that she'd be one to take the deal. Francis, like JJ, keeps to herself. Word around campus is that she began cutting herself in high school as a coping mechanism—something to do with her parents divorcing and the overdose of her brother." The professor knew she sounded callous and distant from the student's pain, but that didn't keep her from finishing her thought.

"There wasn't much to suggest—as far as I could tell anyway—that she'd continued cutting during college, but then again would I have been concerned enough to even recognize the signs?"

Ford thought of Joan. She'd never cut herself.

"I was a bit reluctant initially because of her history, but I had to get the book done and I rationalized it—how much additional damage could this do? It might even give her a way to rethink her past behavior."

As the professor talked, Ford thought about another Francis—Francis of Assisi, the saint who disciplined his body in order to control desires and in that way better devote himself to the work and will of God. Was there anything similar between the two? Did they share a relationship to their bodies, an inability to embrace their bodies as a sign of beauty? One Francis saw his body as a source of distraction, and the other used her body as distraction. In both cases pain became a way to quiet emotional and psychological attachments to the world.

The priest understood the need to control the body, in part that's what he and Michael were doing through extreme penance as well as through their relationships to their own bodies as the tools God used. Yet, he felt a strong desire to distance himself from the professor and the professor's work.

Regardless of how he felt, the priest knew he'd have to continue to listen attentively and measure each word against the demands of his ministry.

"Okay, how did the professor's Francis enter the picture?" the priest asked himself, assuming the answer wasn't far behind the question. He was right.

"Francis came to my office hours because she was concerned about her grades in my courses. She had hopes of going on for an advanced degree. She said she wasn't sure what she'd do with it, but history interested her. Keep in mind, Father, there was no need for Francis to worry about her future. Her father is extremely wealthy and she will have no financial worries ever. So, study history or not, she'll be okay."

Ford thought of Joan and wondered how her life might have been different if she'd had money. Joan's response to her circumstance was to protect her body, to claim her body, through the commission of violence and death. Francis, on the other hand, responded to her circumstances by trying to alter the appearance of her body by tracing her misery through bloody cuts. Ford didn't blame Francis. He wondered how Joan was doing, and what she was doing since that day in the confessional.

"Although she'd be okay, Francis also wanted to show her parents that she could take charge of her life, could arrange some of the details of her life. But her grades in the history department were far from impressive. And my seminar was important because it's the required seminar for majors. It's the one graduate programs look at, and it's the one we use in the department to determine who gets the academic prizes we offer to juniors and seniors. She also wanted me to work with her on her thesis and possibly write letters of recommendation for her."

This was a lot for Ford to take in, despite all the penance he and Michael had measured out.

"I had her. She needed so much from me. I told her I could help her … if she could help me. I stood up, closed the office door and sat down again. This time there was no smile on my face. Hands folded on my desk, leaning forward, I looked her in the eyes and told her that I was running an experiment related to how pain affects the response to war of nonenlisted people, and I was looking for student volunteers. In exchange for her participation, I would give her an 'A' in the class, agree to supervise her thesis, and write her strong letters of recommendation to anywhere she decided to apply."

She jumped at it. "Yes, of course. That sounds great, thanks!" She didn't ask questions, and didn't seem at all concerned about the details.

"Excellent," I responded. "Don't worry about anything. No one on campus will have a problem with this. In fact, part of the experiment involves keeping your participation confidential. Can you do that?"

"Not a problem professor, no problem at all." She was so eager, even more so than JJ who really needed the deal I was offering.

"Okay. I run the experiment from my home. I find it best to remove the campus feel from the experiment and conducting it in a place unfamiliar to the students helps with that."

"Sure, professor. Just tell me when and how to get there." Francis left with a smile on her face.

"I told her to be at my apartment the following evening, about 6 p.m., and I gave her the address and directions. I was confident she'd play by the rules I'd established. And she did. Right at 6 p.m. the doorbell rung. I opened the door and showed her in. The kitchen worked well with JJ, and I saw no need to change locations. We walked into the kitchen, lights down so that the room had a yellow glow, plastic on the table, and the knives positioned as before. Francis wasn't as shocked by the setup as JJ had been. I thought to myself she'd seen knives before, perhaps not exactly like these, but something about it was probably familiar. JJ got loud and agitated. Francis was quiet, still, and seemed mesmerized by the display. I wasn't certain how to talk to her about what was next, so I started by asking her to take a seat opposite the knives."

"Okay, professor. I'm not certain what's happening here, but okay." Perhaps muscle memory kicked in for Francis?

The professor didn't want surprises. She needed to be certain Francis would react properly. "Francis, everything we'll do is related to the experiment and only that. It's not meant to do any permanent harm to you or me. You will be fine."

Francis wasn't frightened. She assumed just seeing the knives might be the full experiment. Maybe the professor would ask her how she felt about knives, and would explain how knives were used in war. She thought the professor might ask her to touch or handle the knives, to cut something. Francis didn't realize that she was the thing to be cut until she was instructed to roll up her sleeves as far as they would go. She was reluctant, but after hesitating she did as instructed.

The professor looked at her arms. They weren't like JJ's arms or even her own. These arms spoke to hard years and emotional stress. It wasn't her veins that were prominent, but the scars from her cuts.

The look on her professor's face embarrassed Francis. She jerked her arms back and hid them under the table, below view.

"I don't want to talk about it, professor. It's none of your business."

She understood this. She knew the rumors about Francis, but now she'd seen her arms and she wasn't certain what to do. Letting Francis go without completing the process could jeopardize her book and that wasn't a good thing. But would going forward create problems beyond her ability to control? After all, Francis wasn't there through force … not really. She'd take her chances. Like Francis, she didn't have a choice.

"I won't ask, Francis. You're right. It's none of my business. But it's okay. We can move forward without saying a word." As she spoke, the professor thought about the scars.

"My legs … umm, my legs too."

Francis didn't say much more than that, but somehow they understood each other. She had taken refuge in the pain cutting brought, and now the professor was affirming pain as the language of life. They didn't need words. Francis had stopped cutting because people insisted it was wrong and dangerous, but here was a professor she trusted showing her that pain could be useful, could be vital … could be a learning process."

Francis stood, looked at her professor with an odd expression she couldn't identify, lifted her shirt to expose her stomach, and moved forward until she was prone. Her back was exposed and clean. No marks, no scars, no cuts.

"Okay, professor," Francis said.

She couldn't be certain what the professor was planning to do with the knives. But *she* was the professor running the experiment, and she'd trust her. Besides Francis figured cutting—if that's what the professor was going to do—had felt oddly good to her in high school, and in college she'd often felt the urge to cut again.

Ford imagined Francis on the table, perhaps arms perpendicular to her body like she's on some type of crucifix.

"I didn't expect her to be so complaint, not after JJ. But really, I didn't know what to expect. How could I? I only knew I needed this, so I pushed her shirt up a little further. The small of her back to just below her shoulder blades was exposed, pale and bony. I told her not to worry. I took one of the knives and left the other in her view. With the tip pointed just to the left of her spine, I lowered it slowly until the tip touched her. Francis jumped a little like we do when something cold touches us. But that was it, she didn't try to get up. She didn't complain—just jumped and then settled in. I cut her from the small of her back to about four or maybe five inches up. She didn't react other than a quieting of her breathing and a slight tremble that could be pain or pleasure."

The professor wondered if the cut took her back to the troubled days of high school. Or, was it something else—a type of pleasure almost sensual. Pain and pleasure can be difficult to distinguish, life and death bound in that way. Isn't that why during an earlier age an orgasm was known as the "little death"?

In a way, the professor was thrown by Francis's reaction to the experience, but she was just as emotionally captured by her own reaction. She enjoyed cutting Francis. If she were honest about it, the professor would also have to say that she'd enjoyed cutting JJ, and also herself to a lesser extent.

She traded in pain, in misery, and found in it both academic and physical enjoyment. Holding the knife firm, she looked at Francis's back and asked herself, "What am I becoming?"

"The cut bled, but she didn't seem to care, and because she couldn't easily reach the spot, I dressed the cut and lowered her shirt. She didn't say a word as she pushed against the table, rose up, adjusted her shirt, looked at me, and walked toward the door. I didn't know what to say either, so I simply followed behind her."

Ford wondered how it felt to move down that hall in silence. Was it anything like his hallway? Were there pictures? If so, of what? Did it smell like perfume?

"When she was down the hallway and in front of the door, she turned and looked at me, then opened the door, and left. I closed it and went to my office to write. I was just about done with the book. My chair's reaction was the same as before; he thought the project had come along nicely, and that all missing at this point was a solid conclusion."

The professor explained the book as first written didn't have a conclusion. There was nothing holding it together, nothing that really made the project hers. In fact, she could see in hindsight that she'd hidden behind the opinions of others, her voice muted by the words of others. Through this embrace of pain as the source of inspiration and muse, her voice came out and she owned the story in that book as never before. Her arms, JJ's arms, and Francis' back had gotten her this far, but what would get her through the conclusion—one more student? And while another student's blood might be enough to satisfy her academic hunger for pain, would it be enough to quiet that growing desire for inflicting pain coming from elsewhere deep in her? First things first she decided. The professor was determined it was better to wrestle with that second question from the safety of a tenured—life-long—job.

She found another student to cut—Peter. He was planning to take her seminar the following year. He was a comparative literature major, and history major, and he'd come to talk about his interest in graduate school. He was driven, determined, and in need of what the experiment could offer. Peter wasn't as resistant as JJ had been at the start, and he wasn't as compliant as had been Francis. He reacted to the kitchen and the cutting of his arms with an expression on his face that

236 · ANTHONY B. PINN

said, "I will do what I must do to get what I want. Cut me."

Peter bandaged his arms, asked for instruction on what he'd need to do now, put on his coat, and walked toward the door. As with the others, the professor followed, shut the door, and went to her computer to work. In a short period of time, just a matter of a few days, she'd written the conclusion. Her chair responded as she'd hoped he would—"Good work. Let's send it to my publisher." The professor was done with the book and the hardest part of the tenure file.

"The file was in, and I thought everything had worked out. None of the students, after that initial challenge from JJ, said anything or did anything that exposed me.

Sometimes I'd wonder about the three students and what they thought about the experiment beyond the grade they'd get. To the extent those questions didn't last long, I relaxed as much as someone thinking about keeping their job could."

Ford rubbed his eyes, and thought the itch was just jitters. The story made him nervous and anxious.

"My department sent an accompanying letter endorsing my request for tenure, but there were other people who had to sign off. And that would take some time. One afternoon while I was in my office thinking about this process, someone knocked. Not wanting to get up, I just called out "come in." The door opened slowly and it was Francis looking tired and disheveled. She apologized for interrupting me in a voice that was weak and drained, like she'd not slept in a while. I was grateful for her pain, so I smiled and told her not to worry and I asked what I could do for her. She stood in the doorway, didn't move in, her body stiff and drawn in on itself—like she wanted to take up as little room as possible. She said she had a quick question. She wanted to know if the experiment was over. I told her yes it was, and I thanked her for playing such an important part in it." The professor sounded distant and professorial.

"She tried to smile, looked down, and backed out the door. It was odd, and I didn't know what to make of it, so I chalked it up to the stuff that goes along with students that age. I went back to my thoughts."

The professor stopped speaking—just a moment to collect

thoughts before continuing.

"The next morning ... when I was checking my e-mail there was a note from the Dean of Students announcing sad news. I opened it, and started to read ... Francis had been found dead in her apartment tub. She'd cut her wrists, and left a note on her kitchen table ... just a few words, Father—'the experiment is over.'"

The priest could sense the spasm of her body as it fought emotion. The story was done—the sin named.

"Forgive me for I have sinned. It has been a long time since my last confession."

She wasn't content; she wanted to say more than that before the priest could respond.

"I am a Catholic, but I don't attend mass as often as I should. I do believe in God, although it isn't always evident, and it may not be exactly the way the Church speaks about God. I have trouble with some of the Church's positions on different issues, but I don't think I'm the only Catholic who does. I hold to the essential elements of the faith ... most of the time. I believe in spiritual life and the need to nurture one's soul. But I also believe it's possible to honor God by using your gifts in your professional life. That's what I try to do. To honor God through my intellectual talents."

He heard in the voice what he wanted to understand as contrition.

"What is your sin?" There was silence except for the faint sound of arms folding and a body leaning forward.

"Pain that kills," the professor responded.

Ford thought about sacrifice, the surrender of someone or something for the sake of others, but where was the professor's empathy? Where was her concern for others? Was there anything about her that suggested people were anything more than a way to meet her wants and needs? Pain that kills ... Who was the professor in this scenario?

He had another thought, the type of wondering Joan had provoked. Where is God in all of this? Then he remembered that in the Book of Genesis God instructed Abraham to sacrifice his son in order to prove his devotion to God. He takes his son, the boy he loves, positions him and is prepared to plunge the knife into him when an animal appears. Abraham is told to replace his son with the animal. The physical death

238 · ANTHONY B. PINN

of his son is short-circuited, but what about the emotional death, the way that experience must have convinced the child he was expendable and that blood is required as a sign of obedience?

Ford struggled with the thought: Is squeamishness to blood and pain a mark of God's grace that negates the need for such sacrifice? Or, is it a sign of humanity's distance (even of the most devout) from God's demands for the proper spiritual life?

The priest wondered if that requirement from God found in Genesis complicated the professor's story and his interpretation of the penance that might be necessary to cover these deeds.

Ford was familiar with the notion that "some things come only through prayer and fasting"—through a discipline of the body; but had the Christian Church, his Church, lost sight of the demand for blood as the mark of purification, and in this way did the Church mock the real meaning of communion and discipleship?

God sometimes requires blood; but what did this mean for the professor's confession? Was she of the same mind as he and Michael, but just a bit misguided concerning the context for sacrifice? He didn't think so. She isn't doing this for God, who hadn't demanded the pain she caused. What the professor said pushed him, or was it something else about the professor that really challenged him?

Father Ford had listened to what the professor said, but he was also mindful of what he felt in his body. There was a tingle, and alertness in his body, that both excited and troubled him. His body was alive to him through the professor as it had never been before.

"What's happening to me?" he asked. The priest remembered the words Michael spoke in response to his question about humanism— "at least more human"—and he feared this meant his body was now responsive to him in ways he could not fully discipline.

Ford felt unprepared for this; prayer hadn't trained him for this because it had only helped him to deny those yearnings he felt by focusing on one—Jesus—who did not know those yearnings so tied to human life. Rituals of the Church had done no better. He felt alone.

Michael did not need to wrestle with his body in the same way; he is married and the Church actually expects him to surrender to urges … within the context of the marriage bed. Not so for the priest, whose black suit is meant to hide the body of flesh and whose white collar is meant to strangle the wants emerging from that flesh. He wanted to grab his robe and pull it tighter around his body to protect it from those questions, but at the same time he wanted to remove it.

Between Joan and the professor, Ford was made more aware of the body involved in ministry. His natural inclination was to privilege the work of the spirit in this regard, but their stories and something about them made that so difficult. The priest wondered, who protects the priest from the confessions in that box, and who protects him from his human self?

Ford was alarmed by his physical response to the professor. He wanted to see her, to touch her, and be touched by her. The priest knew he couldn't, and had no sense of what to do if the opportunity presented itself; but he still felt something both frightening and pleasurable. And at this point the only way to enjoy it was to enter the conversation, although he knew what had to take place.

"You have committed a mortal sin by reducing people to objects. You've denied them their importance in the sight of God."

The professor's natural professorial posture of debate—counterargument—kicked in.

"I understand what you're saying, but I didn't make them do anything, Father. They had options and isn't that all I'm responsible for providing?"

The professor's response was a natural reaction: academics raise questions, push boundaries, and offer alternatives.

"Are you sorry for what you've done?"

"I regret it, but I didn't really do anything wrong. I gave them an option, and I didn't take anything from them, and ... well, Francis had a problem that I didn't create."

Ford countered the professor. "Francis is dead because you showed no regard for her situation."

"She's dead, Father, because she didn't want to live. Maybe the problem is her parents, maybe school culture, but not *me*. Anyway ... it's unfortunate she's dead, but with respect to me, she got something out of the deal. It's too bad, but it's not my fault."

Was she really saying this to a priest? She surprised herself.

"Why did you come to confession?" Ford was frustrated, shifting in his seat.

"I wanted to tell somebody, someone safe. It was a lot on me to have this secret." The professor paused, "Okay, Father. Maybe I did something wrong, maybe I played a role; but I'm not the only one."

Father Ford was silent. He'd been in the confessional enough times to know that type of change was a crack in the defensiveness, a glimmer of empathy that could lead to contrition. He waited for her to continue. There was silence for what seemed minutes in length.

She thought she knew what he was thinking; she'd worked through various scenarios before heading to the church. "I can't tell my chair. No one at the school can know … I could be fired. There's got to be something else, Father. What's another way to deal with this?"

That's what Ford was waiting to hear—a sign of contrition that could lead to penance necessary for redemption. He thought of what should come next. But he also felt something that fought against what he knew his work required. He wanted her to be safe because part of him held a vague hope he would be able to see her, and against his better judgment he thought about what it might be like to have her body. It could be God only wanted him to demonstrate a willingness to sacrifice, but God would ultimately provide another way to show discipleship.

The priest thought about it during those few moments, and wondered if perhaps God was testing him—like Abraham had been tested. Why this woman? He'd not felt so out of control—sexually—before. Why now? Was it a consequence of his growing body awareness? What?

He knew he needed to talk with Michael, but he felt inspired by a thought: God requires not the sacrifice of her life but of the thing that meant more to her than life—her career. Ford was sure Michael would agree with this approach or at least he hoped as much.

"I'm sorry. I know I was wrong to do what I did, and I regret the loss of life."

"Contrition," Ford thought to himself, "now penance."

"What do I need to do?" She spoke these words hoping that her gut feeling was wrong. The priest would require that she tell the chair of her department what she'd done, and she couldn't think of anything worse than having to do that.

"You must tell the chair of your department …"

"Father … that could cost me everything. Please—something else."

"That is your penance. If you want the easing of your conscience, you must tell him."

The professor said nothing as she stood to her feet and began making her way out of the box. As the priest heard the sound of her heels on the floor, he couldn't resist. Once he believed she was at a safe distance, unlikely to turn and look, but still close enough to have her features available to his view, he moved forward and opened the curtain. Ford turned his head in her direction and looked at her body, imagining the feel of the arm she cut, the feel of the chest that must have heaved up and down as she cut, and the color of the eyes that watched the blood as it moved down the cut. The priest looked at her, and without warning she turned and looked back at him. Ford's face convicted her.

CHAPTER FORTY-ONE

"Hello ..."

"Can we meet at the coffee shop? I'd like to talk with you about something."

This isn't the way the phone conversation with the priest started. "What's the problem? Is there something wrong? Is it the Bishop?"

"Nothing like that," Ford said hoping to ease Michael's mind but also suggesting by his tone that there was something serious to discuss.

"Okay. Tomorrow? I'll head there lunch time, say 12:30?"

"That's fine." Ford felt some relief, but he was also uncertain. Would Michael have objections? More importantly, was he acting consistent with the will of God and his requirements as a disciple? Was he acting like Abraham, or like an enemy of God?

At the coffee shop, Michael sat waiting for Ford to start the conversation. He assumed it was important the way the priest played with his coffee cup and avoided eye contact.

After what seemed much longer than it had actually been, the priest told Michael about the professor who'd shown a lack of empathy, had used people like objects, and whose actions resulted in the death of a student. He didn't mention the way his body felt whenever he thought about the professor—that was better left unsaid.

"I gave her penance, Michael. The professor had to tell her chair what she'd done."

There was a death involved, and a lack of empathy regarding what she'd done. Yes. Maybe extreme penance, but he would accept what the priest had done at least while Ford explained.

"She will probably be fired."

"I know—a small price to pay for what she did." Michael responded quickly—as if matching a move in a game of chess. "But ... okay, we will leave it with the penance you prescribed."

The conversation lasted only a few minutes, and with it done they ordered something to eat, and afterward the priest went back to his duties and Michael his.

That night Ford went to bed thinking about the professor, and hoping to encounter her in the safety of his dreams.

CHAPTER FORTY-TWO

It wasn't like her to have lights on through the night. None of her neighbors could remember a time when the glow of the television could be seen from her window at four in the morning, and certainly not for days.

Mrs. Jenson saw everything in the complex, but she couldn't remember this young, attractive woman leave or return to her unit for days. Several people, not good friends, but observant and courteous people, asked Mrs. Jenson about the young professor until finally an investigation was initiated. When she didn't respond to a knock on the door, or a call, nerves were rattled.

It was someone from the condo association who found her body. The young professor had been in the bathtub for at least three days from what the untrained eye could tell—both arms submerged in the water, neck resting against the rim of the tub, the rest of her body blurred by the blood-stained water. A few hours passed before authorities arrived and placed the body in a black bag for removal.

The medical examiner later confirmed the time of death as being 72 hours from the discovery of the body.

The wrists were cut, and there was a note held to the kitchen table by a knife. It read, "Now the experiment is over. I'm sorry. Contrition … my penance."

Before the end of the broadcast, after weather and before the lead in for the next program, a sad announcement was made. Professor Faith Santo was found dead, an apparent suicide, the local news reported. She was a thirty-three-year old history professor at the local university. Her career had been so promising, a PhD from Harvard, and all the intangibles necessary to make it in the academy—and pretty on top of it. Those interviewed for the story commented that she was a dedicated professional. However, it had recently come out that she'd broken university regulations regarding experiments with human subjects, and it was likely her employment would have been terminated pending an internal investigation. A student had come forward with details. According to the chair of her department and other officials, "Professor Santo confessed her misconduct, and was waiting what was likely to be her termination notice, one week before her apparent suicide."

There were rumors of a connection between the suicide of Professor Santo and that of a student some weeks before—a similar note was found with the student. "Such a pity," were the words used to end the report.

Everyone seemed shocked, although her devotion to the job and the likelihood she would lose it made some wonder how she would react. Everything revolved around her life as a scholar, and her colleagues thought she might have a difficult time, but not to the point of suicide. She was bright and could possibly get another academic appointment somewhere.

The news reporter on one of the other stations said she'd tried to get comments from some of her colleagues, those at the same rank, for perspective but they were reluctant to comment "on the record." Off the record they talked about the demands of tenure—the pressure to publish and to be liked by the students in order to get good teaching evaluations. Each one said something about the pressure and the negative effect it could have. Asked if they thought the tenure system was a bad idea, they all looked around before responding, smiled, and said of course not, it's the cornerstone of academic life and intellectual freedom. With some there also seemed to be relief in their expression—as if one more competitor had been bested and their positions were that much more secure. Although polite, the competition is nonetheless brutal—only those with a thick skin, good instincts, and a crafty disposition survive.

Ford wondered if he'd be contacted about the arrangements, and he rehearsed in his head how he might respond if he were in fact contacted. He would want to honor the request, but what he'd say about the professor in light of the situation was more difficult.

Ford turned off the television. While he would normally absolve the sinner, in this case he couldn't. The professor's action prevented forgiveness—mortal sin resolved through mortal sin. It was a theological thicket for which the Church had little compassion. Ford knew it was possible God offered the professor—and Francis—an opportunity to repent before their deaths. This was "salutary repentance," but he couldn't know. He *could* pray. Without moving from the couch, he began to pray for her soul.

Ford started praying out loud to drown the sound in his head of her voice and her shoes on the floor of the church. He didn't want to think about what he felt when he caught that glimpse of her, and what he dreamed about her. Not wanting to believe those dreams, images, and activities in his head—but that he didn't consciously control— were a sin, he felt they could still lead to sin if he weren't disciplined and ever mindful of his larger obligations to God over his body's wants. He fought hard to suppress the memory of her body as it turned toward him before she left the church. And he worked to replace it with images of the crucified Christ—also cut, also bloody, and also dead.

This only helped so much. Theology and doctrine only did so much to render the body docile, even the body of a devout priest thinking about a woman he didn't know. The priest felt a sense of loss, but recognized it wasn't attached to anything real.

Death and death of the young and promising weren't foreign to this line of work. Ford knew all about those tragic situations and had a professional and psyche reserve for addressing them. But this was different. He had only encountered her in the confessional. He knew nothing about her childhood, youth, or adulthood, and nothing about her years as a graduate student and the hopes as well as dreams born and crushed during those years. She was a shadow, but still he felt her death took something from him.

The priest wasn't experienced with this feeling. He hadn't had a relationship end with a pain that required hours in the dark listening to that perfectly sad and knowing song. So he couldn't situate what he felt. There was no emotional boilerplate providing a way to name his response to the evening news announcement. He could only compare it to what he knew of the Church's love and his love for Christ. Caring about people wasn't the issue, but there was something about being religiously devout that can limit the quality of that care.

The closest attachment over the past several years was his shared ministry with Michael, and he wanted to call Michael, but couldn't think of what to say. His partner in ministry was probably watching the news anyway. Ford remembered Michael indicating that he normally watched the evening news whenever he had a chance. It was his way of connecting to the world, of reminding himself of all the misery that needed God's mercy and grace.

The more the priest thought about Michael, the more worried he became. Michael didn't look himself. He was thinner, pale, and seemed to lack energy. Even his eyes looked ill, drained of color, tired, and without their normal luster. Ford thought back and never remembered Michael as a big guy, but now he seemed thin in an unhealthy way. Food wasn't the issue; he knew Michael ate lunch every day and he assumed breakfast and dinner as well. Nothing about their meals together suggested Michael didn't like food. Ford thought maybe it was the stress of his job, or maybe family life, or the demands of discipleship.

"Lord, is Michael okay?"

CHAPTER FORTY-THREE

With each act of extreme penance since Professor Santos, Michael seemed more disconnected and less capable of the physical demands often placed on him. It was like every act of devotion to God drained away some of his life. Ford was worried, but he didn't have a way of starting that conversation. So much time had passed without them establishing that type of bond, and because of this distance he wasn't certain how to bring it up. In his own awkward way, the priest would try to open conversation. "How are you doing?" before moving on to penance didn't really achieve the desired outcome. Michael would respond in a belabored way—"Doing okay. You?"—and they would continue with the work of their ministry.

Michael noticed the changes as well. Looking in the mirror, or even the fit of his clothing, suggested something was wrong. His bathroom habits changed; there was blood and pain. The nausea couldn't be explained away with a quick—"I'm suffering from allergies," or "I ate something that doesn't agree with me." The vomiting was becoming too frequent for that. It was easier not to think about it, to try to lose himself in his job and his ministry. But people noticed, and there were whispers about him. "God would take care of it because God will protect him as a disciple," he thought to himself whenever he caught someone's eye and they had that concerned look. What worried him most was his wife. Susan noticed and commented.

"Babe … is everything okay?"

She tried what she could—vitamins, oils, exercise, self-help books, and anything else she could think of, or someone told her about. And

Michael went along with it. He'd kept so much from her for the sake of his ministry that giving her this little bit of control and comfort seemed right.

"Sweetheart, please take these herbs with your coffee in the morning. I read something about them increasing energy and purging the body."

"Okay, Susan."

"Michael, I bought this tonic that's supposed to get rid of toxins in the body. Let's give it a try. I'll take it with you."

"If you think it will help, sure."

"Babe, let's go for a long walk each evening, I mean when you're not working. Exercise might be the answer. And I bought us both walking shoes that are supposed to be good for the back and the legs."

With a smile, "Whatever you want Susan."

"I'm gonna change our diet—everything organic, not just your lunches. Okay? From now on everything free from harmful chemicals. It will cost more but your health … our health … is worth it."

"That sounds right, love."

In addition to all these changes, Susan and Michael touched each other more often. She'd walk past him sitting in a chair and stroke his hair. He'd see her in the kitchen, walk over, and place his arms around her waist. In his sleep Michael would reach out his hand and touch her, or just pull her as close as his strength would allow. She'd make certain they spooned as they drifted to sleep. They took every opportunity to make contact, to bring their bodies together as best they could with his declining strength. Their bodies seemed to know what their minds wouldn't acknowledge—Michael was ill.

After spending a large sum of money on things that had no effect, and after going through every possible scenario in her head, Susan asked Michael to go to the doctor.

"Michael, I'm really worried. This isn't just a cold, or the flu, or something like that. Please go to the doctor. You're getting worse."

"Susan, I'm certain it's nothing. I'll be fine. It'll be okay; we just need to give it time."

"Michael, please …."

"Okay."

Michael called his doctor the next morning, and described his symptoms. The nurse consulted with the doctor, and later that day he received a call telling him to come in the next day. He was shocked by how quickly this was all happening.

"This can't be good," he thought to himself.

Michael showed up early to the doctor's office. He regretted it once he arrived—too much time to look through old magazines and watch Fox News on the television. "Fox News?! That's reason enough to find a new doctor," he said quietly enough for no one to hear him. Michael read through five magazines, and in turning each page he wondered had someone sick sneezed on that page, or dripped some type of disgusting discharge on it?

"Really doesn't matter much," he said in response to his paranoia. "Who knows what I'm leaving behind on these pages."

After what seemed too many painful stories on the television, the nurse called him to the back, took his weight—he'd lost 30 pounds— took his vitals, and gave him that backless gown to put on. Sitting there with only his socks, underwear—a new pair for the occasion—and the gown on, Michael thought about what would come next. Prostate exam? The doctor would save that for last. Check for a hernia? Sure, right before the prostate examination. Blood work, of course—but that's done in a separate suite. Stress test? Michael was thinking this would be a typical physical—just earlier in the year.

The examination involved everything Michael listed in his mind, but there were also x-rays, and machines he sat in without moving for long periods of time, devices that made a humming sound—not the hum of a projector that always put him to sleep in his art history classes, or the hum of the florescent lights in his office. This was a medical hum—the sound of serious investigation. He had to drink this horrible liquid so that they could see inside particular organs; he didn't really get what was going on with that. The doctor and the technician didn't explain it beyond a few medical terms. Seven hours after he arrived, Michael was headed home with instructions to come back for the results in a week.

"Okay. Do I need to call to schedule that appointment?"

"It's already taken care of, Mr. Thomas. You just need to show up for the appointment."

"9:30 a.m.?"

"9:30 a.m., correct. Mr. Thomas, you'll need to take care of your co-pay. The insurance company may send you a bill for a portion of the cost of the other tests. But for now, it's $35—cash, check, or credit card are accepted."

"Credit card." Michael handed her his American Express card. In an odd way, he was both proud and embarrassed by his platinum card.

"I'm sorry, Mr. Thomas. We don't accept American Express."

"Of course not."

He took back the card and handed her $40, got his change, and headed home.

Ford wanted to call Michael to find out how he was doing. He'd asked at church but he wanted more detail than could be provided at the end of the service as they shook hands. But he didn't know how to ask, and that bothered him—a priest who didn't know how to ask this person about his condition?

"This is ridiculous. I need to know how he's doing." The priest would do that for any other member of the parish, why not the person with whom he shared a ministry?

Finally deciding it didn't matter exactly how he asked about Michael, he just needed to call and ask, he picked up the phone.

"Hello."

"Yes, hello."

"This is Father Ford. I wanted to check on Michael. We didn't have time to talk after service and I wanted to know how he's doing. Can he come to the phone?"

"He's just resting, Father. I'll call him to the phone. Thanks so much for calling. This really means a lot to me."

Susan called out to Michael. He wanted to know who was calling before coming to the phone. Once he learned it was Ford, Michael picked up the phone in the den and asked Susan to hang up.

"Ford, hello."

"Michael, I know we don't really talk much about anything other than our ministry, but this call isn't about penance. I'm just calling to see how you're doing. We really didn't get a chance to talk. But I remembered you said you'd taken some tests and that you're awaiting word. How are you holding up?"

Ford regretted not being closer to Michael. He was embarrassed that he was a priest who didn't know how to talk to the person who understood him best, and who shared his ministry. If he shared emotional intimacy with anyone it was Michael because of this spiritual bond. But the conversation was tortured, with long gaps.

"I'm okay, thanks." He wasn't certain, couldn't know if that was true. "I will know something in a couple of days. Should I let you know what I find out?"

Michael felt as awkward as Ford. He understood his relationship with Ford as disciples, co-laborers. Were they friends?

"Yes, please ... I know you must be tired, so I won't hold you. Just know that you are in my prayers, you and Susan."

"Father Ford, thank you."

"Be blessed."

"Goodnight."

Ford put the phone down, and went to his room. He thought about Michael and Susan until he fell asleep. Some of his thinking was selfish, about him really. "What happens to this ministry, if Michael is no longer a part of it?"

Michael and Susan prepared for bed. It wasn't very late but they were both tired. They found themselves tired most of the time now.

"That was nice of Father Ford to call you."

"Yes it was. I appreciated it, but it surprised me a little."

"I don't know why, Michael. You've given time to the church and to St. Barbara before the accident. He has to appreciate all that, and recognize that you are a special person."

"Maybe ... good night, babe."

Michael wanted to end the conversation with those words, and so instead of talking he just felt the warmth of her body against his. It made him feel alive, and comforted, despite what he feared the doctor might say.

Michael showed up on time, not too early like with the last appointment. It had been a rough week, waiting for the test results. But he told himself it was just a matter of minutes and, if nothing else, at least he'd know. Before he could fully process that thought, the nurse called him to the back. No gown, no weight, or vitals—just Michael waiting in a beige room with framed posters that seemed to be reproduced for every doctor's office in the country. Stock stuff. Those happy pictures were combined with anatomy shots. He wondered why he'd never paid much attention to these posters and pictures before.

"Hello, Michael." The doctor seemed uncomfortable and anxious.

"Hello ... do you have the results?"

Michael saw no good reason to delay the purpose for the visit. Getting it over wouldn't diminish good news, and delaying would increase the pain of bad news.

"Well ... okay ... I wish I had better news, Michael."

"Yes." Michael tensed up. So many possibilities ran through his head.

"It's liver cancer ... I'm so sorry. We will do everything we can, but unfortunately, Michael, my best advice is to enjoy your remaining days."

Michael understood the idea of bad news, but this hit him hard. What he heard was, "You are dying, Michael. And there's nothing we can do about it."

He found it hard to catch his breath. His heart raced, and his thoughts flashed between his wife and his ministry.

"I understand ... ah, is there anything that can be done?"

"There are options, but nothing that will improve quality of life. There isn't a cure. Everything I can offer you will have strong side effects."

"I'd like to think about this. Talk to my wife, and decide what to do."

"That's a good idea. If you have questions you'd like to ask, or if you want a second opinion, just let me know."

Michael knew the doctor had to say that, but did it really make a difference after seven hours of testing? "I don't think I'll need a second opinion. I just need to figure out what to do with my life ... while I have it."

Everyone recognizes human life is short term, but it's one thing to know it theologically and it's another to feel the truth of that reality in your own body.

This was all coming too fast for Michael. He'd prepared for the possibility of them getting caught in their ministry—he thought that through. But he'd not prepared for death in this way—after all, there was always the thought in the back of his mind that ministry protected him from certain things. Theologically he could always imagine himself the exception, the one with a special mission from God that would somehow shift the truth of mortality. And while he'd tried not to give this much thought before, should his ministry, the discipleship he'd embraced as others rejected it count for something—something special, even miraculous?

Shouldn't his devotion give him some type of special favor in the sight of God? After all, he wasn't a priest but he was doing the will of God when the princes of the Church would not. Didn't God need him?

Yes, he at times thought of himself as John the Baptist, but did the end of his ministry have to come like this? Where's the glory in cancer?

Michael wasn't a theologian, and there was nothing abstract nor disinterested about his questions and the angst he felt. He knew about the story of Job and God's use of suffering to prove the glory of God, shrouded as it is in mystery; but why him? Why now? Job's afflictions weren't unto death, so why was he being killed? Wasn't he as devout as Job?

Michael gathered himself, shook the doctor's hand, and left.

"Not like this God. Not like this …"

He'd need to tell Susan, and he'd need to tell Ford about this and he wanted to tell both before the end of the day. No need to delay.

Michael was restless. His body felt heavy. He couldn't go to work. Why ever go back to the job? And he didn't want to go home—couldn't stand the idea of sitting alone looking at the markers of his life spread through the rooms: pictures, books, art, stains on the rug that told the story of one event or another. Needing to be distracted, Michael walked around the city. Just walked, no particular destination—just anywhere that would occupy his thoughts and time, and as far as his tired body could take him. When Michael finally looked at his watch it was afternoon, about the time Ford would be in the confessional.

"Go there, and tell the priest," he told himself. He stopped, turned, and pointed his body in the direction of the church. Better yet, he'd go back, get his car and drive to the church. Michael drove to St. George, parked, and entered the sanctuary.

His ministry, the clear sense of life meaning and purpose started in the confessional at St. Barbara with James Ford. Michael suspected it was only fitting that this ministry—his life with meaning and beauty— also end in the confessional, with Ford.

Chapter Forty-four

Michael looked around at the windows, the scenes of God in contact with humans, pictures of agony and pain, glory and triumph. The beautiful stones that carved out a space for remorse and worship, the altar, the pews, the shine of the floor—he took it all in before entering the confessional.

"Forgive me Father ..."

"Michael? Michael, what are you doing here? I, ah, I understand what you're doing here, but what are you *doing* here?"

"Things began for me talking with you, and ..."

Ford had a sense of where this was going. Today was the appointment with the doctor, and the news must have been bad.

"What did the doctor say?"

"It's stage four liver cancer, James."

Silence. Painful silence.

"Stage four? Are they certain?"

Theological questions about suffering and righteousness flew around in Ford's mind, along with the patent answers. Nothing about this situation was as fixed and certain as he had been trained to believe. His thoughts were disorderly, nothing like the way the questions were presented in church doctrine or seminary classes, and these circumstances were too intimately connected to his life.

Could the priest dare question God about this, simply because it impacted him and Michael? Would doing so be a sign of doubt, and would it damage his ministry, and somehow also harm Michael's spiritual life and soul?

"The doctor seemed certain. His suggestion was to enjoy what's left of my life and not to take any aggressive action to combat a cancer they can't destroy."

Ford was listening but also thinking about the cause of this cancer. This was not a theological "where are you God?" question. He was not pressing divine accountability for human misery; it could be bracketed for the time being, with the answer lodged somewhere in the workings of divine mystery. No, the priest was thinking of a more biochemical question of origin. Was it environment?

Their city was polluted and guilty of environmental racism. With Michael living in the city, in what was once an economically troubled area, it's possible chemicals in the air and soil are unavoidable and caused this. Ford remembered all the mornings the weatherman said it wasn't a good day for those with sensitive systems to be outside— does Michael have a sensitive system? Was it stress induced? Possibly— his job was demanding. Was it genetic? Maybe a family history— possibly—but even so he's young and he appeared healthy. Could it be food? Food! This one stuck with Ford.

"Michael, do you remember Herman? Herman Jackson?"

"Yes … why?" Michael was searching his memory for the connection when Ford spoke again.

Michael caught on and understood where Ford was going with this, but he couldn't say it. Ford would have to fill in all the blanks. "He died of cancer, Michael. And … you buy from Your Food Groceries. Don't you?"

Ford sighed, "Your Food Groceries and cancer."

The similarities between Herman and Michael were too much for Your Food Groceries' chemicals not to be the cause.

Ford was angry with himself and with Michael. They knew about the food at those stores. Why didn't he make Michael stop going there? Michael had similar questions.

"Why didn't I stop going to Your Food Groceries after Herman's death?" Michael wondered if he were guilty of spiritual arrogance. Had his sense of ministry pushed him to assume no harm could come to him because he was doing the will of God, and that this service gained him divine protection from the police and all forms of harm?

He wondered if his faith had caused him to ignore science. He knew about the food; they'd killed because of the food. Why didn't he stop eating it? Why didn't he urge Susan to shop somewhere else? Why did he let Susan eat it?

It hit him. Michael knew why he hadn't stopped eating the food despite what he knew about him. Something Ford had said a long time ago, and that he'd played over in his mind, came back to him. The priest talked about their strength as disciples and alluded to a scripture about the servants of God not being harmed by poison and other things. The exact scripture came to Michael as he sat with Ford. He said loud enough for Ford to hear, "And these signs shall follow them that believe. In my name shall they cast out devils; they shall speak with new tongues; they shall take up serpents; and if they drink any deadly thing, it shall not hurt them..."

Ford caught Michael off, "Mark 16:17-18." The priest remembered what he'd proclaimed about God taking care of them, and he thought of Michael dying.

After saying the passage, Michael was angry and confused for a moment, and then an odd feeling overcame him. This must be God's will. He wouldn't complain, wouldn't seek a legal recourse. Nothing. He'd accept what was going to happen. If God took care of them, as they'd believed and as scripture suggested, he'd have to accept his condition. God could save him, or could have prevented illness so he could continue his work, but God didn't.

Everything about his shared ministry with Ford urged him to this perspective. "Disciples pay a price," he thought to himself.

Ford started to speak, but Michael cut him off. "God knows best," he said.

The priest responded, "amen."

Michael left the church and went home to talk to Susan, but without giving her the details. She took it as well as anyone might—anyone whose sense of life was wrapped in the dying person. She cried, hugged him, questioned God, questioned herself, questioned him—and when she couldn't cry or talk anymore, she sat on the couch with Michael's head on her lap stroking his hair and humming their favorite song—Bill Withers, "Just the Two of Us."

Michael lifted his head as she hummed the second verse. He had to say something to her, "Susan ... don't eat from Your Food Groceries anymore."

Michael paused thinking about his wife's efforts to get them to eat better ... both of them. She'd started buying so much of their food from there. He only hoped her body would fight off the effects of the chemicals, and that she would remain healthy. If not, he'd have to believe her death was also the will of God. "God have mercy," he thought to himself.

"Michael ..."

"Promise me. Please."

"Okay." She didn't ask him why. It didn't really matter. More important to her was giving him some comfort, and allowing him to shield her from whatever troubled him about the market.

"Okay, babe."

His job had always been important to him, he liked what it meant to work, and that would have to stop now. She'd also take off some time to be with him for whatever days remained.

They slept hard that night. Both worried about the other. Would Susan be okay? Would death come gentle?

The night was no easier for Ford. The questions wouldn't stop. Could he provide Michael with spiritual comfort? Could he ease the transition?

CHAPTER FORTY-FIVE

The next three weeks were difficult and full of pain. Michael spent most of those days in bed, trying to be comfortable and provide solace for Susan. Ford came by every day to check on Michael and to just sit with him—no words were necessary.

Sometimes he'd bring dinner for the three of them, although only he and Susan ate—and they did so with great difficulty and disinterest in the meal. Other times, Susan would need the distraction and so she would cook something, but this made eating no easier.

There was medication to control the pain, but it also kept him from being present with Susan and Ford. So he refused to take it the last three days.

There wasn't much of him left. He wasn't the Michael that Ford met in the confessional years ago, and nothing in his eyes reminded Susan of their life together. The cancer ate away everything that was familiar about him.

His body was destroyed, but Susan hoped his soul was refreshed and strengthened. Susan hoped, but Ford believed himself a bit more confident than that.

The day before his death, Michael asked Susan to leave the room and close the door so he could have a private conversation with his priest. He couldn't go to confession, but he thought Ford would be kind enough to bring confession to him. Ford agreed.

"Forgive me, Father ..."

"Michael ..."

Ford hadn't taken confession without the protection of a wall before. He'd never looked someone in the eyes and listened to the thoughts and actions they kept hidden from others. He'd never been this close to flesh trying to purge.

"Ford, please, I need to do this."

Michael raised up on his pillows, his eyes sunken, his skin gray, and his arms thin showing weak veins, and his collar bone exposed by the ill-fitting pajamas made Ford think of the Holocaust survivors he'd seen in so many pictures.

"Father, forgive me for I have sinned. It has been," Michael coughed a body-shaking cough, and continued, "… since my last confession."

Ford had to respect Michael's need. He had to honor the wishes of his co-laborer.

"What is your sin?"

Michael's breathing was loud and labored. His muscles and lungs fought his spirit.

"I don't know, Father. My soul doesn't want to believe it, but in moments of weakness I think I must have done something; I must have sinned—committed a mortal sin that is destroying my spiritual life inside out. Maybe ego out of control? No humility … I don't know, but something, Ford."

"We all sin. Everyone has sinned and come short of the glory of God. That's what scripture and the Church teach."

"I know all of that. But I mean something more. Not original sin, but something more—something that would turn God against my desire for discipleship. I don't know what it is, but there must be something."

Michael stopped talking, looked at Ford and waited for the priest to say something—to pull something from his theological training and his spiritual insights that would help him deal with what was happening. His flesh pushed against what his spirit knew. And so, he wanted Ford to remind him that they had done God's will. He wanted Ford to encourage him during this transition, to recall, as his priest, the good he'd done in the name of God.

"You've given your life to God. You've done what most others wouldn't do. And you did it all for the glory of God. Some things we just can't understand," was Ford's response.

"That sounds nice, but it's theology-lite. There's something to this, and if we listen ... if I listen ... we'll understand ... I don't have much time."

Michael was losing strength, but he needed some type of answer. He wanted something to make this go easy for him. He believed it the case, but he wanted Ford to confirm that his spiritual life was healthy even though his body was not. From Ford he wanted some assurance that his sin, whatever it might be, wasn't a mortal sin that required cancer as extreme penance. He wasn't sure he deserved or should need this assurance, but he was human and he wanted it ... desired it.

There was no need for contrition as far as Ford was concerned. He and Michael were flawed, yes, but which disciple or prophet wasn't?

Michael wanted to know how to distinguish the outcome of a life. How do you know when misfortune or even death is the result of human free will without the stigma of punishment for sin, and when our demise is the consequence of sin punished? Is there a way to distinguish sin, and does that ability extend beyond human knowledge and agency?

He wanted Ford to help him understand that what they had done from the burning of the church to the last act of extreme penance was actually God's will, and that his death is that of a martyr—someone with divine favor—and not the consequence of evil. He wanted something Ford couldn't provide.

"Faith. That's all we have left. We do our best, and the rest is faith and God's grace."

Ford imagined that statement might not satisfy Michael completely. It was what Ford believed in his heart of hearts; it, he was willing to believe, was our last best hope. Faith.

"Is that enough?"

"I pray and trust it is."

At first it wasn't evident to him whether Michael felt comforted by the confession or more convinced by his uncertainty. But after saying these words, the priest felt some assurance. He took Michael's question not as doubt. For the priest, it was Michael's statement of faith in God's work beyond our human capabilities expressed through the limits of human imagination and language. It was recognition of human frailty and that God has final say over human life.

Still things couldn't end with that weak statement. The priest knew better. He had to change his words.

"Michael … it's enough because it is all the soul can offer. Don't forget, we never lacked empathy. You never lost sight of God's will … never."

Michael closed his eyes.

Ford studied Michael's chest to make certain he was still breathing. Confident he was, the priest touched and then held Michael's hand—for the first time—stood, slowly released his friend, and left the room.

The next morning Ford received a call in the office requesting that he get to Michael's home as quickly as possible. He grabbed his communion kit, his Bible, and his coat. On the way there he thought about the work he and Michael had done.

"Is this the end of our ministry? Michael is dying."

Susan opened the door and showed him into their bedroom. He could hear Michael's breathing from the hallway, and he imagined how he might look. Ford walked in and pulled a chair to the bedside to perform the last rites. Susan stood in the background thinking about Michael, and a life empty of him.

They had communion. With each word and movement, they remembered the first time they'd shared that sacrament. Ford made the sign of the cross, lightly touched Michael's forehead, and Michael smiled. The priest took comfort in that.

1:37 p.m.

Michael passed away, with his fellow disciple and wife with him. He'd been in a good deal of pain because he didn't want to take the medication. He wanted to be alert. Ford, however, thought his death was easy. Michael didn't struggle; he didn't resist. He surrendered.

The funeral was a small gathering. Michael and Susan didn't have many friends since he'd become so involved in church, and their families were small and living some distance from them. There were members of the parish, a few friends, co-workers, and some members of their families—but the empty spaces in the pews weren't easy to ignore.

Ford was there to officiate over a fellow disciple's last service,

264 · ANTHONY B. PINN

and he knew the number of bodies in that church couldn't measure Michael's impact. He'd chosen his ministry over his own comfort and enrichment. The spaces in the pews, as far as Ford was concerned, reflected the strength of that surrender to God, and were filled with spiritual energy.

Susan had Michael dressed in his favorite blue suit—one Ford had seen on many occasions in church and at a few of their meetings. For the priest, the outfit was appropriate and meaningful in ways Susan and the others gathered couldn't know and probably wouldn't understand anyway.

When Ford saw the body in that cherry wood casket he didn't think Michael looked peaceful, not as he had during their last moments alone. Not looking peaceful? What would that even mean in this situation?

Ford gave a eulogy for Michael, but he could only tell half his story. The priest started by saying Michael died young, and to us that might challenge faith; but we must understand that God's timing is perfection. The mind of God is a mystery to us, and we can't understand why a powerful and compassionate God would allow such tragedy for one so good.

Ford told them that even in those moments when we wonder about God's will and human destiny, it is important to take comfort in our faith and trust God when our senses and mind tell us to doubt.

"Michael trusted God. He was a hard worker, a serious man, committed husband, and upstanding member of the community."

Ford also reminded them of how much Michael loved St. Barbara and St. George, how much time he gave to both.

Ford couldn't tell them about the new ministry, the divine calling to discipleship that shaped the last few years of his life. It was that work for God that defined his spiritual life, not the things Ford was free to mention. Those things he talked about he knew were just superficial, just ornamentation on the righteous soul.

He prayed for Michael's soul and for his family and friends. The priest took comfort in his belief all was well with Michael. He'd served God with courage and abiding faith, but the time for men of faith, for prophets and disciples, can be short.

While the body was once the material instrument of God and the supple covering for a vital soul, it was now an empty shell, and the substance—the spirit—that could generate a feeling of peace expressed through the flesh was no longer there. Instead, Ford simply thought sometimes the body is just the residue of a spiritual life well nurtured. Michael was more than what he saw in that box, and God would grant him peace because God always gave rest to those who'd devoted themselves to righteousness and God's will. Right? Ford couldn't let that question linger, but others persisted.

Ford wondered about his own body, and how it would respond to the demands of death. The priest hoped his faith would remain strong and that he would enter the grip of death with the same type of grace shown by Michael. As a priest and a disciple he wanted to do that much with his last moments.

Michael was gone, and Susan decided to move in order to be close to her family. There was nothing left for her in this city, just memories and she would have them wherever she lived.

Michael had been her life, and now she'd depend on family to fill that void. Ford helped her pack her things, and they talked about Michael as they filled boxes. The conversation was a bit awkward, but they both needed to say something to each other, about someone who meant so much to them.

Ford had been vulnerable in front of Michael, and he mourned the loss. With death he'd come to recognize that he in fact loved Michael like a brother, and had as high regard for Michael as he had for anyone. The priest never said anything of this closeness when Michael was around, and in his own way he was trying to express it to Susan now that Michael was gone. Recognizing loss and dealing with it as a dimension of his emotional and psychological self was new to him, and couldn't be done quickly. The priest had spent too many years stuffing down those elements of his inner self, and working hard to only acknowledge and cultivate his spiritual life and the connection to his divine commission.

CHAPTER FORTY-SIX

Michael's funeral marked the start of a difficult period for the priest. He wrestled with his ability to fulfill the will of God. Was it still in place? How would God use him now that Michael was gone?

The priest spent evenings pouring over the scriptures, but it seemed to present a world closed to him, and it offered stories coded with meanings he struggled to understand. He didn't want to anger God, to lose God's favor; but he didn't know how to proceed. He felt lost, and he wished he could avoid the confessional now that Michael couldn't be called for assistance.

Each morning he got up, put on one of his dark suits, or appropriate casual clothing, and he worked. But it seemed like he was just conducting business—and it was that reutilizing and deforming of the Christian mission that started his real work at St. Barbara and that secured his commitments at St. George. Purification of spiritual life—fire and penance.

Ford moved through each day carrying out his responsibilities but without the same sense of underlying meaning and purpose. Breakfast, office, schedule given to him by Margaret—it was mechanical. Going through the motions got him through his obligations.

People in the parish, other priests, and members of the community he'd come to know worried about him. They wondered why this particular death meant so much to him.

The priest could never answer that question for them. Some who'd attended other funerals at the church and were bold enough would ask him about his connection to Michael. They knew the two had coffee or the occasional meal together, but that wasn't enough for them to explain away what appeared to be serious depression. Were they really good friends?

There were a few who tried to make a sexual connection between the two men, but it didn't get beyond those few. People didn't think of Ford in that sexual way—with men or women. He just seemed asexual to them: he didn't get too close when he spoke to parishioners; he didn't shake hands and hold on too long; he didn't let a touch give the wrong impression; he maintained eye contact and didn't let his vision wander. He didn't seem flirtatious with men or women.

They didn't know how he'd felt about the professor in the confessional, how his body responded to the thought of her, or how he'd dreamed about her.

Others thought it wasn't about the dead man: Father Ford must be burned out. He was so active in the community, so present and available. These members of the parish would say he must be tired and in need of a vacation—a few days away will fix him up—because church people and community people can be difficult to deal with. They could make this statement because they were some of the difficult people—of course they wouldn't see it that way.

Ford heard some of these rumors. Things travel fast in religious circles, and Margaret had a particular expertise in getting this information to him without implicating herself. And for the look on faces and the way some approached him, he suspected what other things they must be saying when he wasn't around.

Talk didn't bother him.

"They'd talked about Jesus," he'd said many times in response to gossip and rumors. He'd heard it from some of the parishioners at St. Barbara—didn't understand it fully. And he had no intention of putting himself in the place of Jesus when using it—just the idea that everyone, even God, gets talked about. The priest wasn't always comfortable with that line, but there was a song he'd heard during one of the gospel music festivals at St. Barbara and that seemed right on: "You can talk about me just as much as you please. The more you talk I'm gonna stay on my knees."

Yep—pray the hell out of people; get them with kindness. That was the concern for Ford—what to do with people, hopelessly sin-sick people.

There were large and costly issues on his mind. Michael's life was important, but his death pointed out a concern the priest couldn't escape. "Did Michael's death change him, and alter ministry?"

It would take time for him to distinguish grief over Michael's death and concerns regarding his discipleship. Now he gave himself permission to entertain the thought—did love for Michael now distract from his love for God? Isn't this what the Bible implied: you can't serve two masters? When Ford first thought this, it seemed reasonable—consistent with scripture. But the more he thought about it, the more he saw the distinction. It wasn't about serving two masters; it wasn't about Michael. It was about the priest, always about the priest. Could he appreciate both his body and his spirit? Could he serve God through both his body and his spirit? Those questions were the real challenge for the priest. He thought disciples throughout history wrestled with this dilemma—controlling the body, its wants and limitation, and advancing the soul through the body. All for the glory of God!

Ford recognized that with time and continued dedication the spirit would trump the flesh, or at least that was his faith. For him that was the ongoing lesson taught by scripture and Church Tradition at its best.

All this connected his thoughts to his ministry. He realized Michael had provided balance: priest cut off from the world, and man in the world cut off from the stranglehold of Church hierarchy and protocols. Together they had better perspective than either could have alone.

It wasn't that Ford seriously thought about giving up his ministry, or being unable to embrace God's will. How could he when God selected him and only God could read the future and determine when his work was over? No, it was more a matter of the priest needing to regain his composure, and assess how to conduct his ministry without Michael.

"Everything in the right time, and for the right purpose." Saying this gave him some ease during the more challenging moments as he waited for God to reveal what God wanted him to do next.

CHAPTER FORTY-SEVEN

It took months of thinking, reflecting, praying, and working but Ford recovered. His focus was restored and his commitment to his discipleship was affirmed. The need was still present, everything around him spoke to that fact.

His ongoing work in the confessional, although not taking the form of extreme penance, made clear the destruction of spiritual life affecting so many calling themselves children of the Church and followers of Christ.

Christians? Were they Christians? And what would it take for them to be restored to God? He had high expectations, perhaps stemming from the way in which the encounter with Joan made him and Michael more humanistic, more human.

Whatever the case, there was a need for penance, for pain to correct, but he believed God did not want him doing that work alone.

God had a partner in this work for him. Patience and devotion would bring them together in God's appointed time, as it had brought him and Michael together.

He and this new disciple would show God's glory in small but significant ways through pain—redemption through pain. In this way they would revive the Church and restore spiritual life.

Until then, he'd pastor and observe.

"In God's time" was his mantra.

Whenever he thought about patiently waiting, some of the words from a song he'd heard a few times always came back to him.

Children go where I send thee.

How shall I send thee?
Oh, I'm gonna send thee two by two …

The Beginning

ACKNOWLEDGMENTS

This book was almost two decades in the making, and along the way numerous people helped me reach the point of offering you this story. I want to thank them. First, I have had many wonderful students over the course of my career, students who have taught me important lessons as I tried to offer them something worthy of their time (and tuition dollars). Among them is Gregory Colleton, one of my former students from Macalester College and one of my friends. He encouraged me to put this story on paper, and he provided much-needed feedback. Oddly enough, most of this book was written on the beautiful campus of the Huntington Library in Pasadena, California. I am grateful for the hospitality and the unpredictable inspiration to describe death made possible through the colors, sounds, and sights of the Huntington gardens. Numerous colleagues and friends provided kind and encouraging words—despite how weird it must have seemed for me to turn from academic writing to test my hand at fiction (perhaps not so different, really). Thank you to them all, particularly Ramon Rentas, Benjamin Valentin, Eli Valentin, Alexander Byrd, Maya Reine, Warren Reine, James Cone, Katie Cannon, Juan and Stacey Floyd-Thomas, Jeffrey Kripal, April DeConick, Nick Shumway, and so many others. I also thank my biological family for support, understanding, good trips, and good humor. Finally, I must express my great gratitude to Kurt Volkan for his generosity, powerful suggestions, and his willingness to take a chance on a first-time fiction writer. Thanks, Kurt!

ABOUT THE AUTHOR

Anthony B. Pinn is the Agnes Cullen Arnold Professor of Humanities and director of the Center for Engaged Research and Collaborative Learning at Rice University. He is the author of numerous books, including *The End of God-Talk: An African-American Humanist Theology* and *Writing God's Obituary: How a Good Methodist Became a Better Atheist,* and is the coeditor of the collection *Life Sentences: Short Stories.* He lives in Houston.